A View of The Bottom
A Novel by Chaka Adams

D1070372

www.PrettyGirlsRead.com

Published by PrettyGirlsRead™, LLC
Cover Art © 2014 by PrettyGirlsRead all rights reserved
Cover Layout & Design: HotBookCovers.com
Cover Photo: CSB Photography
Author's Photo: Kat Goduco Photography
ISBN 978-0-9887010-0-7
First Printing June 2014
Printed in the United States of America

PrettyGirlsRead
Atlanta, GA
www.PrettyGirlsRead.com

Acknowledgements

You held my hand through the dark days.
Words can't thank you enough.
But I'm a Writer. Words are all I have...

Munira, Denise, Nicole – you pushed me to keep going even when my heart was at its breaking point. Thanks for always seeing the **REAL** *me and loving me just the way I am...*

My **ROCK** *– who wants that perfect love story anyway?*
Yours Forever...

Ly'Nasia & Lyman Green – my reasons for living...

Samlith, Delia, Jeanine, Yirelis – friends come and friends go. Real friends stay. My unwavering loyalty for life...

Shanell "Diva" Grady – you made me see the good in people again and it saved me. Your heart is genuine, never change...

Shari "Dara" Starkes – you deserve the world, don't settle for anything less...

Shana Washington – you never cease to amaze me.
SW Consulting, your time is now...

Spacious, Ivory, Dawn, Kanisha, Keke, Tilly – seasons change but memories last a lifetime. We'll always have 4B...

City Chapters – keep writing...

The **PrettyGirlsRead** *Team – there's no me without you!*
123...

In life, there will be people who build you up and people who tear you down.
In the end, you will thank them both... Thank You!

This one is for Chiggy.
May her little heart now be at peace.

"There's no greater agony than bearing an untold story inside you." - Dr. Maya Angelou

Prologue

Well, here the fuck I go again. You know that saying, "Wherever you go, you take yourself with you"? Well, I must be the unofficial poster child for that shit or something. Sure I physically left the hood but mentally I still find myself neck-deep in the trenches of that six blocks radius that I once called home.

Queensbridge, the largest housing projects in New York City, is at the eroded core of the Rotten Apple. Consisting of 96 buildings and 3,142 apartments, that maze has me trapped like a sewer rat scampering to make it out. The more I run from it, the more magnetic its force becomes. Similar to the woes of Notorious B.I.G., that place is like a drug to me; sort of like what crack did to Pookie in New Jack, except after crossing over - I keep going back.

Queensbridge and I are engaged in what I would describe as an abusive relationship and believe me, I know all too well about those. The more it beats me down, the more I try to make it work. In all reality I'm just a crab longing for the security of my barrel. I clawed my way out only to limit how far I could go. It's like I need that barrel close enough to me just in case I have to jump back in and submerge so the comfort of my familiar surroundings can keep me safe.

That's some backwards ass shit, ain't it?

Here I am, in a whole new story, trying to write a completely different chapter of my life with new characters and surroundings but in the end, it was already written. No matter where the fuck I end up, what's for me – is for me.

Oh, don't get me wrong, my shit is looking real good on paper. I surround myself with what appears to be a better class of people. At least that's how it seems from the outside looking in.

My love for street dudes is still pretty strong. No, I can't live with 'em but I definitely can't live without 'em either. However, I no longer fuck with local nickel and dime hand-to-hand hustlers. The motherfuckers I deal with got guap. I'm talking long money – the type of shit that covers bail, a lawyer, some media coverage and a closet full of Armani suits with wingtip shoes for the court appearance type of money.

Yet even with the glitz, they still have grimy tendencies. The street code of shutting the fuck up doesn't mean much to them when they're facing maximum sentence federal time. You see, when you step above that local hustling shit and start making real money, the consequences increase right along with the size of your stacks. Some get the money but lose the principles and that shit is like mixing vodka and milk; a sickening combination. In my former world, honor was everything. It's obvious these new cats completely missed that memo.

My Bench Dwellers, those nosy ass project people who sit around gossiping all day, have been replaced by bougie debutantes with their noses so far in the air, they can smell the rain before the clouds even have a chance to form. They smile in my face but as soon as I walk away they start clucking like typical project birds.

"She should get some braces. That mouth of hers is all types of jacked up," says one.

Joined in by the other snooty Hermès toting socialite while twirling her hair and popping her gum, *"Oh my God, she's so ghetto. I bet she wouldn't even know what fork to use at dinner."*

I've gone from thinking I was too good to thinking I'm not good enough.

The only real distinction between the girls I grew up with and this new breed I'm hanging with is how quickly they've evolved. My newfound clique completely bypassed that whole hood rat baby mama phase and graduated to being bad broads with degrees who live in non-subsidized condos and master hustles incomparable to any I have ever known.

Ironically, these chicks still have a street smart in them that my secluded ass thought only applied to project girls like me. I was wrong though. From the row homes of Philadelphia to the Bankhead Highways of Atlanta, a hood chick wears many masks. She's a double-threat. Although she can ratchedly survive in the grimy streets of North Philly or the cum-stained champagne rooms of Magic City, she can still button up for corporate boardroom meetings on Monday morning. Her meals no longer consist of four wings and fries from the local Chinese restaurant where they take her order from behind a bullet proof glass. Instead, she dines on sushi, trading in her plastic fork for bamboo chop sticks. She's self-made and no matter what she has to do, she's determined to never go back to being broke.

Like a chameleon, I blend. I watch my surroundings with wide eyes so that I never miss a beat. Most importantly, I learn. I take what I already know, add in a splash of some new shit and before long, I've buried my past just deep enough to make it disappear from the surface. But it's still there and anything buried in the dark has a way of coming to light.

Biggie called it, *"Life After Death"*, but I wonder if there really is a way to come back. Is it even possible to reinvent yourself after going through the fire? To this day, I'm still not sure. Outwardly my life has changed but the blood running through my veins is the same. My heart still pumps loyalty and love from the crown of my head to the soles of my feet. I was just bred that way. Like my mother used to say, I'm cut from a different cloth. Unfortunately, they don't make that fabric anymore.

My type of love, however, fosters a dangerous weakness. A weakness I should never show. I remember there was a time when I did and it forced my story to come to an untimely end. Or maybe, just maybe, that's when my life really began.

Shit, I still don't know my damn self and perhaps I never will. But fuck it. Here's the rest of my story...

Chapter 1

I looked around, realizing the United States Navy Recruit Training Command in cold ass Great Lakes, Illinois, felt more like a prison cell than what I had previously envisioned. At least that was my first impression of boot camp based on the many stories I heard about Riker's Island. A life consisting of three meals, a cot and scheduled lights out sounded extremely similar to the Rose M. Singer Center for Women that my best friend Ta-Ta's mother continuously warned us about. With the way she described it, that was the last place I ever wanted to end up.

The windows were so high up on the chipped gray cinder blocked walls that I couldn't even get a clear view outside of our dorms without stepping on my tippy toes. Even then I was straining just to see beyond the large bronze statue of a fallen soldier that stood right outside our building which we called the barracks. There wasn't much to look at anyway besides other hopeless recruits stoically marching down the street singing cadence, *"Left – right – left – right."* The sounds were a far cry from the brainless chirping of the Bench Dwellers to which I had grown so accustomed.

Rows of bunk beds were stacked and lined up against either side of the room with enough space in between to place two six-foot rectangular tables which were used for writing letters or studying Navy training manuals. Other than that, we weren't given any personal time to just sit on the rusted folding metal chairs and chill. Which, since I grew up in the hood, had undoubtedly become my favorite past time.

Although it felt claustrophobically small, it was big enough to fit about sixty other women ranging from as young as seventeen to as old as thirty-four. Most were from the redneck backwoods and never lived around Black people or even saw them except while riding their confederate flagged pick-up trucks through town. Boot Camp was the culture shock of my previously uncultured life.

Any expectations of privacy were quickly eliminated. We couldn't even take showers by ourselves. The bathroom looked more like an above-ground cellar. Double doors, one for entering, one for exiting, led to a large open room with five door-less stalls on the right, directly across from the same numbered sinks and mirrors. Whatever business you had to handle was done in public where even the people who weren't looking directly at you could see your reflection while brushing their teeth. Five shower heads were stacked against the left wall with just three drains that kept getting clogged from the White girls who had to wash their hair every single day. Shit, I was lucky if I shampooed twice a month.

My mother always told me how nasty White people were but it wasn't until I was stuck living with them that I realized how right she was. They were constantly shedding wet stringy hairs all on the bathroom floor, walking around barefoot and actually sitting on the toilets. Calling them barbaric would be putting it nicely. Funny, some of them had the nerve to not want to live around Black people. Shit, we did them a favor by integrating with their trifling asses. I'm sure they learned a lot from us.

I had only been there for about a month and was already allowing my slick ass mouth to get me in all sorts of trouble. There was something about the whole discipline thing that just wasn't sitting right with me. I didn't give a fuck if I was in the Navy or not, I still wasn't about to let anybody tell me what to do.

I was reprimanded for everything from wearing my Navy-issued baseball cap cocked to the side instead of pointing the brim straight forward to asking for the logic behind making us spit shine our boots before going to fill sandbags. I'm still not sure how either made me a better person or a better sailor. I mean, damn, what did America gain by the way I wore my stupid ass baseball cap? It was small things like that which made every day in boot camp a living hell. I was always getting yelled at for having, what they referred to as, a 'New York Attitude'.

Naturally, I wasn't sitting back and allowing that shit to happen.

Some of the other girls might have been cool, I suppose, but I wasn't there to make new friends so I pretty much kept to myself for the first three to four weeks. I didn't say anything to anybody and I gave less than two shits about what anybody tried to say to me either. Despite my change in geography, my motto stayed the same - guards up at all times. Besides, all the other recruits had cherub angel faces with dreams of protecting America and shit. My reasons for joining the military had nothing to do with serving this unjust country and everything to do with getting the fuck away from the injustice facing me every single day.

Regardless of how hard I tried, I couldn't completely get away from my former life though. Every time I closed my eyes, I relived my last encounter with my much older and former drug dealing boyfriend, Malik. He warned me that I would see him again so I should have known he would go ballistic after realizing his five-minute dick game wasn't enough to keep me hooked after all he put me through with the cheating and the abuse. On that last occasion, I only gave him some pussy out of a temporary moment of weakness. Still, that motherfucker was like a recurring nightmare causing me to fear any form of sleep – even my day dreams were on some *Elm Street* shit. And if it wasn't him haunting me, it was Ta-Ta. I could still smell her putrid blood as it gurgled from her mouth.

Although I called Ta-Ta's house every chance I could, she wasn't speaking to me. Her mother assured me that she was recovering well and would write when she could. She said she moved down to Charlotte, North Carolina with her aunt and was trying to get back on her feet which was why she hadn't contacted me yet. I knew she was lying because I had already spoken to wild ass Dana, our mutual friendand from what I heard, Ta-Ta was right back in the projects once she got released from New York Hospital and didn't want to have anything to do with me after realizing I skipped town. But what other options did I have besides getting the fuck away from there? Manny, with all his Columbian drug ties and penchant for killer dogs, told me I had to get the fuck out of New York or risk feeling his wrath. After Ta-Ta and I fucked up all his money, I wasn't willing to stick around and take my chances. I already saw him in action so I knew his Tony Montana sounding ass was about his business. I wondered how long it would take before Ta-Ta really understood the seriousness behind Manny's warning for us to break the fuck out. Because she was still in the hospital while shit was really going down, she wasn't forced to bear witness to his form of retaliation. On the other hand, I had a front row seat to that shit and believe me, I wasn't sticking around to catch an encore. One day Ta-Ta would understand and if she didn't, I would have to say 'fuck her'. I was on some fight or flight shit; and let's just say, when the going got tough – Chaka got going.

Amid my boot camp chaos, combined with my Queensbridge memories, I did manage to make friends with this one chick. Well, it was a little too early to refer to her as a friend but she definitely had a swagger about her that made her stand out from the rest of the recruits. First off, she was Asian with an ass that looked like she could balance a cup on it. Before meeting her, I thought all Chinese people acted like the little quiet smelly motherfuckers named Ping or Wong who rode the 7 Train to Flushing, Queens–the unsanctioned Wonton capital of New York.

But this slanty-eyed broad wasn't typical by any meaning of the word. I could tell she was in a league of her own from the first time we spoke. Coincidentally, we were both being forced to clean the toilets with toothbrushes as punishment for mouthing off, so we had nothing but time to literally talk some shit.

"Yo, these motherfuckers is straight tripping," she said, sticking her brush back into the soapy water bucket.

That was the first time I heard her talk beyond the usual scream outs we had to do during daily exercise. She didn't sound meek like the stereotypical math geniuses from elementary school. If I closed my eyes, I would have thought she was Black. Come to find out she wasn't even Chinese, she was from Thailand. Shit, they all looked alike to me. Except for the ones who did my nails and she reminded me of them. I swear I wanted to ask her if she knew how to do a manicure and pedicure but I didn't want to seem all racist and shit.

"They don't even know me like that to be telling me what the fuck to do. I ain't sign up for this shit." She continued.

"Yeah, me either."

My response was brief and my eyes never left the corner of the tile behind the toilet that I scrubbed for dear life.

She brushed off my cold shoulder as if it meant nothing to her. "What did you say your first name was, again?"

"I didn't," I mumbled under my breath before checking my attitude and pointing to my last name which was embroidered along the top right pocket of my shirt. "But my name is Chaka. Chaka Adams."

"Oh damn, I gotta get used to using the whole government and shit. Where I'm from, we don't ever let people know all that." She laughed. "Well in that case, I'm Piper. Piper Cheng." She paused as if for dramatic effect. "And I like my martinis shaken not stirred."

"Ha!"

Her reference to James Bond left me with an opened-mouth laugh as her sharpness caught me off guard. I was usually the quick-witted one among my friends back home but she was on some smart clever shit too.

Piper lived in Philadelphia and was heavy into the streets according to her stories. Although we were about the same age, it seemed shit in her world moved a lot faster than I knew anything about. Her voice spoke volumes much larger than her stocky five-foot stature. With her full lips and pronounced features, she looked like she had some Black in her. I chuckled when she explained the only Black going up in her was the type that had green in their pockets. *Yup, I was digging her from the start.*

Her chinky eyes and jet black hair was practically the only Asian thing about Piper. Her silky tresses were like the type that Reece, my bald-headed former friend turned foe, who occasionally hopped up on my ex-man's dick every now and then, wore. All the hood chicks would go broke just to rock a Malaysian ponytail or a sew-in bundle of weave. They would have been in awe if they saw Piper's hair. Her shit was the real deal. She complained about having to get it cut for boot camp but she was singing to the choir with that one. My strands were chopped to right above my shirt's collar as well. I'm sure hers would have grown back much faster than mine so her whining went on deaf ears.

We hit it off after that initial conversation and for the next four weeks, we were inseparable. Nobody fucked with us or even said more than what was required in our presence. It wasn't as if we'd listen to those lames anyway. Piper and I were on some *'team us'* shit. When you're away from real life, like we were, you need a support system and Piper was that for me. I'm sure I was the same for her too. We had things in common like both remembering every lyric to Wu-Tang's "C.R.E.A.M.". We sang it every day while envisioning Method Man butt naked, wearing nothing but a pair of tan suede Timberlands and ruggedly banging us out doggy-style. Piper and I had a thing about roughnecks. We loved them.

The other recruits didn't seem like they had experienced half the things we did in our short lifetimes. They just didn't have a clue. In many ways, I envied that about them. To be young and naïve was the perfect veil which hid the real ugliness of the world.

During the middle of the night, when most of the other women were sound asleep, Piper and I would meet in the bathroom and chit-chat for hours on end. Because there was always at least two other recruits standing watch, we made sure to hit them off with a couple dollars so they would let us sneak away. Ten bucks here and there was enough to give us free realm of the barracks when all lights were supposed to be out.

Piper showed me pictures of all the Philly dudes she claimed were getting money. Besides their Muslim looking nappy beards, which she called a Philadelphia Sunni, they didn't seem so different from the Queensbridge guys. I guess the drug game was just as prevalent in other hoods as it was in New York.

"So why did you come to the Navy?" I asked Piper during one of our bathroom sessions.

Her mother had somehow managed to sneak a cigarette into the care package she mailed. So that we wouldn't get caught puffing, which was strictly forbidden, we each took a pull, put it out and then lit it back up once all the smoke evaporated into the dense bathroom air. We were taking a chance, especially with the tattle-taling snow bunnies in our barracks, but fuck it. That wouldn't be the last time Piper and I broke a few rules.

"Girl, it was either the Navy or go to jail," she said matter-of-factly.

Of course this struck a chord with me and I had to know more so I dug deeper. "What you mean the Navy or jail?"

"It was nothing. I was making a run to bring some shit to these dudes up north; to your part of town actually. Well, it was somewhere in Queens. I just got off the Tri-Boro Bridge and was about to get on the Grand Central Expressway before I got stopped. It was like that motherfucker was sitting there waiting for me. When he pulled me over, I had a few pounds of weed in my trunk. Well, to say a few, is putting it lightly. I got bagged with fifty fucking pounds. But I wasn't gonna say shit about who I got it from or where I was going. So, I just had to take that. Loose lips sink ships, you know?"

"DAMN, fifty pounds?"

My lower lip dropped and my eyes grew wide at the thought of all that ganja. Clearly Piper wasn't fucking with small timers at all.

"So, what did they do when you got arrested?"

"Who said I got arrested?" She rolled her eyes at my quick assumption. "I told you it was either the Navy or jail. The cop who pulled me over was mad cool. He gave me an ultimatum. He said I could go to the military or I could take the weight." She paused, plucking split ends from the bottom of her hair which she somehow managed to pull into a ponytail.

"And then what happened?" I asked, tapping the palm of my hand against my leg to get her to keep going. If there wasn't anything else I hated, I couldn't stand a slow ass story teller.

"Girl chill, I'm getting to it. Damn." She flung her tiny ponytail to the side and lit the cigarette, inhaling deep before putting it out again. "Then the cop told me he knew some people in the Navy and I should go get my shit together or he would arrest me. Now I'm not stupid so of course I said yeah. He let me go right then and there. Then last month he called me and set it up. My recruiter picked me up the next day."

Instantly, I was reminded of Salerno. I laughed to myself at what seemed to be the new NYPD pick up line. *See a girl in distress and send her ass off to war. How romantic.* With all the police in New York, I knew the odds were slim that her cop was also my Knight in Shining Armor so I ignored the comparisons.

And what a Knight he turned out to be. Detective Paul Salerno, with his younger version of Andy Garcia looking ass, kept in touch with me by sending care packages. I had a new delivery nearly every other day at mail call. Before I left, he told me the recruiter would give him my address so he could stay in touch but I didn't really believe him until I saw it with my own two eyes. Since I still had the ivory-colored business card he gave me when I was in the hospital eons before, I tried to call him every chance I got. Sadly, his personal number was disconnected and I didn't have the heart to call the precinct.

I wanted to stay as far away from the police as possible. The only way I knew he sent the care packages was because he left a card in every one of them. It was simply signed *L.E.S.* – clearly an homage to his hometown, the Lower East Side. Since he was the only person I knew from that filthy ass cesspool section of New York, I was about ninety-nine percent certain it was his sexy self.

The packages were filled with magazines, note pads and money orders. I wasn't allowed to cash them so they just piled up. Although I had only been in boot camp for a couple of months, he already sent me almost three thousand dollars which was a lot considering a cop's salary was chump change any damn way. Since I was starting from the very bottom once I got out of there, that money was definitely a welcomed surprise so I didn't give a fuck where he got it from as long as he kept it coming. I just wished I could have thanked him for it.

Even though that paper was probably the most important thing to me at that point, I can't even front, the highlight of his packages was that they were also stacked with junk food. He sent me all types of cookies, cakes, caramel popcorn bins – every weed induced munchie you could think of was in there. Even the Funyuns, because hell, ya' gotta have the Funyuns, man.

I wasn't sure what I was going through but I was craving everything imaginable. I would eat anything in sight, including the mashed potatoes we were served everyday at chow despite the fact that I always hated the taste of them, even as a kid. It didn't matter, I sopped up every last morsel. All the meals, all the snacks – I didn't care, I was eating it. I blamed my appetite on my impromptu cocaine detox. Shit, every fiend I knew who stopped getting high would eventually blow up from finally sitting down long enough to eat a full meal. I figured I wasn't any different.

"So, why did you join the Navy?"

Piper's question shook me out of my Salerno haze.

"Oh, me and my boyfriend broke up and I just wanted to get away. I had to get my life together."

Although it wasn't completely the truth, it wasn't a blatant lie either. I didn't know Piper well enough to divulge all my secrets just yet. Besides, some of it was true. I did manage to get my GED while I was in boot camp and I did get the fuck out of Queensbridge. And finally, I did break up with my boyfriend.

I'm sure it wasn't in the way his sorry ass expected but it was still a breakup nonetheless. So I wasn't telling Piper the truth, the whole truth and nothing but the truth – but it was the only reality I was willing to share with people who didn't already know my story. Besides, Piper wasn't the fucking District Attorney and I wasn't under oath. So the less she knew, the better it was for the both of us.

"I hear that, girl." Piper passed me the cigarette which was so close to the brown filter that we called it 'Smoking on Brownsville'.

"Leave it up to a man to hurt us enough to make us wanna do something better for ourselves. Ain't that some shit?"

"Damn, I never looked at it like that," I replied.

She had a point that I never acknowledged until then. If you can't have a pot of gold at the end of your rainbow without first having some rain then perhaps Malik was the black cloud that would eventually lead to my treasure.

"Anyway, let's go back to bed before we get our asses in trouble," she said.

"You mean get in trouble...AGAIN?"

She grabbed my hand and pulled me up from the floor, then we snuck back into our bunks. As usual, falling asleep was a task for me. Instead, I laid there, looking up at the metal bed frame looming above me. Even though I hadn't completely grown to trust her yet, I was happy I met Piper. With all the craziness going through my head, I don't think I would have made it without her by my side.

Piper would later introduce me to a whole different world though. And just my luck, that world would eventually be both a gift and a curse.

Chapter 2

"Argh," I grunted, clenching my teeth while trying to force myself to crawl out of the bottom bunk.

From the sounds of bustling recruits, who were quickly putting military corners along their crisp white bed sheets, I knew the 5AM daily wake up routine was going on around me. My brain told me to get to my feet but the pain in my stomach made it impossible to move.

"Let's go recruits. Get up and get moving," the pint-size Petty Officer First Class, similar to an Army's Drill Sergeant, yelled out causing girls to scatter about, spit shining boots and wiping down their lockers in time for daily inspections.

Still, I couldn't move.

At first I thought I was just having one hell of a battle with cramps or more like a UFC kick-fighting match was going on in my uterus. My insides were grinding together so tightly, I could barely breathe in between the dagger-type stabs.

"Chaka, come on girl. Your ass is about to get us in trouble," Piper said while lazily jumping down from the top bunk right above me and rubbing her red crust-filled eyes.

I tried to respond but the only sound to resonate was another shriek, that one much louder than the first. The pain was getting worse by the second.

"What's the matter?" Piper quickly knelt by my side after she caught a glimpse of my face; my eyebrows scrunching together in agony.

"I got cramps," I said. "Go get me some Motrin."

No matter what the ailment, from a toothache to a paper cut, the military kept us stocked with 800-milligram horse pills which they cleverly disguised as Motrin. I guess they had to keep us numb to the underhanded shit this country does in the name of honor.

While Piper scrambled to the First Aid box hanging far across the room on the bathroom wall, the Petty Officer noticed I was the only person still in my bunk.

"Oh, you must think you get a special invite, Prima Donna," she snarled, approaching me with her yellow brick road munchkin-like wobble.

She hated me as soon as I walked off the van and onto that military base. Her type always did. I was young, light skinned and cute – her complete opposite. Supposedly she thought she was a bad ass because she was from Detroit. As if that was some shit to be proud about. Although the military enforced short hair on women, I knew her nappy-headed broke down Halle Berry cut wasn't by choice. Hair options were obviously slim for her. Either braid it up, get a wig or settle for rocking those broom sticks that poked out from her scalp. She had the type of face that looked like she was half a chromosome away from having down-syndrome. Top heavy, with a square waist and short legs, she resembled Sponge Bob Square Pants which seemed fitting since she spent her career at sea.

True to the ugly girl affliction, she was a bully who popped off just because she could. I knew if she didn't have the safety of the barracks on her side, she would have immediately lost all that bass in her fucking voice. But what could I do? Believe me, I wanted to bust her ass but I was not trying to end up in nobody's military jail. So, I just let her get her rocks off by ordering me around. However, that day was a completely different story.

I leaned forward on the bed, hoisting myself up on my right elbow and yelled back through gritted teeth, "I can't."

"Don't talk back to me little girl. Get up now recruit." Her voice barked like an enraged Tibetan Mastiff.

My panic-stricken eyes darted feverishly around the room, honing in on Piper who was already making her way back to the side of my bunk.

"Don't you see something is wrong with her?" She shouted while embracing me like a lioness protecting her pride.

"Yeah, the only thing wrong is the fact that you two little high yellow heifers think y'all better than everybody else. You won't city slick me, I'm from Detroit. Now I said get up and I mean that," the Petty Officer snapped, saliva spouting from her mouth and spraying on us like bullets.

That evil cunt was really feeling herself and completely out of line. Her first mistake was undoubtedly that foul attitude but her next mistake was like opening Pandora's Box once she grabbed Piper by the t-shirt and tried to force her to stand. Without giving it a second thought, Piper pounced on her so fast that nobody even saw it coming. Before I knew it, her hands were wrapped tightly around the Petty Officer's neck rigorously choking the shit out of her.

I don't know what got into her at that moment. I mean, I could tell she wasn't a slouch but I didn't expect Piper to go all Jet Li ninja on her either.

By that time, the rest of the recruits started surrounding us while Piper continued clobbering D-Town's finest to a bloody pulp. I winced in pain but nobody noticed. All eyes were glued to the brawl going on right in the middle of our dorm. Funny enough, not one of the other girls tried to stop the madness either. In reality, I think they were happy to see that Wicked Witch of the Mid-West get her ass handed to her on a silver platter. I guess the saying was true, "People with short arms shouldn't box with God". Well in her case, she shouldn't have boxed with an untamed chop-suey eating jawn either.

A warm liquid streamed down my leg as I tried to squeeze my pussy lips closed. My Kegel exercises weren't doing shit to stop the downpour trickling beyond my thighs.

"Ugh!" My body jerked upright and my back arched after feeling a knot, the size of a lemon, slide through my walls, transforming from a hard mass to a watery substance that flowed down to my ankles.

Somehow I managed to move my legs. First the right foot hit the floor with a thud. Then, I used both hands to swing the left foot around before planting it next to the other. With a deep inhale, I grabbed on to the top bunk, pulling myself up off the bed.

"Ugh!" Another cringe went unnoticed.

Once I finally mustered the strength to stand and prop myself against the bed railings, I realized the white sheet I had been lying on was stuck to my ass. Before I had a chance to push it aside, everything around me came to a stand-still. The other recruits turned toward me, looking on with their hands covering their mouths. Piper, with her fist paused in mid-air, cocked her head to the side, staring at me with her mouth agape. Even the usually loud Petty Officer looked on with a bewildered expression. I had no idea what caused the stupor until I turned to see why the sheet was still sticking to my back side. Burgundy globs of blood were plastered on the sparkling white sheets causing the material to practically glue itself to my behind. I reached between my legs because it felt like my heart was going to push its way through my fallopian tubes. It didn't help. The blood gushed, spraying all over the polished floors.

"Chaka." Piper gasped in horror while dashing toward me.

Her reaction was about ten seconds too late. After my first two feeble steps toward the bathroom, my body began to sway from side to side. My head spun around in circles while I watched the room rotate, making me dizzier by the second. As I lifted my foot to take a third step, my body had already gone limp. Unable to balance, I reached for the metal locker in front of me but it was a finger tip too far away. There was nothing to break my fall as I felt myself get closer to the floor. Finally, I just closed my eyes and let go.

I don't really remember much after that. By the time I came to, I was on a stretcher being hauled off into an ambulance while the fatigue-wearing military police were putting restraints on Piper.

Flashbacks of my past vividly reappeared in front of me before drifting back into an unconscious realm, primarily created from the morphine shot into my arm by the trauma nurse who asked, "Seaman Recruit Adams, when was the last time you had your menstruation?"

Malik's face, with a smug smile exposing his crooked choppers, appeared in front of me as I shamefully recalled the last time I had sex. *Fucking bastard* – I knew that pathetic tryst across my dining room table would come back to haunt me. That little motherfucker always had a way of squirming back into my life.

Chapter 3

I heard the nurse talking and although my body was there, my mind was traveling somewhere else. It was like it was when I was a kid. When things got crazy back then, I would imagine I was another person who lived a life in a far away land with horse carriages, fairy-godmothers and a whole bunch of other make believe shit that Disney tricked me into thinking could really happen. The Chaka in my head was way better than the Chaka in reality. So when the nurse asked questions, instead of facing the truth, I did the only thing I knew how to do. I closed my eyes and imagined I was somewhere else - drifting off, back to a time when life was so much simpler.

CHIGGY

"Prr-rr-ro," I stuttered.

Even at six years old, my sassy attitude was front and center. After sucking my teeth out of mere frustration, I tried to pronounce the unfamiliar word yet again. "P-ro-hib-i."

Standing on the Queens Plaza train station platform, my mother knelt by my side as she rubbed my shoulders like a basketball coach schooling a star athlete on how to make the game winning shot.

"Chiggy, don't rush it," she said.

I loved when she called me Chiggy, even though my childhood nickname sounded like it should have been used to describe a fat kid, which was the complete opposite of my skinny-mini self. It seemed like a term of endearment when my family said it though so I didn't mind.

"Try it again. Just sound out all the syllables, one letter at a time. Remember what I told you Chaka, pretty girls read."

What? Did she just call me pretty?

My mother always knew how to get my little conceited ass to act accordingly. I took a long deep breath and attacked that word like a Spelling Bee champ.

"Pro-hib-it-ed," I said, before completing the entire sentence. "Entering the tracks is stric-a-tal-ly prohibited."

My head was gassed. In my eyes, reading that sentence automatically made me pretty, which caused me to smile from ear to ear, exposing a full row of gapped teeth.

"Mommy, what does prohibited mean?" I asked, that time mastering the word like a pro.

"It means, 'not allowed'. Like, 'something you can't do'," she explained.

Placing my left finger into the small dimple of my cheek, I cocked my head to the sky and pondered her definition for a minute, repeating the sentence in my head, *"Entering the tracks is strictly prohibited."*

To make sure I understood it correctly, I looked back at her and asked for confirmation, "So, that means that you can't be on the tracks, right?"

My mom nodded in agreement and smirked, surely with an admiration for the light bulbs going off in my prepubescent head. The wheels were spinning. I stayed quiet and allowed my brain to work its magic. In order to comprehend what that sentence really meant, I had to act out this long dramatic scenario in my head. *Eureka!* A ringing bell chimed and I finally got it.

"Well, I guess Ramón didn't read that sign," I said, pointing toward the plaque that clearly had the words spelled out.

My mother, with her eyebrows raised, looked at me all confused-like and asked, "Ramón? Who the hell is Ramón?"

I shook my head in disbelief.

"*Beat Street*, Mommy. Don't you remember?" I paused to give her a chance to catch on while waving my hands for her to hurry it up. "Ramón from that movie, *Beat Street*. 'Member? He got electrocuted on the tracks 'cuz he was doing graffiti. But if he woulda just read the sign, he woulda knew he was prohibited to get on them."

I explained it to her, shrugging my shoulders like, *Duh! Why couldn't she put that together herself?*

"Yeah, I guess he didn't read it Chiggy."

She agreed but I could tell it was more so just to appease her little smart ass daughter than actually remembering the cult-classic movie or its main character. Her memory wasn't like mine, which was almost photographic according to my pediatricians. I'm not sure if I was really smart or if I was just able to remember everything. Either way, there wasn't too much stuff that went over my head.

Things came easy to me; at least when it came to school. When I was in the second grade, I read on a sixth grade level. By the time I got to the fifth grade, I was reading high school books like *Macbeth* and *To Kill a Mockingbird*.

Even though mastering that classic literature at such a young age might make me seem all learned and whatnot, my love of books came from constantly reading *Dopefiend* by Donald Goines. I'd sneak the pocket sized paperback into my bed at night and read it cover to cover at least once a month. My parents had all his classics like *Black Girl Lost* and *Whoreson* but my first affair with word play and storytelling came from his brutal tale of a young and turned out fiend named Terry. Donald Goines was a writer who could make you smell the ooze of a puss-filled abscess as a heroin laced syringe slid deep through a heartless junkie's corroded artery.

He was ill.

Because I read a lot, I was exposed to all types of characters. My knack for surviving the streets undoubtedly came from a little piece of all of them. This was evident in my parents' world where split-personalities played a major role in their hustle. Luckily, my bipolar ass fit right in.

As we waited on the platform, the downtown N train bound for Manhattan's 14th Street Union Square pulled into the station. Our hours of hustling had reached the climax which meant the grinding part was done. Earlier that day, we were in and out of local pharmacies from sun up to sun down. My parents stayed one step ahead of the typical cons and dopefiend shenanigans. Their street game was on some smart and sophisticated shit. Actually, they were way ahead of their time if you ask me.

My mother, raised by a Bahamian immigrant, was brought up with a sense of entitlement. Non-American Blacks always thought they were better than Blacks or African-Americans or whatever politically correct racial description we're using this year. Either way, her elitist upbringing was the perfect complement to my father's schemes because she added an heir of class regardless of how grimy the action.

On the flip side, my father was a mastermind of the jook. If there was a Nobel Prize for street smarts, he would have won hands down. It wasn't only his education from the South Bronx School of Hard Knocks that helped him succeed, he was also an intellectual in his own right. Daddy could recite every speech Malcolm X ever made, then in the same breath turn around and sing his favorite folksong, "The Signifying Monkey".

As kids, we rode the trains chanting every verse as loud as possible, *"Said the signifying monkey to the lion one day, there was a great big elephant 'round the way."*

The White people would look at us like we were characters from the *Amos 'n' Andy* minstrel show but we didn't care. We kept signing our song anyway, *"He goin' 'round talkin' I'm sorry to say, about yo' mama in a scandalous way..."*

But Daddy knew more than just carrying a note or two. He was also a mathematic savant who could look at numbers and immediately calculate them to a percentage without pen, paper or a calculator.

Their new hustle put us in the medical profession despite not having a PhD. My father was ill with his handiwork and could recreate doctor prescriptions which he'd use to supply Valiums, Xanax and Codeine to all the White yuppies down in Greenwich Village, which was the Mecca of New York if you let a WASP tell it. We'd go to the doctor for some bullshit sickness or another and then once we got a prescription, usually for penicillin, my father would work his artistic magic. He'd carefully white-out the patient's name and prescribed medication, then adjust the lighting of the corner store's five cents per copy Xerox machine just enough to make the duplicates look authentic. Before you knew it, he had a whole pad of hospital approved, doctor administered scripts.

You would have never known Daddy lacked formal pharmaceutical training because he studied medical school books just like he was reading *The Daily News*. He knew the abbreviations for drugs and how to measure correct daily dosages based on sex, age and weight.

Despite his skills, it was my mother's chameleon like

charm that made people comfortable enough to lend her their government issued Medicaid cards which were used to cover the costs of all the medicine. Of course she'd give them a few dollars for their troubles and seduce them with dreams of lucrative returns but if they ever got caught, they'd be facing federal time. It didn't matter though. Once they realized the consequences, my mother was already walking out the door with the ghetto's American Express card that could be used for both legal drugs and late term abortions.

I was just included for assurance. Inherently armed with both their traits, I was the icing on the cake. When we were hustling, I had to always be on my best behavior and play which ever role we had come up with like I was auditioning for a role in a Broadway play.

Lights. Camera. Action.

"Yes, she's getting much better but she still can't be too mobile just yet. When she's able to get around, I'll definitely bring her here to meet you. I always tell her how good you treat us," my mother said, smiling at the Jewish pharmacist behind the counter.

"Yup, Mr. Horowitz, we're going to see her once we leave here so I can read her my favorite book from school. I can't wait either. I'm in the second grade now, you know," I bragged to the pharmacist, melodically annunciating all my words like some dramatic soliloquy.

Of course I knew there was no patient and my mother wasn't really a home health-aide, despite the green city-issued medical scrubs she wore that were stolen during one of our routine hospital visits along with a stethoscope and the emergency room doctor's prescription pad. But I also knew White people had a hard time denying the little pretty Black girl who was all so 'articulate'. I was simply giving those crackers what they wanted and their dumbasses ate it up every single time.

"Well, that's very nice of you. I'm sure she'll like that," Mr. Horowitz's nasal voice spoke out from above the sounds of pills pouring into bottles as he filled our prescription.

I felt like a little Lolita – unsure if he was impressed with my intelligence or secretly wanted to give me some candy in the back of his brown van with the dark tinted windows. Either way, I'd use his weakness to my advantage.

And just like that, I knew we had him. All I had to do was play pretend and it always worked. My short legs swung back and forth as we sat in the waiting area and I chomped on my gold aluminum wrapped Cadbury chocolate candy bar. I looked over at my mom to gauge her reaction. Winking her eye, she threw me an underhanded smile. She approved of my performance and that was all I really wanted in the first place.

"Seaman Recruit Adams," the visiting nurse whispered, her voice thrusting me from my stroll down memory lane and back to reality where I was lying in a military hospital.

I looked in her direction, blankly staring beyond the stumpy woman standing in front of me. I forced myself to pretend like I had this shit under control but deep inside, I only wanted to whimper underneath my bed sheets.

"Adams," she repeated, roughly jabbing her index finger into my thigh. "I came to talk to you about your options."

Her voice provided no comfort. The surgeon already delivered my diagnosis before she even entered the room. Apparently all that blood was way more than just my period, which had somehow managed to skip two months without a worry from my dumb ass. I'm usually good at keeping track of my cycle but with boot camp and all the shit that was going on back home, I just thought my body was under stress or something and that it would eventually get back on schedule. I couldn't have been further from the truth.

In fact, I had an ectopic pregnancy which caused the egg to plant itself in my tubes where it grew like a normal baby. Once it got too big, it ripped me apart from the inside out. If I didn't get to the hospital when I did, the doctors said I would have died from infection. To make matters worse, the tube was ruptured beyond repair. By the time I regained consciousness, it had already been surgically removed. There I lie, with a reproductively destroyed womb, while this stupid ass nurse wanted to discuss options. I'm sure that bitch had all of her female organs intact so what the fuck did she know?

According to the doctors, I probably had an undiagnosed case of Chlamydia which fucked my tubes all up. Of course that nasty shit had to have been courtesy of Malik's trifling ass as a result of him running up in random chicks. I should have left him the first time he stepped out on me. Perhaps my life would have turned out much better if I did.

"We were able to keep your other tube so you can very well get pregnant again someday." She smiled like she was delivering word to Mary that unto her a man-child would be born.

"You act like that's good news or something. How do I know this won't happen again?"

"Well." Her voice was terse. "You only have that one fallopian tube left and about seventy percent of it is blocked with scar tissue. Maybe you should have been more selective with your sexual partners, Miss Adams. But I'm not here to judge you. God already did that. See, the way it looks now, you might never get pregnant again if you keep that attitude up. I swear, you people need to be more optimistic."

With that, she sashayed her arrogant ass out of my room.

And that's what that bitch called options.

Chapter 4

"**S**ignature here, please."
I signed it.
"And here."

Again, I signed as the redheaded nurse, wearing a too tight for her cleavage Navy dress blue uniform, requested. It was all a formality really. It wasn't like I was in the Navy long enough to be considered a veteran so sitting there at the Veteran's Hospital, signing discharge papers, was really a waste of everybody's time. However, the bosom buddy in front of me, with her triple-D boobs nearly popping out through her buttoned up blouse, kept passing me the forms. With no other options, I just kept signing.

Once I ended up in the emergency room, only one week before graduating from basic training, the military had to let me go. There was no way I could finish boot camp and possibly go to war after the shock my body suffered from that tubal pregnancy. My condition was too much of a liability for America. I mean, I was on welfare my whole life and the government never denied footing my medical bills any other time. Apparently, it was a different case when it came to the Armed Forces. They had no intentions of being responsible for my well being. The funny thing was that I received better care from a Medicaid clinic than I ever did at the Veteran's Hospital.

The recovery rooms were extremely small with dreary off-white paint that cracked along the walls. In addition to mine, there were three other lumpy mattresses on rusty bed frames lined up around me. One stack of pillows belonged to a very familiar face. Somehow my right hand accomplice, Piper, had earned herself a spot right next to me.

After the fight, she was brought into the hospital where they feverishly pumped her stomach of the same 800-miligram Motrins that I begged her to get for me. According to the medics, she tried to commit suicide. The stunt landed her a one-way ticket home and an administrative discharge under honorable conditions.

"When you ever heard of somebody dying from some fucking Motrin? Come on, Chaka. I ain't stupid," Piper whispered one morning while we both awaited our walking papers.

I laughed in amazement, knowing full well that conniving trickster did that shit on purpose. Once the military found out about the fight, they would have dishonorably thrown her ass out after forcing her to spend thirty days in the brig which was much worse than civilian jail. Her alleged suicide attempt saved her from a lifelong blemish on her record and afforded her a respectable discharge.

"What you gonna do when you get out of here?" She asked.

I heard her question and up until that point, I hadn't even allowed my thoughts to get that far ahead of me. What the fuck was I going to do when I left there? It wasn't like I had anywhere to go. Queensbridge was out of the question for more reasons than just Manny. I mean, shit, my mother had a two bedroom apartment and I'd be damned if I was about to shack up on a pull-out couch with my brothers again.

Grunting, I slapped both hands on my forehead, rubbing my temples in deep thought.

"I don't even know, Piper. This shit is all types of fucked up."

If it wasn't one thing, it was a motherfucking 'nother. I was beginning to think I had a dark cloud just sitting above my head, constantly following me despite any new direction I traveled. Every time I tried to do right, I somehow managed to fuck it up and go left. Whether I was in the wrong place or with the wrong people, I was a bullshit magnet and regardless of how hard I tried, I could never get away from it.

"What you gonna do when you leave here?"

I figured thinking about my dead-end wouldn't have changed matters much, so I turned the tables on her.

"Well," she replied with a nonchalant shoulder shrug. "I'm going back home. I still got my apartment. Maybe I could still get my job back."

Her sudden employment status shocked me. I didn't figure her to be the working type.

"Get your job back? I thought you was hustling before you came here?"

"Umm, hello, you always gotta keep a legal gig even with a side hustle. Where the fuck you been?"

Obviously I hadn't been in the right places. Before joining the Navy, I never had job. Shit, I didn't even work for the Summer Youth programs where the city gave out bi-weekly minimum wage checks to all the teenagers in the hood. Matter of fact, my lazy ass never had working papers, which were required for employment before the age of eighteen. It didn't matter to me because I knew how to get money so the thought of a nine-to-five never crossed my mind. I figured that as long as I had a gold mine between my thighs, there'd always be a money-getting man on my heels ready to pad my pockets.

"Oh, well I mean, you made it seem like you were getting paper. I didn't know you had to work for it."

"I never said I *had* to work." She snarled her upper-lip. "But I ain't sitting on my back waiting for a check every month either. You can't meet money if you ain't somewhere making money."

Damn, she was right. How the fuck would I ever meet somebody outside of the projects if I never had a reason to venture beyond my comfort zone?

"Well, what type of work do you do?"

"A little this and a little that." She chuckled. "But mostly, I work at a club. It's cool. The money is good and I meet a lot of people who know people, who know people."

"So, you're a bartender or waitress or something?"

"Yeah, something like that."

She didn't offer any more explanations and I didn't ask. Anytime I ever went to a club, the chicks were either serving drinks or taking orders. It didn't seem like it took too much experience to do either and all the ballers I knew were heavy tippers so perhaps she did have a good job, once I thought about it.

"And you make good money doing that?"

I had to ask. I mean, I'm not really the one for all that serving people and shit.

"You have no idea, boo!" She held her hand up, rubbing her fingertips together. "You can come to Philly with me if you want.

My job is always looking for a new face."

"Philly? What the fuck? I don't know nothing about no damn Philadelphia. Girl, bye."

I looked at her, turning my lips up in disgust. I was going through some serious shit and there she was, talking about some damn place that I had never even visited. Besides, we were cool but I didn't know her like that. For all I knew, she could've been living in some damn roach motel.

She immediately snapped back. "Hold up, I was just trying to be nice. It ain't like you got a whole bunch of other choices. I heard you on the phone and I don't think anybody is waiting for you back home with open doors. So, excuse me for keeping it real. My bad. By all means, rock the fuck out boo-boo."

I knew I hurt her feelings once she snapped her fingers, got up and stormed her way to the bathroom, slamming the door behind her.

Even though I hated boot camp, meeting Piper made it a little more tolerable. My time in the military was too brief to qualify for any type of discharge with money. So she was right, the only thing I was getting was a bus ticket to anywhere within the contiguous forty-eight states along with a letter of recommendation for time served. There I was, right back where I started. Except this time, I was completely on my own. My friends had scattered like roaches being hit with a light switch in a project kitchen. Once things blew the fuck up, they all vanished like shadows in the daylight. They say, "Misery loves company", but in my case, misery didn't have any company left to love.

Ta-Ta wasn't fucking with me in the least bit. I kept calling. I kept writing letters. I even talked to my recruiter to see if he could work his magic and get her in the Navy right along with me. I did everything I could do, short of going back to that dreadful night and trading places with her. Had I known that Malik was going to wild out, I would have never let her be so vulnerable. But who knew that motherfucker could hold so much hate in his heart for me and anybody close to me? My battered brain couldn't predict how an occasional punch in the face or choke of the neck would lead to premeditated murder; or at least an attempt at that shit.

I guess since I didn't pack my bags and get the fuck out or get gully and bash that motherfucker over the head with a metal skillet, I should have known it was only going to get worse after the first time he beat my ass.

"If this bitch don't leave me after this, she ain't never gonna leave me."

I'm sure that's what Malik was thinking and honestly, he was absolutely right. My acceptance gave him power. Once I made my move to get away from him, I should have been prepared for the fight of my life. Unluckily for me, I didn't know that back then. My fear was his lifeline but my strength was his lethal injection. In a way, I killed him long before he tried to do the same to Ta-Ta.

My mother always told me, "When you take away a man's power over you, you take away his balls. And if he doesn't have any balls, then he ain't a man."

I wrapped Malik's manhood around my pinky finger the day I told his sorry ass to get the fuck out of my apartment. His pride wouldn't let me get away with that.

Still, Ta-Ta blamed me for her attack and because she did, the Thelma to my Louise was gone. I laid there, gazing at the gravel ceiling in the cold of my hospital roomand thought back to the last time I saw her. She had been my side since the day she came to check on me in my old apartment, which because of all the bullshit that had transpired within those walls, I referred to as my *Little Shop of Horrors*. People in the projects joked that we were each other's better halves. Where ever they saw one, the other wouldn't be too far behind.

When I was struggling with hand-me-downs, after Malik's downfall, she was right there picking me back up with shopping sprees at the Woodbury Commons Outlets in New York and local shit like Macy's Herald Square. Falling from the top in the projects sets off an imaginary alarm to every ravenous scavenger within hearing distance, letting them know there was fresh meat on the chopping block. They longed for the opportunity to peck at whatever sense of self-esteem I still had lingering after my man fell off. Although there wasn't much left, those trolls were happy to devour whatever they could.

After everything I went through, I barely had the strength to do anything more but ignore their little snide remarks. My role as a self-centered hood princess evaporated in the blink of an eye. How the fuck was I supposed to show any confidence after that?

But Ta-Ta wasn't having it and had enough cockiness for

the both of us. The moment a broad turned her lips up or even looked at me with a hint of disrespect, my best friend was quick to pop off in my defense.

The whole Thelma and Louise shit took on a life of its own. Beyond what everybody saw from the outside, we shared bonding moments that would stay with us for a lifetime.

Back in the day, we made a pinky swear to never wear sneakers. We really thought the ladies wearing the highest heels were the ultimate vixens so we swore to wear nothing less than three-inch pumps or leather ankle boots. Our transformation to womanhood would be evident through our choice of shoes or so we thought. This code of honor lasted for about two seasons, winter and spring. By the time summer rolled around, we each snuck off and copped a pair of white classic K-Swiss sneakers, the ones with the metal circles around the shoe string holes. Our sneaky asses waited until the first hot day of the year before either one of us rocked them – coming outside looking like some Bobbsey Twins. We laughed once we realized we both broke the pinky swear at the same damn time. There was nothing we could do but happily switch our asses around the hood in our rubber bottoms. Great minds thought alike and Ta-Ta was like the left side of my brain. When I went right, she went left but somehow we always managed to be heading in the same direction.

Despite the fact that we grew up and became women together, she wouldn't even speak to me. Although it hurt, I had to accept the fact that there was nothing I could do to change that. Shit, I was half-way across the country. It's not like I could have spoken to her face to face.

As for Carmen, the only hot-blooded Latina in our clique, she finally bagged herself a money-maker. Riding in BMWs and wearing full-length chinchillas was an everyday occurrence in her world. I heard the dude she was fucking with had ties to Alpo, who was at one point in time, the King of Harlem's drug world.

She was another one who didn't respond to my letters or phone calls. As she told Dana, who later told me, joining the Navy was my first step toward a life full of lame shit. She chose to distance herself from that by keeping her interactions with me at a bare minimum. Actually, they were non-existent.

Zakia, who was Ta-Ta's older sister and the crew's Mother Hen, was working on her next baby as was my Afrocentric turned born-again Christian friend, Sophie. I didn't really expect them to stay in touch. It's not like I wanted to talk about diapers, formula and colic remedies anyway. So, I didn't bother reaching out to them either.

However, I still had Dana, the wild-child drunk who claimed that 'maintaining her sexy' meant rocking linen suits and designer penny loafers. She was there to accept every one of my phone calls and I counted on her to send me weekly letters, updating me on all the shit going on in the hood. Although I wasn't in boot camp for that long, it felt like a lifetime.

It's not like she had anything better to do. By her third letter, she admitted to being five months pregnant. It was too late to get an abortion at that time so she kept her baby; not that she would have gotten rid of him anyway. Despite her buck wild antics, she had moral beliefs that didn't include a pair of forceps and a vaginal vacuum.

Her baby's father wasn't shit though. After finding out she was pregnant, he dropped her like a bad habit. That was fucked up because he was probably the first dude she really loved. Or at least what all of us young, dumb and full of cum, chicks thought was love anyway.

In retrospect, he did her a favor by not stepping up to his responsibilities because he later turned out to be a non-productive alcoholic who clearly wouldn't have been a good father any fucking way. Her son was better off without him.

I hadn't yet had the opportunity to tell her that I was pregnant too. Well, that I had been pregnant. Actually, I didn't want anybody back home to know. Not my mother. Not my cousin, Taylor. Not Dana. Not anybody. I felt like a failure and in all reality, I was. I left Queensbridge with every hope of finally making something of myself. Yet, there I was, getting kicked out of the one place that gave me an opportunity to escape that maze of six blocks and ninety-six buildings.

My life was always fifty shades of fucked up.

"Miss Adams."

The fire-crotch Dolly Parton looking nurse had already dropped the Seaman Recruit shit, being as though my enlistment was coming to an abrupt end.

"You're being discharged tomorrow morning. You need to let us know where to book your ticket."

I knew the time was coming but I wished they would have

waited a little longer. Shit, my abdomen still clenched tightly every time I moved. Though the blood had somewhat lightened up, I was still soaking through the thick old lady sanitary napkins they had given me. Clearly I wasn't in the best position to leave but I sure wasn't going to be able to stay there. They made that crystal clear.

I looked over at Piper, who had returned from the bathroom and was packing her toiletries in a black duffle bag. Finally, it hit me. The couple thousand dollars Salerno sent me would be just enough to get on my feet. It wouldn't last long but with the right moves, I could make it work. And the only person I could trust at that point was right there beside me.

"Philadelphia," I said, pausing long enough to watch Piper's reaction. "Get me a ticket to Philadelphia."

Piper turned toward me while shaking her head no and rolling her eyes.

Jokingly, she teased, "Umm, who told you that you could still come with me with your 'I'm too good for Philadelphia' ass?"

"All I know is you better not be living in no dirty ass apartment," I said, throwing my pillow toward her bed and catching her right in the face.

She shrugged and threw me a smirk. "Girl, it ain't much but we gon' grind together. Gotta get on our grizzy like the new Wolf Pack. Early."

"What? I don't understand all that mumbo jumbo."

Her slang was so different than the shit we spit in Queensbridge but once I got beyond her word choice, I knew exactly what she meant. She was starting from the bottom just like me. Together, we would build as counterparts. I know some people might put a time span on a new friendship, as if knowing someone longer makes them a better friend or something. **Wrong!** I learned enough about people to know that it's always the closest ones to you who shit on you the fastest. The bitch patting you on the back today is the same one looking for the softest spot to plunge her knife tomorrow. Once you expand beyond the people you knew all your life, you just have to take chances and trust your instincts. For all intents and purposes, Piper was good people to me from the very start. Although I didn't know her for that long, she would prove to be more loyal than most of the females I had know from my childhood. We'd definitely have to travel a long road before I came to that conclusion but Piper made sure it was a ride I would never forget.

"Don't worry, girl, we got this," she said, as she plunged on my bed, hugging me tightly. "Buckle up, we on a mission."

"Come on, yo." I slapped her arm away, while covering my aching stomach. "My shit is still fucked up."

"You gon' be aight." This time, she gently placed her hand on top of mine. "Fuck it. Friends 'til the end."

Before I knew it, the sun was rising and we were both getting dropped off at the Greyhound station in downtown Chicago about an hour's drive from the Recruit Training Command. That was the last of my Navy careerand truth be told, I was ready for whatever awaited me. I copped a squat in a seat near the back of the bus and the driver took off. Who the fuck knew where this ride would lead?

Chapter 5

The nineteen hour trip from Chicago to Philadelphia was about the most uncomfortable thing I ever had the displeasure of sitting through. Cramped between crying babies, welfare mothers with black plastic garbage bags for luggage and dirty trailer trash who smelled like a bottle of moonshine mixed with Jean Naté body spray, I popped a few of the pain pills I had leftover from the VA Hospital and tried to sleep. It didn't help because as soon as I nodded off, the little brat behind me would kick the back of my chair. I turned around and gave his mother a look which I hoped would've prompted her to control her offspring of Satan. Clearly, she didn't see anything wrong with his behavior because he kept on kicking and she kept on jamming to her broken headphones that blasted music loud enough for the whole bus to hear. The disrespectful apple didn't fall far from that rotten tree.

Piper sat across from me and laughed every time I scratched my arms with the thought of bugs jumping on me from one of the other passengers. We were seated in the back of the bus where the stench of the bathroom caused a gag reflex every time somebody opened the door. Apparently she was used to these long ass bus rides as she so happily admitted to making runs up and down I-95 on a regular basis. Not me though. Riding through Detroit, Cleveland and then Pittsburgh, I nearly flew out of my seat once we pulled into the Filbert Street Greyhound Station in Philadelphia.

"Excuse me," I yelled at some slow ass lady as she grabbed her bags from the overhead compartment.

She was old and I should have helped her but all I wanted to do was run the fuck out for a breath of fresh air.

"Nah, I can't wait," I snapped at Piper who moved at a snail's pace while telling me to slow down.

I felt claustrophobic and couldn't wait to get off of that germ-ridden bus.

"Ahhhhhh." I exhaled loudly once my feet hit the concrete.

Immediately, I realized Philadelphia was kind of like a little New York. The station was smack dab in the middle of downtown and right outside the doors were crackheads begging for money along with homeless people sprawled out on the corner. A line of yellow cabs stretched down the block and we jumped into the first one available. If I didn't know any better, I would have thought I was in Times Square. Except, there were no bright lights or knee-high boot wearing prostitutes posted up outside of a 24-hour Peep Show Theatre.

"633 West Rittenhouse Street," Piper yelled to the African cabbie who smelled like he never heard of deodorant yet alone rolled one along his armpits.

The address sounded fancy to me. *Rittenhouse Street.* Hell, at least she didn't live on Martin Luther King Jr. Blvd because regardless of what hood you're in, any street with that name is bound to be located in the most ratchet part of town.

We drove through the city and it felt like home. There weren't as many skyscrapers as Manhattan but you could definitely tell it was a major metropolitan with lots of people and cars bustling along.

"That's where they filmed that movie, *Rocky.* Remember when Sylvester Stallone was running up the stairs?" Piper said, pointing to the steep steps of the Philadelphia Museum of Art.

I peered out the window like a kid on a field trip "Oh shit, they even got a statue of him up there."

A nostalgic feeling came over me once I saw the bronze boxing gloved replica standing at the top of the steps with his arms raised above his head in victory. As a child I would watch that movie over and over again. Actually, the one when Apollo Creed was killed had given me a long standing hatred toward Russians. So looking at the Rocky statue, in all his glory, gave me a little vindication.

That was my first time out of Queensbridge, in a big city, with absolutely nobody but my damn self. Besides Piper, I had never even met anyone from Philly. Thoughts of starting a new sent chills up my spine.

We drove down a long narrow road, with the Schuylkill River

flowing along the driver's side of the car. Across the river were more lights and highways. As we approached a curve, the driver made a sharp turn along the two lane strip. We barely swerved quick enough to dodge the oncoming car as its horn blared loudly.

"Yo, chill out. Where's the fire?" Piper snapped at the driver before turning toward me. "You gotta be careful over here. This is Lincoln Drive, girl, this shit ain't no joke. This is where Teddy Pendergrass got paralyzed."

"How the fuck you know about some damn Teddy Pendergrass?"

I turned toward her, picturing her non-English speaking parents jamming out to "Turn Off The Lights".

"I told you, I'm really a Black chick trapped in an Asian girl's body."

"You ain't lying."

By the time I gained enough courage to open my eyes again after that treacherous ride, we were pulling up to her red bricked twenty-two story apartment building. White letters that read *Rittenhouse Square*, were plastered along the green awning which lead to glass double-doors. The doorman, fully clothed in a green uniform and hat, sat at the front desk.

"Miss Piper, you're back," he said, tipping his hat in our direction.

"Yes, John. Unfortunately, things didn't quite work out like I had previously intended."

Piper's voice switched to some proper shit at the drop of a dime. Stunned, I looked at her to make sure I wasn't imagining the words coming out of her mouth.

Where the fuck was the hoodrat I came to know in boot camp?

"John, this is my friend, Chaka. She'll be staying with me for awhile. Chaka, this is John."

"Hello Miss Chaka. Nice to meet you."

We shook hands but I didn't verbally respond. For one, I wasn't used to doormen or people calling me Miss. Secondly, I was scared some ghetto shit would come flying out like diarrhea of the mouth. Sure, I knew how to turn on my White girl charm, just like Piper did, but I was so rusty that I didn't know if I still possessed that ability. The last time I used proper English was in high school and even then I made sure my Queensbridge friends were nowhere around. From as far back as I could remember, I was always chastised and picked on for 'talking White'. In my feeble attempts to fit in with the people closest to me, I'd use more slang so that I talked their talk and walked their walk.

"If you need anything, just let me know. I'm always here." John was reassuring as he buzzed the side door, letting us into one of the two sections of Piper's building.

"This is nice," I finally said, while walking along the carpeted corridor leading to the mirrored elevator.

"Oh, don't get gassed, girl. I live in a studio but the building will make motherfuckers think I live in a penthouse."

And just like that, she was ghetto again.

The elevator stopped on the ninth floor and opened up to a long hallway that looked like a scene from *The Shining*. Piper stood in front of apartment 918 and unlocked the door. Once we entered, I realized she wasn't exaggerating when she said she lived in a studio. The queen-size bed was across the room, adjacent to a computer desk that held her nineteen inch television. By the time I got all the way into the apartment, I felt like I was already at the foot of her bed. There was hardly any room to drop my bags.

"This is the kitchen." She pointed, while opening two French doors revealing a hidden kitchenette. "And the bathroom is right around that corner."

With a few steps, I had walked through every inch of her apartment.

Where the fuck am I gonna sleep?

"I cut the cable off before I went to boot camp but I got some movies if you wanna watch something. My ass is tired so I'ma hop in this shower and crash."

She started to undress right in front of me which made me turn away. Her lack of inhibition completely shocked the hell out of me. I sat on the folding chair and started to rummage through my bags looking for some pajamas. Shit, I was exhausted after that long ass bus ride as well and all I wanted was a good night's sleep.

"You got some blankets or something for me to lay on?" I asked, trying to seem like I wasn't staring at her naked body.

"Chaka, you don't have to sleep on the floor. There's enough space for both of us in that damn bed. Here." She passed me some sheets from the linen closet beside the bathroom. "I don't remember changing them before I left so you can make the bed while I get in the shower."

As she closed the bathroom door, my eyes welled up. Here I was, with a new friend who didn't know me from a can of paint, yet she was willing to open her home to me without any questions or expectations. She didn't have much but the little bit she did have, was shared without a second thought. Once she got out the shower, I hopped in right behind her. Tomorrow would start a new day for me, full of new opportunities, in a new city with a whole new game plan. Eventually, I would have to tell my mother that I got kicked out of the Navy but for the time being, I would just let her think I was still enlisted. What she didn't know, wouldn't hurt her.

Piper was already snoring by the time my head hit the pillow. Tossing and turning, until I found a comfortable spot, I said a prayer for God to direct my steps because Lord knows I had no idea what the fuck I was getting into. However, as long as I had Piper by my side, I knew I wasn't going to be alone. From that day forward, she was my new ride or die chick. My mother always told me that I would find my real friends once I left Queensbridge. Like the saying goes, "Mother knows best".

"Piper." I nudged her lightly.

"Whaaaaattttt?"

"I just wanna say thank you. I really appreciate this. For real."

"Don't sweat it, Chaka. That's what friends do for each other. You good. But if you wake me up one more time, we got beef."

Before I could say anything more, she was snoring again. I shut my eyes and pictured how my new life was going to pan out. It would be a struggle but my mother didn't raise a quitter. Failure wasn't an option.

Chapter 6

Shit was a lot rougher than what I expected. Three months flew by as I quickly blew through Salerno's money. Piper's rent was nine hundred a month and I offered to pay the first two months upfront. Although she hesitated to take my money at first, I wasn't taking no for an answer. It was important to me that I held my own weight. Once those months passed and I still hadn't found a job, or met up with some dude who would sponsor my pockets, I had to really hit the ground and hustle up some sort of income.

Piper never made me feel any bad vibes though. If she went out for drinks, she brought me along and paid for me. Whenever she cooked, she made sure there was enough for both of us to eat. I wasn't used to paying for lights and water but she covered my portion of those bills as well. Everything was free in the projects. Besides paying for cable and the phone bill, we didn't worry about utilities so those new expenses came as a surprise to my non-budgeting ass. I kept telling Piper that I'd pay her back as soon as I could but she never sweated me about it. She had my back way more than I could have ever expected from a new friend.

I still couldn't bring myself to tell my mother that I had gotten kicked out of the Navy. To the best of her knowledge, I was on a top secret mission and couldn't divulge my whereabouts. Yes, that was my story and I was sticking to it. Had I told her the truth, she would have given me a long drawn out song and dance on how I needed to come home and find a job or some dumb shit like that. My mother didn't understand the street shit I was going through. Things were different from when she was growing up in Queensbridge. There was no loyalty anymore. No camaraderie. There was no way in hell I could go back there again. My pride wouldn't allow it. So, every time I called her, I would block the number and make up some quick excuse on why she couldn't call me back. The lies were mounting up and I knew eventually I would have to tell her the truth, but for the time being, I was riding with it.

As soon as we got to Philly, Piper went right back to work. She said she would talk to her boss to find out if there were any openings. In the meantime, I learned how to ride the Philadelphia train system, which they called SEPTA. It wasn't that difficult, really. If I could navigate the New York subways, I could surely master the two trains they had the nerve to call mass transit. Because we lived in Germantown, which was one of Philadelphia's suburban areas, they also had a regional rail system. I had to take those trains to get to the underground ones that eventually led me to the heart of Philly. I only took the twenty dollar cab ride to the city when I was feeling lazy which didn't occur often since I was also trying to live off of my last couple of dollars.

After my constant inquiries, Piper finally talked to her boss and scheduled an interview for me. I thought shit was about to change for the better. I thought wrong.

Now, I should have known something was up because Piper would leave for work around seven in the evening and not return until like four in the morning. By the time she walked through our door, she was pissy drunk with a face full of make-up and smudged mascara. She told me she worked at a club so I didn't really think twice about her hours but I should have looked more closely at the duffle bag she carried with her every day. I'm not the nosy type but if I were, I would have definitely noticed the six inch platforms and g-string bikinis she toted along with the garter belts and make-up bags. For some reason, my slow ass didn't put two and two together until the day I went in for my interview.

Using my last twenty dollars, I took a cab to the city. It pulled up in front of a discreet brick building with a simple sign on the front that said, *SIGNATURES*. Located on Locust Street, in the heart of Philly's prosperous Center City, the entrance of the club was full of White businessmen in crisp suits and expensive shoes. The valet dude, a young boy with blonde hair and freckles, opened the cab door and let me out. I saw money all around me but I didn't know how they would be spending it. I walked through the club's doors despite the strong whiff of Victoria's Secret body spray almost knocking me off my feet.

"So, what do you want your stage name to be?" The head bartender asked when I told her I was there to see the manager.

"Huh," I answered, "my stage name?"

"Yeah, how should the DJ announce you?"

It was the sort of question that should have made red lights go off in my head but this shit was still pretty new to me. I had never been in a club as fancy as *SIGNATURES*. Looking around made me optimistic about the types of tips I could get from waiting on tables.

The waitresses wore skimpy black vinyl shorts with half their butt cheeks hanging out. They all had on white wife beaters with the club's name outlined in rhinestones along with a black bow tie. My little bee-sting titties were nothing compared to the obviously silicone enhanced bimbos strutting around but I was pretty enough to definitely stand out. I hadn't seen Piper yet so I just assumed she was probably in the back somewhere.

"Well, they're about to do the showcase so just sit right here and I'll be back to talk to you about the position."

Showcase?

Again, I felt like I was in the twilight zone with absolutely no idea of what was going on.

The club was enchanting. Gaudy gold mirrors aligned the walls along with red velvet booths. There was a stage in the middle of the dance floor which seemed odd to me at first but then I thought it must be for performers because it was oval shaped without any obstructions blocking a customer's view. I wondered if this was a hip hop club that brought out an occasional rapper or two. Then again, since I was in a White club, they probably catered to those types of singers who played acoustic guitars and covered Eric Clapton songs. Besides, the stage wasn't that big so I doubted they could fit a rapper's entire entourage of groupie friends. I scanned the room but still, no Piper.

Suddenly, the lights went out and a bright spotlight shone causing the crowd to quiet down and focus their attention to the middle of the dance floor. As the DJ started playing some rock and roll song that I had never heard of, he began to yell into the microphone.

"For your viewing pleasure, please allow me to introduce the beautiful ladies of SIGNATURES. Don't worry, fellas, there is a lot of sexy to go around so pick one, two or maybe even three. They love applause but they love money even more so don't be shy. Please welcome Bunny to the stage."

The crowd went wild as a petite blonde, with big boobs and a slinky evening gown, cascaded from the back door onto the stage. Followed behind her was yet another make-up plastered stunner, this one stood about six feet with long legs and waist-length red hair. As the DJ called out name after name, each girl walked onstage and strutted around, throwing a coy eye to any man who looked interested.

"Give a loud round of applause for our very own special delivery hot off of the Oriental Express, Chyna."

My jaw dropped as Piper took the stage.

In a transparent gown, her erect nipples stood at attention. Her thick hair was bone straight and glistened with glitter as the stage lights glared down upon her head. While her body swayed seductively to the music blaring from the speakers, I looked around in utter shock as she blew kisses to the men sitting at the foot of the stage waving crisp dollar bills. That's when it finally hit me, Piper was a stripper.

Now, I know it seems odd that it took me that long to catch on but honestly I had never been inside of a strip club before. Where I'm from, we weren't into that sort of thing. At least not back then we weren't. As a matter of fact, we looked down on strippers like they were the scum of the Earth. Before meeting Piper, I would have never even sipped out of the same cup as a person who got naked for money. But that was because I didn't know people who lived outside of my own little circle. I wasn't privy to other types of hustles. The only thing I knew was drugs. Therefore, the only thing I ever got was drug money – which, by the way, really ain't shit once it stops clicking. But being in a new place required me to see things differently. Sitting at the bar while watching my roommate squirm her way out of her gown, exposing a black g-string and perky titties, was totally different than anything my small mind had ever experienced.

"The showcase is over, so they'll be calling for open auditions next. What is your stage name?" The bartender asked again.

Of course, I still hadn't a clue about a stage name or any type of audition. Shit, I thought this was an interview. I couldn't even remember if I had shaved my bikini line so how the fuck was I supposed to get on some damn stage and strip? My shit might have been looking like I had Buckwheat in a leg-lock or something.

"Umm, can I speak to Piper? Ur, I mean, Chyna. I'm her roommate. I only came to see her real quick."

"You said you were here for an interview. Make up your mind."

She walked off with an attitude as if I had somehow stopped her from making an extra tip. I spotted Piper as she headed toward me.

"You ready, girl?" She asked with absolutely no fucks given.

"Ready? Piper, you didn't tell me this was a strip club. How the fuck am I supposed to be interviewing? I got on some slacks and a blazer, not a fucking negligee."

"Come with me," she yelled over the music, grabbing my hand and pulling me into the back dressing room.

Half-naked girls stood near the metal lockers while painting their faces and discussing the club's dance floor full of potential tricks.

"That fucker will spend a grand tonight if I just sit there and let him jerk off while I play with my pussy," said the blonde waif who rocked a bob, glasses and boy-shorts. I guess she was going for the tomboy look.

"Honey, my customer has been here every night this week but if he doesn't give me his credit card number by tonight, he can kiss this sweet ass goodbye," said another who was checking herself out in the full-length mirror as she zipped up her thigh-high boots.

My head kept spinning round and round with voices that made me think I was stuck in a really bad porno movie and Ron Jeremy would somehow magically appear with a circle of white smoke around him.

"Come on now Chaka, you had to know."

She was right. After all, how else could I explain all the single dollar bills she spent on an everyday basis? Sometimes we block out the shit we don't want to believe instead of seeing what was staring right in our faces.

"I can't do that Pipe. I mean, I don't knock you but I just can't get up there and shake my ass. I can't do it."

She pulled a stack from her hot pink lace garter belt and started peeling dollars off as she handed them to me.

"You'll never know if you don't try," she said. "Here, this is for a cab. I know you don't got it like that to be running back and forth. It's way too late to be getting on somebody's train."

As she placed the Bath & Body Works Cucumber Melon scented bills in my hand, I looked down at them and felt like a chump. There I was, depending on the next chic to get me from point A to point B. With no work experience under my belt, I doubted if I would have ever found a decent paying job. Shit, I still had to maintain the necessities like my hair, my nails and my occasional splurge on shoes. I wasn't thinking about running home, at least not yet anyway. I knew that place was full of motherfuckers just waiting for me to fail. The last thing I was about to do was give them that satisfaction. My life flashed before me as I weighed my options. Either I continue to live like a homeless derelict sleeping in my friend's bed at her studio apartment or I, quite literally, put my big girl panties on and make that money. I didn't have to think long. I knew what I had to do.

"Well, I don't have anything to wear," I said, holding my head down already ashamed at the path on which I was about to embark.

She strolled to her locker and pulled out a pair of red patent leather platform shoes that buckled right above the ankle. As she passed them to me, she also threw me a little red teddy with matching red panties.

A fucking devil in a red dress.

"Put this on and I'll tell the DJ that you're coming out. Just dance sexy and pretend that nobody's watching. Block all those thirsty motherfuckers out of your head and just see the dollar signs, boo. That's what I do. Don't worry, you'll be aight."

Piper's voice was reassuring but did nothing for the butterflies swarming around in my stomach. After I whispered the moniker I had chosen as my stage name in her ear, she was out the door and I was left standing in front of a full-length mirror with nothing but my reflection staring back at me. Gone were the sounds of the other girls and their hoe'rific tales. Nothing else mattered at that moment but me and what I was about to do.

Sometimes I think back to that night and wonder where I would have ended up had I never gone on stage. Money is a motherfucker. That mean green can make you abandon everything you believe in without a care in the world. I'm not sure if it's the thought of being without it or the addiction to getting it that kept pulling me back. Either way, I was all the way in.

"Please welcome **Charlie** to the stage. She's new so make sure you take good care of her tonight."

The DJ made the announcement to a packed room full of suit wearing Caucasian men with deep pockets and Black girl fetishes. Malik used to call me Charlie whenever I would get on my sexual freak mode. So, I figured this was the perfect environment for her to make a grand reappearance in my life. My legs moved with a mind of their own. Chaka was gone. I had a new role to play. Introducing Charlie.

Lights. Camera. Motherfucking Action.

Chapter 7

Who the fuck was I kidding? In my mind, I was about to step out there on some Queen of Sheba type shit. But once I got onstage, reality set in as the glare of the lights practically blinded me. I could barely see the steps leading to the platform which had a silver pole dead smack in the middle of it. The girls who performed before me knew how to slide up and down, some even did acrobatic flips where they'd manage to get all the way to the ceiling before seductively inching back down to the floor. Not me though. I was lucky I didn't topple over especially when my six inch heel got stuck on the hem of another girl's dress. It was a disaster to say the least but I kept on swaying side to side with about as much rhythm as a honky-tonk cowgirl at a hip hop concert. Maybe a drink or two would have helped to loosen me up but it was too late for that. All eyes were on me. Since the dollars were finally getting thrown on stage, albeit very slowly, I had to give the crowd what they wanted to see.

Reaching behind me, I untied the skimpy string from around my neck and the dress fell to the floor, exposing my two little 34A mounds. They stood at attention, more so out of nervousness because I was anything but horny. Luckily, the club was only topless so I didn't have to come out of my panties but I still felt completely naked on that stage as the audience gawked and cat-called. An older Black man stood alone at the end of the bar with a large stack of bills. He immediately caught my attention. For some reason, I've always had a thing for older guys. Especially those with a little salt and pepper mixed into their facial hair. Men who resembled him.

Like a cat ready to pounce, I got on my knees and crawled toward my prey. He was wearing a grey fedora with a crisp white shirt. As I got closer, I noticed the faint tan line around his ring finger. Slowly, I rolled my head in circles, allowing my hair to softly fling from side to side. This must have aroused him because he lifted the side of my garter belt just enough to cram a few dollars in before snapping it against my thigh. The other men in the club became invisible to me. My Smooth Operator had all of my undivided attention.

Although I was only supposed to audition for one song, it felt like the DJ was playing the extended version with a ten minute instrumental remix. When it finally came to an end, he repeated my name and reminded the horny onlookers that I was a newbie. It must have worked, because I – well, I mean, Charlie – was in full demand. As I exited the stage, men were flapping dollar bills in the air, trying to summon me for a private dance. Ain't nothing like fresh meat.

"You did great, girl," Piper screamed over the loud music as I scurried to her with both hands full of loose dollars that I managed to accumulate.

"Oh my God, I can't believe I just did that," I squealed, relieved that it was over. My stripper cherry had officially been popped.

By my visual count, I had about a hundred dollars. I was ecstatic. Surely I had enough funds to keep me interested in my newly found profession. I mean, who wants to do manual labor for eight bucks an hour when I could make way more than that just by shaking my little ass? Money was a hell of a motive.

"Uh-oh, you got a little stalker over there," Piper whispered while pointing toward the mysterious gentleman who was all so generous during my performance.

I slid him a flirtatious smile and waved briefly before turning back to my friend who had subsequently become my stripper coach.

"What am I supposed to do now?"

Nodding her head in the direction of a dark walkway just to the side of the main stage, she said, "You see that room over there? That's the Champagne Room. Anything goes in there."

My eyes nearly popped out of my head.

Anything goes?

Piper, sensing my hesitation, added, "I mean, you ain't gotta fuck him but he can touch you more back there than out here. The best part about it, is that you can charge the shit out of him."

She looked over my left shoulder as her eyes scanned up and down before delving deeper into her instructions.

"He looks like the type who'll spend, so tell him you want five hundred for an hour and see if he goes for it. Make that money, boo."

With Piper's directions, I sashayed my way toward my new customer with a sudden surge of confidence. He was expecting me, I'm sure, because he already had his money in his hand.

"Hi, I'm Chak – I'm Charlie. What's your name?"

I almost said Chaka before reminding myself that I was playing a role, starring as some high priced whore in a swanky night club. *Always the actress.*

Extending my hand to shake his, I figured that might have been too proper for a stripper's introduction but hell, I didn't know any better.

"I'm Gus," he said.

His voice was deep like that guy from the Allstate Insurance commercials. Actually, he kind of looked like him too with his Hershey's Dark Chocolate complexion and pearly white teeth.

"Umm, do you want a dance?"

I spoke loud enough to be heard over the blaring music and giggling girls who were desperately trying to con some poor schmuck for the night.

"Only if you're dancing just for me," he replied.

His hand began to massage my right shoulder. I flinched at his touch. After all, I wasn't used to strangers feeling all up on me but I shook it off realizing this was part of the hustle.

There was a hefty guard standing in front of the private room that Piper had pointed out to me. I peeped one girl slide him a few dollars as she exited on the arm of a chubby red cheeked White guy whose zipper was halfway down. I had no idea what to expect beyond the black velvet curtain that hung in the doorway but whatever it was, I was about to find out.

Grabbing Gus' hand, I led him toward the entry way. His palms were soft as if he had never worked a hard day in his life. The guard gave me a nod before looking my customer up and down. I suppose that was his way of letting me know he was legit. Truthfully, I felt safer with him standing watch. He looked like a six-foot tall Hell's Angel biker with a bald head and a long scruffy beard. Tattoos covered both his arms and neck. His biceps were about the size of my thigh so I knew if Gus got out of hand, I wouldn't have to run too far to get him put back in his place.

Once beyond the curtain, there were four private side rooms with soft red lights, giving each space a sensual vibe. We walked past the first room which was occupied with some bare breasted blonde sitting on a guy's lap. He was playing motor boat with her titties as she bounced up and down like she was riding a mechanical bull. With the mammoth size of her boobs, he's lucky he didn't get a concussion from them shits knocking across his head.

We continued walking down the hallway and I looked down at my breasts. I was barely out of a training bra so I hoped Gus didn't think he was getting that sort of action.

I peeked into the next room to see if it was empty. Embarrassed by what I saw, I quickly turned away. I ended up stepping on Gus' feet since he was so close behind me trying to catch a glimpse too. It only took me a minute to figure out what that dancer was doing with her butt cheeks in the air and her head buried deep in some dude's lap. Shit, I was about to turn in the other direction and head back to the dance floor until Gus squeezed my hand.

"It's your first night. I don't want all that."

His smooth baritone voice was convincing enough for me. I'm sure he could feel my palms sweating profusely as I got more and more nervous. So, I pulled my hand away from his and rubbed it against my sheer dress; leaving sweaty palm prints along the way.

We finally arrived at the third doorway and it was empty. Besides a lacquer coffee table, the only other thing in the mirrored room was a black leather couch. Gus sat down like he was already accustomed to the antics that went on where no other eyes could see. As for me, I looked in the mirror and hated the person looking back at me. My reflection was a constant reminder of everything I had done that brought me to my current state. I didn't need to be reminded of all that so I tried my best to avoid looking at myself.

My body stiffened. My heart raced. My mouth went dry. Sweat beads popped out of my forehead. I was supposed to be back there with him for a full hour yet I could barely make it through the first couple of minutes.

He grabbed my hand and pulled me close as he tossed the stack of bills on the table. "This is for you."

"It's five hundred for umm, for an hour. Y-y-you know that, right?"

I stuttered, nervously regurgitating Piper's instructions.

"I know. It's all there. Go ahead, count it."

He grinned like a Cheshire cat.

I'm not sure if I was too embarrassed to count it in front of him or if I was just naïve enough to believe he wouldn't short me. Either way, I did a quick calculation in my head and by the looks of it, it all seemed to be there. With that, I stood up and used my knee to spread his legs apart so I could dance between them. At first, I just moved side to side like I had done on the stage moments before. Hell, it worked well enough to get his attention then, I didn't think I had to put too much more effort to keep it. However, he must have expected more because he reached up and firmly grabbed my waist.

"No, move slower. Let me see you grind, baby."

Inside, I was shaking to the core but I did as he said. Slowly, I arched my back and squirmed like a snake charmer. He must have liked it because the bulge in his pants started to grow.

"Now take off your top," he said.

I obliged. If all I had to do was a sexy two step and show some titties, surely I could do that. Shit, for five hundred dollars, I figured I'd give him a little bit extra. Cupping my small breast in my hand, I bent my neck far enough forward so that my tongue could slide around my brown areola, occasionally flapping across my hardened nipple.

"Yeah baby, I like that," he moaned.

My confidence grew with every beat of the music coming from the speakers. Slowly, I turned my back toward him and bent over placing my hands on the coffee table in front of me. My tight little ass jiggled when he slapped my cheeks. The first time, it was a soft slap. By the third or fourth time, he got heavy handed with it. I was starting to regret turning around but I stayed in that position. Hell, it beat having to look at him or risk seeing my reflection in the mirror again.

"Come sit on my lap," he ordered.

Before I could respond, he had already pulled me down by the string of my thong. Those fucking shoes I had on were too high for me to really hold my balance enough to put up a fight any damn way. So, I plopped on his lap with little resistance. As I tried to regain my footing enough to grind him, I reached back in horror. While I had my back turned, that nasty motherfucker somehow managed to unzip his pants and pull his dick out.

"What the fuck?" I shouted, trying to scramble to my feet.

My attempts at getting up were useless once he pressed firmly against my shoulders, holding me still without much ability to wiggle my way free.

"Come on baby. Don't worry, I won't put it in. Just rub on it."

He started humping my exposed butt cheek.

"Just like that," he groaned.

His dick began to harden even more and if I'm being honest, it kind of aroused the freak in me although my brain was throwing up all kinds of warning signals.

Glancing at the five hundred dollars sitting on the table in front of me, I second guessed escaping his clutch. All I had to my name was the little twenty dollars Piper had given me to catch a cab home along with whatever I got from dancing on the stage. I still hadn't counted it so I wasn't sure how much it really was. If I complained or made a big spectacle out of this Champagne Room romper, I knew I wouldn't have been allowed to dance again. So, I closed my eyes and did what the fuck I had to do. I danced. Actually, I rode the shit out of his dick, still wearing my panties, of course. I hoped he'd get off quickly so I could take my dough and get the fuck out of that chamber of perversion as fast as possible.

"Yeah, baby, just like that."

I wasn't even listening to him at that point. His voice made my stomach turn so I ignored the sound of it altogether. As he reached up to run his fingers through my hair, I smelled the faint fragrance on his sleeve. It was a smell I'd never forget. The scent was Hugo Boss. The first time I smelled it was in 1986. I was only nine years old.

CHIGGY

I believe the children are our future...

Whitney Houston's voice sang like a hummingbird through the speakers of my silver portable tape player. I begged my mother to buy me the whole album but she could only afford the ninety-nine cents single cassette. Hey, that was enough for me. Shoot, I just knew Whitney made that song for me anyway so it didn't matter if I had to listen to it over and over again. I had it playing on repeat that day. Once the tape stopped, it automatically flipped to the other side and then played again. I memorized every single word. After all, I was going to sing it in my third grade assembly the next day so I had to make sure to have my routine completely down pact. Over thirty other girls auditioned for the chance to sing that song at our annual talent show but my teacher, Mrs. Rosenberg, chose me. It was my first step toward having my star placed on the Hollywood Walk of Fame.

My mother and father had just left to hit the streets with my brothers in tow. Who knew when they'd return? Sometimes we didn't stop hustling until the middle of the night. Since they knew I had to rehearse for my grand performance, they let me stay home with my big sister Camille, who was seven years older than me. At sixteen, she wasn't too excited about being left with her bratty kid sister. As soon as my parents walked out the door, she was gone to meet up with her friends leaving me with strict instructions to keep the door locked and to never tell my mother that she left me alone. As long as I had an audience of imaginary people watching me perform, I didn't care if she was there or not.

All my Barbie dolls, my Cabbage Patch Kid and my best teddy bear were seated on the couch as I stood in front of them, using my wooden hard bristled brush as a microphone. Since this was a dress rehearsal, I wore a big pink bow in my hair just like the one Whitney donned in her "I Wanna Dance With Somebody" video. I even rocked a white body suit and pink tutu, similar to the one she had on as she pranced across my television screen. From the first moment I laid eyes on her, I knew I wanted to be just like her. My bedroom was full of Whitney pictures despite my brothers constantly ripping them off the walls to make space for their WWF wrestling posters. It didn't matter to me. I just taped them right back up every chance I got. Whitney was my idol.

They can't take away my dignity...

That was a strong note so my tiny self dropped to my knees, pumping my little fist against my chest, really giving my dolls a full dramatic concert. I belted every riff through my one missing front tooth. As my tongue flapped through the opened space, I wondered how long it would take before it grew back. My mother called me her Snaggle-Toothed Lollipop. I giggled at the lollipop but frowned at the snaggle-toothed. That didn't sound too pretty to me. Still, I was star. And I wasn't about to let that one missing tooth dull my sparkle.

I just couldn't wait to be on stage and show the whole school that I was famous just like Whitney. I was never the nervous or shy type. Actually, performing made me more comfortable than anything. It was my chance to be somebody else.

The knock on the door interrupted my show. I know I shouldn't have answered it but for some reason I thought it was my best friend, Nicole. She was the only other kid from the projects who was in my class. Although there were a few Queensbridge children who attended PS166, Nicole and I were the only Black students selected for the top classes in our school. We were smart enough to learn aside all the rich White kids but once we got bussed back home, all our project friends teased us for being smart. As if that was something to be ashamed about. So, we didn't fit in with the Leahs and Bonnies of the world, who could afford dinner at Central Park's Tavern on The Green and performances at the Metropolitan Opera. But we had nothing in common with the Shaniquas and Latoyas who were still reading *The Berenstain Bears* while we were studying *Silas Marner*. Luckily, Nicole and I had each other and that was more than enough for me.

So, when I heard someone knocking, I just knew it was her. After all, she was the only friend who ever came to play with me anyway and there she was coming to be my back-up singer. She was definitely the *la-de-da* to my "Greatest Love of All" melody.

I opened the door without propping my dining room chair up so that I could stand on it and be tall enough to look out the peephole. That's usually how I did it. Instead, I unlocked the locks quickly so Nicole could hurry up and get to rehearsing with me.

"Oh, Mister Danny, I thought you was Nicole," I said, after

realizing it wasn't my fellow snaggle-toothed bestie waiting in the hallway.

"Hi Chaka." He knelt down, his hazel eyes looking directly into mine. I was instantly mesmerized. "I just saw your mother and father downstairs. They said I could come use your bathroom."

He smiled, showing his gold capped tooth. It had a star cut out in the middle of it. His teeth weren't really that white to begin with, so I could hardly tell where the gold stopped and his tooth started. His flat-top haircut was fresh. I know because I could smell the same powder the barber used whenever my brothers went across the street to Mr. Joe's Barbershop for a shape-up. Mister Danny's gold rope chain looked like barrels with a sparkly cross that draped along the chest hairs sprouting out from under his white tank top. The tight red velour sweat jacket he wore matched his pants and covered his arms. I knew he was really strong by the way his muscles were flexing in the jacket's creases. He had on some loud perfume. Well, since men don't wear that sort of thing, it must have been cologne. It smelled good but he wore a lot of it. So much so, that my nose twitched up as the heavy scent flowed from the hallway and through my door.

"I can't let nobody in. My sister's not home," I said through the cracked opening.

My foot was placed firmly against the door from the inside. I saw my mother do that on occasions when she didn't really want somebody to come in the house.

"It's ok, cutie. I'm only gonna use the bathroom, all right? You don't want me to have to go out here, do you?"

He smiled even more that time, opening his arms and looking around the hallway. His tooth sparkled. It sort of made me melt. I always thought Mister Danny was cute. Like, for an old man type of cute, though. He was always nice to me. Whenever he saw me playing outside, he'd give me a dollar or buy me an ice cream cone from the Mister Softee truck as it rode up and down the streets. Surely, my parents would have let him use the bathroom. They always talked to him when were outside. I even overheard them say he had the best *boy* in the projects one time; although I never actually saw his son before. Still, he was their friend. And well, he did tell me that my parents said it was ok. I believed him. Besides, I didn't want him to pee in the hallway. That was just gross.

"Ok, Mister Danny. Come in."

I opened the door with slight aggravation that he was ruining my Broadway performance.

Because the greatest love of all is happening to me...

Whitney continued to sing.

"What you in here doing, little Miss Super Star?"

He didn't head toward the bathroom. Instead, he sat on the couch. I didn't give that a second thought.

"Umm, nothing," I giggled, blushing with embarrassment while rewinding my song to the beginning. Messing with him, I missed the best part.

He put Maximus, my favorite teddy bear, on his lap. "Let me see," he said.

What? Was he giving me a chance to perform in front of a real live audience? I was hyped. Even at such a young age, I longed for the spotlight.

As the tape started to play from the beginning, I walked to the center of my living room as if I was finding my mark on stage. My tiny hands flapped furiously as I tried to evoke the spirit of Whitney through my pint-sized body.

Give them a sense of pride...

My eyes shut tight as I imagined I was in Hollywood with an auditorium of people cheering me on, loving my talent and clapping at the sound of my voice. This was, after all, my Grammy award winning shot and that only happens once in a lifetime. At least that's what it felt like to me.

I didn't know what keys I was supposed to be hitting but I continued to serenade into my wooden brush, flinging my thick hair that fell to the middle of my back, from side to side. Even though my voice cracked at times, I thought if I just kept going, it wouldn't even be noticed.

I found the greatest love of all...

My eyes stayed closed as I sang, increasing the volume of my voice one octave at a time. Maybe if I would have opened them up, I would have seen what Mister Danny was really doing.

But I didn't. I just thought he liked my talent because he kept saying, "Yeah, yeah". He must have been super proud of me for sounding just like Whitney and that was his way of letting me know.

When I finally decided to look out into my audience, I saw what he was really doing. Instantly, I closed my eyes back even tighter and held my wooden brush like a vise grip.

He had his pee-pee out.

Well, none of my teddy bears ever did anything like that before and they watched me sing almost every single day. For the first time ever, in my short life as a performer, I got nervous which caused me to stutter through my lyrics as if I hadn't had the whole song memorized.

I'm not supposed to see pee-pees anymore.

My mother told me I couldn't use the bathroom with my brothers and I listened. I was a good girl. My Daddy even said he couldn't wash me up anymore because only my mother could see my stuff. I knew I wasn't supposed to see what Mister Danny was doing but I don't think anybody ever told him that because every time I opened my eyes, just a little, to take a peek, he was still rubbing his private parts.

People need someone to – someone just to...

Every syllable I uttered sounded choppy as it made its way up my throat. The words were hard to get out amid the tears that started streaming down my face. I felt like I was choking. Everything was closing in around me. I couldn't even see Maximus sitting on his lap anymore. At that moment, it was just me and Mister Danny. My whole audience had somehow disappeared.

"Come here, baby."

His voice was soft. It flowed with the song's harmony. I shook my head no. I didn't want to go to him. I just wanted to sing.

"No, no. I'm Whitney. I just want." I paused, trying to catch my breath from the heavy sobs escaping my mouth. "I just gotta finish my song."

I closed my eyes again and dropped the brush to my side as I clasped my hands together tightly, twiddling my thumbs. I continued to sing at the top of my shaky voice.

I DE-DE-DECID-ED LONG A-A-AGO...

I thought if I sang louder and better, he wouldn't try to stop me. It didn't work though. And Whitney didn't save me as Mister Danny leaned in. His big chest looked even larger, like Goliath's, as he got closer. Reaching up under my tutu, he grabbed the panty part of my body suit and pulled me close until I landed on top of his lap.

"No, Mister Danny. I'm just a singer," I cried, hoping he would let me go.

"I know. You my little Super Star. Just sing right here. Just move like this," he said, while placing his hands on my tiny waist and forcing my butt to rub on his pee-pee.

The wood paneling in my project apartment, which was normally brown, looked gray and blurry through my teary eyes. The sun shining through the blinds that I had previously imagined was my spotlight had transformed into a glimmer of shame. I felt nasty. Where was the greatest love? Surely, it wasn't in the living room with me despite Whitney repeating the lines over and over again.

"Mister Danny, please. Please stop."

"It's ok, baby. You a star," he whispered in my ear as he yanked my panties to the side, harshly jabbing his index finger inside of me and scouring my tiny insides.

"AGGGGHHHHH," I scream. It feels like a rusty nail scraping against a dry chalkboard.

Where's Nicole? I thought to myself. *She was supposed to come and help me sing. Not Mister Danny. He wasn't supposed to be here.*

"Keep singing," he ordered, despite covering my mouth with his hand. I could taste his cologne on the tip of my tongue.

Through my cries, I tried to remember the words. It was no use. Nothing I sang sounded anything like Whitney. But I kept going because I was afraid of what he would do if I didn't. My imagination briefly allowed me to escape the torture going on in Apartment 4A. In my head, I was on stage at The Apollo. There was somebody standing at my feet with a bouquet of roses just like they did for Patti LaBelle every time she performed. Well, that's how it happened on television and that was the only thing I ever wanted. I didn't want to be there with Mister Danny but I couldn't get away. It was my fault. I shouldn't have opened the door. My sister told me not to and I didn't listen. I was supposed to be practicing by myself and I shouldn't have tried to show off by singing to Mister Danny. I was the reason this was happening. *Why did I always have to show off?*

Mister Danny got rougher as he shoved his finger inside of me, pumping faster and harder. Moving his hand from my mouth, he used it to spread my legs further apart with me straddled on his lap. I tried to squeeze them back together but Mister Danny's muscles were too strong. My legs just kept opening wider and wider. I thought they would pop off of my body.

"Oh, you so pretty. Like a little angel. Oh, baby girl," he kept saying over and over again.

"Stop. PLEASE. It hurrrrrttttssss Mister Danny. Please, STOP."

I couldn't even pretend to sing the song anymore.

"Shut up. Just wait a minute."

I kept praying my sister would come home. Every time I heard the ding of the elevator approaching my floor, I thought it was somebody coming to my house to save me. Anybody. But nobody ever came.

"UUUUUGGGGGHHHHHHHH," he yelled.

He pushed me off of him so hard that I nearly bumped my head on the wooden Hi-Fi stereo across the living room. White water shot from the top of his pee-pee. He cupped it in his fist as it overflowed and dripped down to his three-finger gold nugget ring. From the floor, I watched him stand up and finally head to the bathroom. I couldn't move.

I heard all the stories in school about not letting adults touch you but those types of people had no resemblance to Mister Danny. He didn't wear a trench coat and he never gave out candy. He was somebody I saw every day.

He came out of the bathroom and walked toward me. I was still sitting on the floor, Indian style, with my hands in the center of my legs. I tensed up so much, my shoulder blades nearly touched my ears. I didn't want to do 'it' anymore.

"If you tell anybody, they gonna put your mother in jail for being on drugs. You know that, right?"

I finally looked up at him. I'm not sure if it was because he said my mother would go to jail or if it was because he said she was on drugs. I knew what she did but I never heard anyone else say it before then. That was my secret.

"She ain't on no drugs."

The words meekly quivered out. They were barely audible as my lower lip trembled. That wasn't anybody's business. All the needles. All the baggies. All the burnt up silver spoons I found around the house. They were things I kept hidden. And because I didn't listen and I opened the door, now everybody would know about them. I couldn't tell. I had to protect my mother.

"Well, you just keep this between us, ok?" He held out a twenty dollar bill. "This is for you."

My eyes darted back to the floor. I didn't want his money. I just wanted him to leave. Instead, he threw the cash on the couch. It landed right next to Maximus. He rubbed my cheek with the back of his hand one last time before he walked out the door. On his sleeve, I smelled the scent of his cologne.

And if by chance that special place...

Whitney's voice echoed throughout the apartment before I finally found the strength to stand up and turn the radio off.

"I HATE YOU, WHITNEY," I screamed, while pulling the pink bow out of my hair, throwing it to the floor and ferociously stomping it over and over again. "THERE AIN'T NO SPECIAL PLACE. THERE AIN'T NO SPECIAL PLACE."

I pretended to be sick the next day and never performed at my assembly. Every time I used the bathroom, it felt like there was fire shooting out of me. I wanted to scream in agony but I tried my hardest not to make a sound because I didn't want my mother to know something was wrong. I went about my days doing everything I could to avoid Mister Danny but I didn't really need to do all that. He ignored me when he saw me and never bought me another ice cream cone. His rejection was like a double edge sword through my heart especially when, in passing, I heard him call another little girl his Super Star.

I must not have been good enough.

From that day forward, I never listened to Whitney again. Fuck her for lying to me. The children weren't our future. They sprang from a past that I wanted to forget. One that was deeply buried until I got a whiff of that fucking Hugo Boss. It was the same scent Mister Danny wore. And ever since then, I've always hated that smell.

The tang of Gus' cologne, as he wrapped his hand around my neck, brought me back. I opened my eyes and all of a sudden, the Champagne Room was a blur. My heart began pumping furiously while I was still grinding on his little bare dick. The more I inhaled his stench, the tighter my teeth clenched together. My breaths got shorter and shallower, causing my whole body to tense up. Unable to focus on anything in the room, I just kept picturing Mister Danny's face and smelling that God forsaken Hugo Boss.

I looked to the right and tears quickly formed as my eyes caught the mirror and I watched my reflection morph back to myself at nine years old. I was Chiggy again. She was there, looking back at me with a desperation that I had never seen. She wanted somebody to protect her. She was scared. I saw it in her eyes. For once, I couldn't let her hurt anymore. Somebody had to save her.

"YOU NASTY MOTHERFUCKER," I screamed, leaping from Gus' lap and turning toward him.

When I looked, it was no longer Gus sitting on that black leather couch with his raw dick exposed. Instead, the face looked even more familiar. It was the face that appeared in so many of my nightmares. I was finally eye to eye with Mister Danny. Only this time, I was big enough to protect myself.

My movements were too swift for Gus to react. Before he could do anything, I had already lifted my leg up and stuck the heel of my six inch stiletto right into the middle of his balls.

"I HATE YOU," I yelled. "I FUCKING HATE YOU."

Continuously, I stomped my foot on his dick. He grimaced but his battered posture could do nothing to stop the barrage of kicks that continued. Finally, I had the upper hand.

"I'm Whitney, you piece of shit. I'm." **Kick.** "Fucking." **Kick.** "Whitney." **Kick.**

He balled over into a fetal position, his hands cupping his manhood as tight as possible.

Tears continued to pour as my hair flung back and forth. I was a mad woman with absolutely no control over my actions. Gus grunted but all I could hear was Mister Danny's voice telling me that I was a Super Star. Soon, every man who ever hurt me appeared at once. I thrust my stiletto into Gus' testicles even harder once Malik's face came into view.

In the midst of the ruckus, the bouncer ran into the room. His strong arms swooped me up while my legs dangled frantically in the air. I glanced back at Gus who looked like a fraction of the man he was when he first walked in. The slight drops of blood on his trousers were crimson red. I could see it clearly. It matched the color of my dress.

"What the fuck is going on here?" The bouncer shouted.

"HE TOUCHED ME. HE TOUCHED ME. YOU PIECE OF SHIT. I WAS A BABY."

Clearly, I was still in a distant memory.

"Get your stuff and get the hell out of here. Now."

The bouncer pointed toward the black curtain as he tended to Gus who huddled over in pain.

Quickly, I ran in the direction of the exit sign. I didn't even grab the money from the table. Fuck it. Just like I didn't take Mister Danny's twenty dollars, I sure as hell didn't want a dime from that repulsive motherfucker. His painful moans echoed throughout the hallway as I made my way back to the main club area. My body trembled but the clickity-clack of my heels gave me strength to keep going. It felt like Chiggy was walking beside me. And for once, she didn't have to be afraid.

As I emerged from the Champagne Room, all eyes were on me. Ignoring the stares, I wiped the tears from my face and headed to the dressing room where I quickly put my clothes on and threw that cheap stripper shit in the gray plastic garbage can on my way out.

Piper rushed toward me as I headed for the door.

"What happened back there? Chaka, what's the matter?"

I couldn't find the words to explain. Shit, I could barely figure out where I was let alone what had just occurred. Besides, she wouldn't understand. Nobody ever understood anything about me. They never did.

"FUCK YOU, WHITNEY," I yelled as I raised both middle fingers in the air before the club's glass door slammed behind me.

Silently I vowed to never look back. Ever again.

Chapter 8

Salty tears stung my eyes as the brisk breeze ripped through my small leather jacket. I don't know how long I was walking or even where I was going for that matter. The memories kept flashing in front of me. Memories I had hoped would never resurface. As long as I kept walking, I wouldn't have to stand still long enough to clearly envision it all. The fear of reliving every moment that I wanted to forget, forced my legs to continue moving.

Since I barely ventured out beyond Piper's apartment and the occasional bar or club, Philadelphia was still very new to me. Before I realized it, I was in a completely different environment that looked so barren in comparison to the posh neighborhood where SIGNATURES was located. The streets, aligned with row house after row house, were abandoned and deserted, like the South Bronx in the late 1970's. Black garbage bags were strewn along the sidewalks, with rats, the size of cats, scurrying from one to the other. Still, I kept walking.

Finally, I looked up and noticed the street sign. It said, Broad Street, but that didn't matter much to me because I still had no idea where the fuck I was going. I just felt alone, as I always had. Lost and alone.

Sure, I put up a good front for the world to see. On the outside, I was this pretty girl who smiled and portrayed a role. Nobody ever took the time to get beyond that façade. Honestly, who gave a fuck, really?

Truthfully, I was sick of living a lie – always being who the world wanted me to be. I was never allowed to be myself. The only time people liked me was when I performed. Whether I was the street chick with the baller boyfriend or the stripper on stage – shit, I got more attention playing the role of Whitney Houston than I ever did when I was just Chaka. Everything I was had been built on a fantasy of who I wanted to be. The girl everyone loved.

My brain started jumping from one thought to the next. Things I wanted to forget appeared with clarity. The view was too much for me to bear. Here I was, with my last dime in my pocket and nobody, besides Piper, to call for help. I wasn't about to stick my tail between my legs and go back to Queensbridge. For one thing, I still had nightmares of bumping into Manny in a dark alley. After witnessing his canine brutality, even the sight of a Chihuahua sent chills up my spine. He never said I couldn't come back home but he was adamant that I couldn't make any more money on those streets. Without an ability to hustle, how else would I be able to eat? Then I wondered what would happen to me if people found out about Malik. It was only a matter of time before someone was smart enough to piece that puzzle together. It sure as hell didn't take a rocket scientist to figure that shit out. I was the missing link; the only connection Manny had to Malik. On top of all that, I wasn't about to give those Bench Dwellers and every other gossiping ass hoodrat the satisfaction of knowing I failed – yet again.

The lonely street gave me enough silence to hear my inner thoughts and they told me that I wasn't worth shit. And if I was gone, nobody would even miss me. Well, except my mother of course, but I didn't even want to face the fact that I had to tell her I got kicked out of the Navy; another disappointment. Voices started filling my brain until I couldn't even hear the sounds of the cars speeding along beside me.

Just end it all.

The words gnawed at the pit of my heart. Finally, I would shut them all up. All those stupid questions that went unanswered in my head would finally stop replaying over and over again. I had made my decision. I just couldn't take it anymore.

I remembered seeing a bottle of pills in Piper's medicine cabinet. They were some form of Oxycodone, which I knew were generic Percocets. At least I learned a thing or two from being submerged in the prescription drug underworld throughout my entire childhood. Those shits were some serious pain killers and since I was in pain, even if it was just the emotional kind, they would help alleviate all of that. The bottle was still full because she never took them. Piper said she had gotten them from her dentist but they made her stomach queasy so they just sat there, unopened and beyond their expiration date. I just had to make it to her house and then all my pain would go away. The bottle of Absolut Vodka sitting on the kitchenette counter appeared clear as day. It would be the perfect chaser. No blood. No rope marks around my neck. There'd be nothing that would give my mother nightmares when she was forced to identify my body. It would be like I was sleeping. But finally, I'd have a peaceful sleep.

The narcissistic side of me wanted a pretty death. I'm ready to die and all I'm thinking about is looking good enough for an open casket. Vanity – one of the seven deadly sins, for sure.

My body stiffened with thoughts that I'd never see the world again but the writer in me was already inscribing the words of my suicide note. In it, I would tell my family that I was sorry. I would let them know that I just couldn't go on anymore. I was tired of being a fuck-up.

I must have looked like a stark raven lunatic, staggering through the bleak streets of North Philly while talking to myself. I didn't care though. I was oblivious to everything going on around me until some rugged looking derelict felt at ease to ask me if I was looking for anything. That shit brought me back to reality real quick.

"Huh?" I was taken aback and somewhat scared of his brolic stance.

He asked again, with lips so white and dry it looked like he'd eaten a dozen powdered donuts without a sip of water in between. His eyes protruded from his forehead so far it was as if I was looking at them shits in 3D.

"Yeah, umm, where's the train station?"

By that time, I was tired of walking. My mind was made up. I knew what I was going to do.

He pointed north and as he lifted his arm, a gust of funk flew out from under his dusty Carhartt jacket. Shit, forget about a suicide, I almost died from the smell of it.

"Just keep walking that way. The Cecil B. Moore station is right over there. You can't miss it."

"Thanks," I replied, trying not to take another breath in his direction.

Clutching the opened collar of my jacket, I headed toward

my destination and away from the foul odor emitting from his body.

"But you good though? You don't want nothing?"

I ignored his question yet again and put a little more pep in my step.

"Yeah, aight. Fuck you too then, you stanking bitch," he yelled.

By then, I was already crossing the busy intersection and had no intentions of responding. My mental state couldn't afford to pay him any mind. Hell, I done been called a lot worse by a lot better so who the fuck cared what a bum had to say about me.

It was only about a five block walk before I started seeing signs pointing toward the station. I paid my little two dollars and went through the turnstile. The train was full of Philadelphia's finest and by that I really mean the grungiest people I had ever seen. It made me take another look at my life. Maybe, shit wasn't as bad as I thought.

"Bitch, snap the fuck out of it. Suicide? What the fuck is wrong with yo' dramatic ass? Only White people jump off of rooftops and shit. You done survived everything life has ever thrown at you. You better deal with this and keep it the fuck moving."

There was a miniature-sized Chaka perched on my right shoulder and she was yelling in my ear. She would come to me every now and again, whenever I was at my wit's end. I always pictured her wearing a black leather biker jacket with high leather boots and possibly a chain-linked leather hat. She was my subconscious and she was bad ass for sure. Of course nobody else could see her but as I looked at the disparate commuters, who seemed like they had no other choices in life, I realized how fortunate I really was. My mother didn't raise me to be a quitter. I had been reared with a touch of etiquette and that could open all types of doors for me. Not everybody from the hood had that ability. Those were the stuck motherfuckers. Not me. I could always find an out when I needed it. If opportunity didn't knock, my mother taught me to kick that fucking door off the hinges. Failure was a fate I seldom accepted, if ever. When the odds were stacked against me, I might have made a detour here and there but eventually I always got right back on track. This time was no different than any other times in my life when the road seemed like a dead-end. I would just have to create my own lane.

"Now stop feeling sorry for yourself and man the fuck up."

It felt like my mini-Chaka had just slashed her leather whip across my ass. My upper lip snarled as the train approached the Chelten Avenue station and I got off. As I walked toward Piper's apartment, I thought about Mister Danny's punk ass and remembered the last time I saw him. He was sprawled out in front of my building with a bullet between his eyes. Everybody around me was all hooting and hollering about him getting shot but not me. Inside, I laughed. Although I was only thirteen by then and barely old enough to exact my revenge, the streets caught up to his ass in a far worse way than I could have ever imagined. One way or another, I was victorious over every last bastard who ever stood in my way.

As soon as I walked through the door, I opened the Absolut bottle and took a shot straight to the head. And then another and yet another. I needed courage to make my next move which would be one of my hardest. Finally, it was time to call my mother and let her know what happened. Well, at least some version of the truth because I sure as hell wasn't about to tell her I got knocked up let alone that I had just been center stage with my titties all out. Some things were better left unsaid. But I knew I had to make the call. Fuck it, I was sick of all the lies anyway. For once, I was ready to face the truth and all that came along with it. I just hoped my parents wouldn't be too disappointed. Oh well, no time for all that now. I took another swig. Que será, será!

Chapter 9

Hesitantly, I dialed my mother's house stopping in between numbers for a quick sip of liquid courage - **718** *(sip)* **482** *(sip)* **7844**. Finally, the ringing sound on the other end meant there was no turning back. I didn't block the number so it appeared clear as day on her caller ID. Even if I chickened out and hung up, my mother would have called back ten times just to find out who was calling her from a 215 area code.

"Heyyyyooo."

A child's voice came through the receiver causing me to move the phone away from my ear and look at it as if I could see the person on the other end. I knew I wasn't that drunk to forget my own damn telephone number. My mom had the same one for years so I could have been straight twisted and still dialed it with my eyes closed.

"Heyyyyooo. Heyyyooo. Heyyyooo."

The constant baby talk was quickly getting on my nerves and I was just about to hang up until I heard my mother's voice. "Boy, give me that phone. Hello."

"Ma?"

"Hi Chiggy. You finally decided to call?"

"Well, yeah. But who was that?"

"Get down from there," my mother yelled out to someone in the background. "Come sit down, right now and finish your food."

"Ma, hello, I'm on the phone."

Usually, I had her undivided attention whenever I called so I was getting frustrated that some Bébé kid was stealing my shine.

"I'm sorry baby, these kids are driving me crazy. How are you?"

"What kids?" I asked but never gave her a second to respond. "Anyway, I'm fine but I have to talk to you so can you pay me some attention?"

"Talk about what, Chaka? What is it now?"

My mother's callous demeanor was a shock to me. Typically, she was appreciative of our little talks but now she seemed too preoccupied to give me the time of day.

"Well, it's about the Navy."

"Chiggy, I already know." She sighed with exasperation as if she had been holding that in for the longest.

"Know what?"

"I know you're not in the Navy anymore. I was just wondering when you were going to tell me yourself. All your mail comes here, remember? They sent your discharge papers months ago."

POW! I could've smacked my own damn self for being so stupid. Here I thought I was dotting all my i's and crossing all my t's but apparently, despite all my sneakiness, I missed the most obvious thing. *Oh, what a tangled web we weave.*

Now that she knew, I felt like a burden had been lifted off my chest. Lie after lie kept building up to the point where I couldn't remember the last lie and before you knew it, I was confused my damn self. According to my stories, I was on a covert submarine mission in the middle of Desert Storm. The next lie had to be more elaborate than the first. All the while, my parents knew I was full of shit. Never mind the fact that the Navy didn't allow women to serve on submarines and the conflict in the Middle East had long been over, they just sat there and let me tell one story after another until I was ready to finally speak the truth.

So now that she knew, I went on without divulging too many details. She was happy that I was living in Philadelphia and didn't come running back to the projects. I burst out in laughter when she asked if Piper knew how to make chicken-fried rice. Her reaction was completely different than what I had expected. Seriously, I thought she was going to tell me to bring my Black ass home. But by that point, she had too much drama of her own to be concerned with mine.

My sister Camille was dragging them through the pits of hell and back. As the eldest of my siblings, she was the one who was able to pretty much do whatever the fuck she wanted. I used to be jealous of her freedom because my parents were so strict on me. I couldn't do shit. I had to check in every hour. My curfew was no later than nine on school nights and eleven on weekends, despite my friends being able to stay out until they felt like going home. But my sister didn't have to deal with any of that. She practically set her own rules.

Since the rest of us were younger, we didn't fully understand what it meant to have parents who were heroin addicts when we were growing up. But my sister did. She was the one who had to pick up the slack while they were in the streets. Instead of hanging with her friends, she had to make sure my hair was done, our dinner was cooked and we all had school clothes ironed out for the next day. Looking back on it now, I'm sure the responsibility of all that had a lot to do with how she ended up.

Once my parents got clean and sober, Camille went buck wild. It started out as just partying or getting caught smoking a joint on the bench with her friends. Soon enough, she was coming in pissy drunk and throwing up all over our shared bedroom. I remember cleaning her up in the tub and changing her clothes. After all, that was my sister. I had to help her.

On the other hand, my mother simply turned a blind eye. Assumingly, she felt guilty for all the shit she put her through as a child who watched from the shadows while her mom battled her own demons. As for me, I knew something wasn't right especially when Camille started staying gone for days at a time. Her pit stops back home came few and far in between. When she did return, she was wearing the same clothes she had on when she left, except by the time she reappeared, they were filthy and smelled like stale cigarette smoke. Everything about her looked dirty and musty. You would have never known it by looking at her but my sister used to be one of those fly girls back in the late 80's. She had sheepskins, leather bombers, every color Lee's Jeans, fur coats, Gucci tote bags and gold bamboo earrings – at least two pair. That shit was popping in her era and she had all of that. Once she started hitting those streets though, all her stuff suspiciously came up missing. She'd say she 'lent' her Louis Vuitton bag to her friend or that she 'lost' her herringbone necklace. My mother never had a chance to delve further into my sister's stories because as soon as she came home, she'd sleep for days. And I'm not talking about a little nap. She would literally sleep for two days before finally getting out of bed to at least wash her ass or get something to eat.

By that time, I was almost fifteen so I heard the rumors

swirling around about her doing a lot more than smoking weed. Even back then, the streets were always talking. That hood gossip was like an alpha and omega; no beginning and no end. But once I was old enough to run the streets my own damn self, she had already moved to Virginia with my uncle. My mother kept the reasons for Camille's swift departure real hush-hush but I had a feeling they knew the road she was going down and tried to stop that train wreck before it even happened.

Camille and I kept in touch with letters and phone calls although I was much closer to my cousin Taylor. Once I got grown, I needed somebody to look up to who was still in the trenches just like me. I could care less about what the fuck my sister was going through down there with the hillbillies. Shit, I was too wrapped up in my own useless world to get caught up in hers.

From the outside looking in, Camille was living the good life in the boondocks. I mean, she had a house, a husband and two kids – a boy and a girl. What the fuck else could a hood chick need? But wherever you go, you take yourself with you. One day, out of the blue, my uncle called and from what my mother was telling me, she and my father drove down south to scoop up my niece and nephew from a crack house where my sister had abandoned them for days. And just like that, they had their hands full trying to care for a four year old and a baby who was already addicted to crack. My little bullshit and all it entailed, took a seat on the backburner. They had way bigger fish to fry.

After hearing my mother drop that load on me, I couldn't help but take another gulp of Absolut. Although Camille and I hadn't communicated with each other that often, she was still my big sister and part of me was crushed.

"So, you don't know where she is?"

"Nope. And I can't even care about that right now."

In spite of my mother's attempts at sounding hard, I could tell she was worried. What parent wouldn't want to know if their child was somewhere dead or alive? This was just my mother's shell – her way of dealing with the bullshit.

"Well, I need to go get these kids ready for bed. I'll tell your father you said hello and that you're ok. This number that came up on the caller ID, is that Pippy's number?"

"It's Piper, Mommy. And yeah, that's her number. I love you."

"I love you too Chiggy and be careful, ok?"

"I will, Ma. I'll come see y'all soon. I promise."

"Don't rush it baby. Get yourself situated out there first. Queensbridge ain't going no place. Oh yeah, before I forget," she said and then paused.

"Forget what?"

"Hold on, I was getting the number. Here it is. Detective Salerno called here the other day looking for you."

"He did? What did you tell him?"

The name made me light up. My Knight in Shining Armor hadn't forgotten about me.

"I told him you weren't here. What was I supposed to tell him?"

"No, that's fine. I mean, what did he say?"

"He just asked for you and left a number for you to call him."

I was like a school girl with a crush. Excitedly, I asked, "And then what did you say?"

"Girl, I don't have time for all that. Write this number down and find out for yourself."

She quickly recited the number and then hung up before even giving me a chance to say goodbye. If I thought I was going to be her number one concern, as I always had been, she quickly changed my mind.

"Salerno."

I said his name out loud while leaning back in my chair and picturing his sexy ass. That olive skin and jet black hair. Those smoldering eyes. Memories of the first time I saw him went skipping through my mind. It was the night I had a fight with Reece's trifling ass. Even though nobody else peeped it, I noticed him winking his eye at me from the driver's seat of his unmarked police car and I never forgot it. Then, every time I turned around, he was somewhere popping up. Whether it was at the store or walking through the blocks late at night, he'd just magically appear out of the blue. When everybody else turned their backs on me, he set up my Navy recruitment and even made sure I was all right while I was there. Now look, he's right back in my life leaving contact numbers for me. All of this and I had never even given him some pussy. After all, he was a White guy. I hadn't yet pondered the possibilities of a swirl. Project girls seldom went outside of our race. Even Puerto Ricans were a stretch.

Since he went through all that trouble, I figured reaching out to him was the least I could do. Fuck it, what did I have to lose? Of course, I pressed *67 before dialing the number. Secrecy was embedded in me whether it was a conscious effort or not.

"Hello."

He picked up on the second ring.

"Umm, hi. Can I speak to Detective Salerno?"

Slurring my words a little, I finally got the full sentence out of my mouth. Shit, I been *dranking*. The four shots I had already drowned were just appetizers. By the time I called him, I was working on my second glass mixed with Ocean Spray cranberry juice.

"Who's calling?"

"Who do you want it to be?"

That was the liquor talking, not me. But I knew his voice from anywhere. It was smooth with a New York Italian accent like John Gotti or Tony Soprano. In fact, he should have just said bada-bing when he answered the phone.

"Chaka?"

Apparently he knew my voice as well.

"Yep, that's her. I mean, that's me. How are you?"

"Wow, I've been waiting to hear from you. I'm good. Now. How about you?"

His response made me blush and my eyes flicker. I wondered if my gap-toothed smile could be felt through the phone.

"I'm ok. I've just been..."

"No need to go into detail right now." He spoke before I had a chance to finish my sentence. "Why don't you tell me all about it over dinner? Come see me."

His quick demand came out of left field. I was expecting to flirt a little bit but here he was with a call to action. The timing was perfect because that liquor had me ready for whatever.

"Come see you? Now, why would I do that?"

"Because I said so." He paused, the silence felt like an icicle rubbing across my nipples. I was intrigued. "And because you want to see me just as bad."

Whoa, he was a different Salerno altogether. His newly exposed dominance was a hell of a turn on.

"I can come this weekend."

"I'll send for you. Where are you?"

"I'll tell you when I see you. And just so you know, I don't get sent for, I do the sending. Call you when I get there. Bye,

Detective Salerno."

"Bye, Miss Adams." He chuckled. "See you soon."

My heart did a little pitter patter. Was it the vodka or did I genuinely have the hots for a cop of all people? Honestly, those hypnotic eyes of his had me hooked from the first time I saw him but who would have ever thought we'd be all flirting on the phone like that?

Giggling, I realized my night had completely turned around from that moment in the Champagne Room. In an effort to keep the vibe going, I blasted the radio to the highest and most ignorant volume. They had the nerve to be playing some of my old school favorites like, Evelyn Champagne King's, "Love Come Down". The Gods must have been in my favor.

"Awww shit now."

I sang out while snapping my finger to the beat and pouring yet another glass. It was a Wind Back Wednesday on the radio so for the next hour or so, they played all the jams from back in the day. Every time they spun the next song, I was pouring another drink.

Completely in my own little world, I didn't hear Piper as she entered the apartment which was unbelievable considering the place only consisted of one big ass room. But hell, I was getting my boogie on. It wasn't until the music went mute that I turned around and caught her standing there. Her expression was somewhere between confusion and comedic relief.

"What you doin' herrrrreee girrrrrllll?"

My neck rocked back and forth like a bobble-head doll. Tipsy would have been putting it nicely. Actually, I was White girl wasted. Usually, I'd drown my worries in a bag of cocaine but I didn't know where to score in Philly so I had nothing to balance out the liquor which at that point, had me looking like Ned the Wino from *Good Times*.

"Well, I came home early to check on you," she said, while dropping her duffle bag on the floor and walking over to the Absolut bottle. "But you seem aight to me so I'll just pour me a drink."

"Ain't nothing." I raised my glass and did a little two step. "Fuck Gus, that stupid mother." *Hiccup.* "Fucker." *Hiccup.*

"Yeah, what the fuck happened there? That wasn't too cool, yo, whatever it was."

"What they gon' do Pipe? Arrest me? Come on!" *Hiccup.*

"Come and get me!" I did a complete turn while patting my palm on my chest. "I'm right here."

Piper sucked her teeth and flicked me off with her wrist. "Whatever. So, he can explain to his wife why he had a stripper in the Champagne Room with his dick out?"

She shrugged and shook her head. "Hell nah, they gave that fool free entry for the next three months."

"Then he shoulda be giving me a thanking me then." *Hiccup.* "Rat bastard."

My speech was completely incoherent. I slammed my drink on the table, breaking the glass into pieces. Liquor spilled everywhere as I started an impromptu rendition of *The Five Heartbeats.*

"Nights like this, I-I-I-I wish that raindrops would f-a-a-a-a-llllll."

"Come on, you need to lay it down. It's over for you, boo."

Piper led me toward the bed where she pulled my shirt over my head. As she unbuttoned my jeans, I grabbed her hand and shook my head.

"No, no, no." I teased, while waving my index finger back and forth. "That's gonna cost ya. Five hundred dollars for an hour."

"Girl, it's time to night-night your drunk ass."

She paid me no mind and continued dressing me, finally getting one of her large t-shirts onto my skinny body.

"Piper, I ain't wanna do it. You know that, right?"

"Do what?"

"With Mister Danny. I told him to stop. I said it. Clear as day. I said to him. I said that I was Whitney. He ain't believe me. You know that, right? That I was Whitney."

She hadn't a clue what the hell I was talking about but she acted as if every word I was saying made sense.

"I know, Chaka, I know. Just go to sleep."

And sleep I did. My ass was comatose before she even turned the lights out. I'd be going home in the next few days and believe me; I needed all the rest I could get. There was no way I was re-entering that battlefield unprepared. In time I would realize, I was stepping into the ring for the fight of my life. No TKO's. No referees. Just a full on brawl where there would only be one person left standing. Hopefully that person would be me but even then, I wasn't too sure.

Chapter 10

Good thing Greyhound only charged fifteen dollars for a one-way ticket to New York from Philadelphia. Piper lent me that little chump change without a second thought especially once I told her I might be hooking up with a potential sponsor. In a world or 'Get Money' a sponsor's role is everything. If chosen wisely, his endless supply of cash could make the right chick be ready to marry him. She'd do anything to stay on that payroll. Whoever said that money can't buy love must have been broke without two nickels to rub together. That almighty dollar made the world go round, even more so when dealing in that street life. Luckily, Piper completely understood that and made sure I had enough dough in my pocket to get there, see Salerno and cash-out.

The bus pulled into Port Authority on 42nd Street. Native New Yorkers called it Forty-Deuce. Visitors called it Times Square. Although I didn't have to leave the terminal to catch the train to Queensbridge, I wanted to breathe the city air despite how rancid it smelled. It had almost been a year since I walked those streets of broken dreams and what better way to get my heart pumping than with a stroll down the Avenue of Lights which was also the number one tourist attraction in the entire country.

Swarms of people covered nearly every inch of each Manhattan block. Some were stopping in the middle of the street to take pictures of where the New Year's Eve ball dropped every year. Others were standing on the sidewalks watching the street performers dance, mime and draw wack ass portraits that never quite looked like the people who were posing for them. Though I had been gone a while, I still hadn't lost my New York swagger as I pushed and shoved my way through the crowds.

Finally reaching my destination, I bought a MetroCard and hopped right on the F train which had a direct route to the recently remodeled 21st Street Queensbridge station. That stop was both the best and worst thing the New York transit system could have ever built. The best because it meant we didn't have to walk too far from the projects to hop on the train. Ironically, it was also the worst because it meant our lazy asses didn't have to walk too far from the projects to hop on the train. It was as if the hood was architecturally designed to be a trap. Every single thing we needed, from a clinic to a beauty salon to a pizza joint was all right there, spread out among six little ass blocks. Who would ever have a reason to venture too far away at all?

Once I got off the train, I had to walk up the escalator because that shit was broken. Of course the one going down worked perfectly; as if anybody needed help with that. All the transit workers had to do was flip the switch to make the down escalator go up but no, that would have been way too much trouble for them, I suppose. Besides, they didn't give a fuck about us. Practically everybody coming off that train was heading to the projects anyway and as usual, the city could care less about the people living there.

By the time I was done lugging my heavy suitcase to the street level, I was breathing all hard as if I had just spent an hour on a treadmill. Who needed Lucille Roberts when that broken escalator gave me a full workout in a matter of seconds? I couldn't understand why so many Queensbridge heifers had big guts. If they rode the train more often, they could've had their daily dose of exercise right there.

Before I had a chance to cut the corner and enter my block, I heard my name being called. I was tempted to keep walking but the "Chaka's" got louder until I had no other choice but to acknowledge them. Tentatively, I turned around. They looked like twenty years had passed since we last saw each other. Time had definitely not been too kind to any of them. Every word came to mind but as they got closer, I had no idea what to say. Ta-Ta, Dana and Carmen – three of the original Sexy Six, were right there in the flesh. However, Ta-Ta didn't actually stop. Instead, she kept walking across the street in the opposite direction without even looking my way.

"Oh, you gonna act like you ain't hear us?"

Of course Dana would be the first to speak up. After all, until a few months ago, she was the only one who stayed in contact with me. Then, once I moved to Philly with Piper, I just stopped calling her. I wanted to stay in touch but I didn't feel like explaining my Navy disaster to anyone so I kept my distance. Anyway, I thought she'd be too busy in her role as a new mom to be bothered with all that. Since they were walking in the direction of the liquor store and were already holding plastic cups in their hands, I quickly acknowledged the fact that, baby or no baby, not too much had changed.

Usually stick thin and model-shaped, Dana had put on a little weight. Well, actually, a lot of weight. She was looking like an Oompa Loompa, albeit, a very tall one. It wasn't that McDonald's Extra Value Meal type of fat either. Her rounded face and poked out belly was surely a result of too much liquor combined with left over pregnancy pounds. She was wearing a t-shirt that had the GUESS logo, outlined in rhinestones, smack dab in the middle of it and a pair of Old Navy jeans. Typically, she was the one who always wore shoes but that too had somehow changed because she had on an old pair of Air Max that I remembered her sporting the summer before. Gone was the little glow in her cheeks and sparkle in her eye. She looked tired as though her youth had reached its expiration date. I'm almost positive that if I had taken a good look in the mirror, I would have seen the very same thing in my own reflection. Unfortunately, my self-perception was too skewed to accept reality.

"No, I wasn't. I didn't even hear y'all. Wassup?"

I faked a smile and leaned in for a group hug.

"Wassup with you Mami?" Carmen's exaggerated Spanish accent was still in effect.

Purposely flinging her wrist back and forth while she spoke, she made sure the princess-cut boulder on her ring finger was noticed. With the way it sparkled, even under the fluorescent street light, she didn't have to go the extra mile because there was no way I could miss that Rock of Gibraltar. Clearly, she wanted me to make some big hoopla over it so of course I did the opposite and said absolutely nothing. Hell, I was still salty that she called me a lame for going to the Navy. I didn't bring it up right then and there but I sure as hell hadn't forgotten about it either.

As I gave her a discreet once over, I could immediately point out the differences between her and Dana's lifestyles. Carmen's footwear alone, some chocolate Manolo Blahnik Timberlands, cost most than everything I was wearing including the clothes I had stuffed in my suitcase. She rocked the shoes well with a pair of army green cargo pants, a white tank top and a cropped acid washed jean jacket. Her blue-black highlights shimmered as she flung her hair so much in the past thirty seconds that I'm surprised she didn't get whiplash. Yeah, she was on top all right and she made sure everyone else around her knew it.

"Awww, we missed you." Dana's breath smelled like she gulped a whole bottle of Tequila for mouthwash. "I'm happy my boo is back. Get over here damnit."

She hugged me again, only this time she was so sloppy with it that one of my earrings went flying off my ear and rolled down the sewer. They were some ninety-nine cents hoops from the Korean beauty supply store so I wasn't going to make a big deal about it. Still, talking to Dana had reminded me that there was nothing worse than being one hundred percent sober and having to tolerate a belligerent drunk. As a result, I needed a drink just to continue that conversation so I grabbed the plastic cup from her hand and took a little swig.

"I missed y'all too. For real though."

Memories of the year before, when we were all inseparable, came creeping into my heart. Deep down, I truly loved my friends. All of us, with the exception of Carmen, had parents who grew up together. Shit, our grandmothers used to drink gin tonics in each other's apartments while listening to Lena Horne and talking about their husbands who were off in the Korean War. We were part of the Queensbridge legacy and inevitably every one of us had ties that would lead us right back here regardless of wherever life had us traveling at any given time. No matter how far we grew apart, Queensbridge would always be the one commonality we shared.

"So, what's going on with the Navy?" Carmen asked as her eyes looked me over from top to bottom and then back up again.

Her tone made it seem as if she already knew I wasn't in the military anymore. She said it like she was testing me instead of being genuinely concerned. Obviously, she wanted me to know that she knew my situation was all fucked up.

Smiling as if it was no sweat off my back, I replied, "I decided that wasn't the best thing for me but I'm working in Philly now.

So I guess everything happens for a reason."

"Oh, good. That's what's up Mami."

I'm sure she knew I was lying. Hell, Stevie Wonder could see that I was lying. But I'd be damned if I admitted it to her.

"Well, anyway, you and Ta-Ta need to talk."

Even in her drunken state, Dana was still the peacekeeper.

"I don't have a problem with her. She's not speaking to me so I'm not about to kiss her ass."

Of course, I wanted nothing more than to have my best friend back. She was the Ying to my Yang. My heart broke a little bit when she bypassed me and walked to the store. Even a slight head nod in my direction would have been better than her completely ignoring me. Instead, she looked right through me like I wasn't even there. So she gave me no other choice but to blow her off as well. Surely I wasn't about to sweat anybody to be my friend.

"Well, come over to my house after you go put your bags down. You know I got my own crib now."

Dana brushed her shoulders off with pride. There was no doubt in my mind that Housing was going to give her an apartment once she had her son. After all, that was one of our major goals in life. Get knocked up. Get our own crib. Life was simple for a project chick. We were born into a cycle.

"Oh shit, party at Dana's."

I did a little Cabbage Patch Kid dance to show some sort of enthusiasm for her recent come up. Carmen then butted in with a need to brag about her financial ability to sponsor the night.

"Cool, because I just gave Ta-Ta a hundred dollars to get some liquor so we about to get bent."

I wasn't feeding into all that so I just ignored her, allowing the sound of her boasting voice to go in one ear and right out the other.

"Give me like an hour and I'll be over there."

Ta-Ta was walking out of the store as I was saying my goodbyes. In order to avoid yet another uncomfortable confrontation or lack thereof, I gave them each a hug and moseyed on toward my building. The heat of their stares damn near burned the back of my neck so I straightened up and put a little diva-esque switch in my hips. If they were talking about me, I might as well give them a little something good to look at while they did it.

There I was again, starting from square one. As I got further away from my friends, I made a mental note to completely knock Carmen out of my spot as the HBIC – the Head Bitch In Charge. She didn't know it then but she'd soon find out, there was only enough light for one of us to shine and that one wasn't going to be her for much longer. Not if I had anything to do with it. Like Oprah Winfrey said in *The Color Purple*, "Sophia home now. Sophia home."

Chapter 11

40-05 12th **Street**. The red address above the building should have been wrapped in flashing neon lights. No matter how far away I went, it drew me in every single time I saw it. This would always be home. So many memories – some good, some bad – but every last one of them contributed to the woman I became.

I thought about yelling up to my mother's window because more than likely, the intercom was broken and she would have to come downstairs to open the door. But I was sick of tugging that suitcase around and I surely didn't want to bump into another damn person while walking around the corner, so I took my chances and tried the door myself. Luckily someone had propped it open by sticking a bottle cap between the door and the magnetic lock so I didn't even have to use the intercom. Unsurprisingly, it had an 'Out of Order' sign taped to it.

"It figures," I murmured under my breath.

I waited on the first floor for the coffin-sized elevator to come down. Once it did and I opened the door, the strong stench of urine came rushing toward me all at once. Whoever did that nasty shit must have never drank a glass of water in their entire life because the smell was so rank I almost threw up in my mouth a little bit. Since there was a bunch of soaked through newspapers scattered all around the floor, I could tell it had just happened; probably by the person who was riding in it right before me.

"Nasty Motherfuckers!" I yelled to whoever might have heard me.

For a moment, I contemplated my options. Either take the steps or ride in that trifling shit. It didn't take long before I did what any other self-respecting hood chick would have done. I inhaled deeply, held my breath and pressed the fourth floor.

Standing in the corner, in what seemed to be the only dry spot, I realized how tiny the elevator was. When I was younger, there'd be at least five people in there along with a shopping cart and if squeezed in correctly, a baby stroller. Now, there was barely enough room for me and my suitcase. My floor couldn't come soon enough.

Apartment 4A. The metal door had dents all over it from years of being banged on and kicked. People go crazy when they get locked out. Chipped green paint along the side of the door exposed another layer of blue paint that had been there before. The gold plated knocker was now rusted and looked like a fungus was growing all over it. I was almost too afraid to use it but I didn't feel like digging in my suitcase to find my key. So I balled up my fist and started banging.

"Who's knocking on my damn door like that?"

I could hear my mother yelling from inside the apartment. I stayed quiet and kept banging. All she had to do was look through the peephole to find out who it was. As her voice got closer, her yelling got even more irate.

"Nobody got time to be playing on my goddamn door. Knocking like you crazy. Who the hell is it?"

Her mood quickly changed once she opened up and saw her gap-toothed baby girl.

"CHIGGY!"

Immediately, I wrapped my arms around her. She had no idea I was coming home and her surprised response was everything I had anticipated.

"Honey, I'm home!" I yelled as she pulled away to take a good look at me.

Grabbing my face by my cheeks, she planted a kiss right on my lips. "Look at you. Get in here."

We finally made it beyond the front hallway when I noticed two little people running up on us. Both of them held on to her legs and stared up at me. Although my niece was already four and my nephew was almost out of pampers, this was the first time I had ever seen them in person.

"This is your Aunt Chaka," my mother said.

I knelt down and opened my arms. Only my niece came diving into them. My nephew was still checking me out from behind my mother's leg. My niece's name was Kyla, which she so eloquently spelled out for me as she said it. She started going on and on about everything under the sun. Even though she was only four, her speech was so clear and she didn't have a shy bone in her body. She looked just like my mother. And I do mean she was the spitting image of her. Had I not known any better, I would have thought my mom had a lovechild in her golden years. Then the thought of my parents still having sex made me nauseous so I quickly erased that vision from my mind.

In complete contrast to this little social butterfly in front of me, my nephew didn't say a word. In fact, he showed no emotion whatsoever. He didn't smile, didn't cry – he just looked indifferent. I heard about crack babies before but I never thought I'd have one in my family. Camille sure knew how to fuck shit up. Even worse than me.

"Oh my God. Look what the cat dragged in."

Those hazel eyes came peeking around the corner.

"TAYLOR!" I screamed and ran to my cousin who was equally as excited to see me.

Yeah, I know it seems extra but being away for almost a year felt like an eternity to me. Before then, I had never left the projects for more than a week.

While my mother bent down to lift my nephew, it finally dawned on me that she was only using one arm to do everything. Even when she walked, she had to practically drag one of her legs to take the next step. The Multiple Sclerosis hadn't gone into remission at all. In fact, it looked like it had gotten worse since the last time I saw her.

As she struggled to scoop up my nephew Taylor came rushing to her side.

"I got him, Debra. Just get Kyla."

She lifted him up and my mother grabbed my niece's hand. "Come on y'all. Time for bed."

"Where's Daddy?" I asked while following them both to the bedroom.

"He had to work tonight so I came down to help your mother get the kids ready for bed."

After raising five kids on her own, I would think she could have handled it by herself. Why the hell did she need assistance in that department?

By then, my mom was in the bathroom with Kyla who was standing on a step stool at the sink and brushing her teeth. I heard her singing the same song she sang to me when I was that age as she snapped her fingers along.

"Up and down and round and round. Now, spit."

The sound of my niece actually spitting with the song's rhythm brought back some funny memories that made me smile. I used to be up there jamming while moving my toothbrush across my teeth as the lyrics had instructed. My mother always made a grand spectacle over everything. She was definitely the one to blame for my dramatic flair.

"Camille is a hot ass mess," Taylor whispered.

Her voice forced me to put those flashbacks to the back of my head.

"She knows Debra can't take care of these damn kids."

She laid my nephew down on the bottom portion of the daybed. Once all the kids moved out, my mother had gotten rid of the bunk beds that I shared with my brothers. Little did she know, she'd have a whole new generation to raise. What was supposed to be her guestroom, was more like a nursery with toys all on the floor next to a box of pampers and a container of wipes tucked away in the corner.

"Where is she?"

My voice was just as low as Taylor's. Obviously, this wasn't a conversation that my mother should have heard.

"Her ass is out here smoking. I didn't see her myself but a couple of people told me she be coming around all hours of the night. They know to come get me the next time she pop up in a crack house some damn where because I got a whole bunch of shit to say to her. She's lucky I ain't bump into her yet."

Helplessly, I shook my head. How could a woman leave her kids to run the streets like that? It was so different from when I grew up. In my day, a lot of parents were on heroin but they didn't abandon their children. Yeah, their houses might have been shooting galleries on the low, at least I know my crib was, but I don't ever remember anybody's mother leaving out one day and never coming home. That crack shit changed the dynamics of the Black family like a motherfucker. There had never been another time in our history, where so many grandmothers were stuck raising their daughter's children. My family was no different because here my mother was, taking care of some toddlers, despite all her children being grown and out of the house. This should've been her time to live for herself but I guess a mother's job is never done.

Our conversation stopped as soon as my mom walked in the room.

"Mama, we gotta pray. Come on, Auntie."

Kyla grabbed my hand and we all bowed our heads while she chanted.

"God bless Mommy and Daddy and Mama and Grand Daddy and my bother and my Auntie and Taylor and my family and the whole wide world. Amen."

Whew! I thought she was about to call out every name she knew.

As she crawled into bed, she reached her hands out, pointing toward the toy chest.

"I know, I know."

My mother's words lingered in the room as she walked toward the toys. To my surprise, she pulled one out that I hadn't seen in years. It was my favorite guy, Maximus. Apparently, my niece was digging my main man just as much because as soon as she got a hold of him, she turned right over and fell fast asleep. Funny, he had the same effect on me when I was her age.

After making sure they were down for the count, I joined Taylor and my mother in the living room. Looking around the wood-paneled apartment, I couldn't help but see the noticeable changes. When I lived there, everything was spotless. The black tiled floor stayed wax. The wooden furniture always shined with a Pledge varnish. There was a place for everything and everything was in its place. If she didn't know anything else, my mother knew how to keep house. Now, there were piles of clean clothes covering the loveseat awaiting somebody to come and fold them up. An opened jar of Dax grease sat on the end table next to an old container of Country Crock butter that was full of barrettes and colorful rubber bands. *Barney* was playing on the television and there was a random Cheez Doodle or two in the middle of the floor. Impulsively, I grabbed the broom and started sweeping.

"Chiggy, don't worry about that. I'll get it later. Come and tell me about Philadelphia," my mother said as she patted the spot next to her.

"I know how to talk and sweep, Mommy. By the way, I can also chew bubble gum and walk at the same time too."

Sarcasm was how I dealt with uneasy situations and by that point, I really wanted to cry. Observing my mother in the past hour, exposed just how bad the Multiple Sclerosis was eating away at her body. When I left, she warned me that she would get sicker. I just didn't realize it would have happened so fast. She was moving slower than normal and could barely see things that were right in front of her. In her condition, she shouldn't have been taking care of someone else's kids. In fact, she needed somebody there to take care of her.

"All right, smart ass," she snapped back jokingly. "And how long are you staying in the city?"

I gave the apartment a once over before responding. There was no doubt about it – she needed me.

"I'ma stay for a minute and help you out."

Taylor wasn't too supportive of my decision because she responded quickly with her disapproval.

"Well, I hope you don't start being a project bunny like your friends. Sitting outside on them benches all day. And that Carmen be walking around like she's running the projects or something."

"I just saw them when I got off the train," I said as I walked toward the garbage can and poured out all the dirt I had accumulated on an envelope which I was using as a make-shift dust pan.

Taylor had started folding the clothes on the couch. "Well, just be careful."

"Ta-Ta came here the other day," my mother announced as both Taylor and I stopped doing our little duties and looked at her. She caught us both by surprise.

"For what?"

My attitude couldn't have been more obvious as I sucked my teeth and rolled my eyes to the back of my head. The code of the streets dictates that if you aren't speaking to me, then you lose all rights to speak to my family. I guess Ta-Ta didn't get that memo.

"She always stops by to check on me. Whatever y'all got going on won't faze me. My name is Paul and that's just between y'all."

There she goes again, making a rhythmic gesture about everything.

Taylor looked at me and shook her head. "Like I said, just be careful."

By the time I finished straightening up, they had hipped me to all the hood gossip. It was just like old times. The only difference was that my name wasn't wrapped up in the street rumors. But knowing me, that was all about to change.

Chapter 12

My mother finally dozed off around eleven o'clock and by then Taylor was long gone. With nothing else to do, I decided to make my way over to Dana's house. She only lived one block over, on the 40th side of Tenth Street, so there was no need to get all dressed up for a stroll through the hood. Wearing the same pair of jeans I had on all day, I tied up my gray New Balance Classic 574's and grabbed a white jean jacket from the closet. I forgot I still had some old clothes left at my mother's house, lucky for me because my gear was scarce.

As I walked through the projects, it felt like a ghost town. During our gossip session, Taylor told me how the Feds swept through with some secret indictments that nearly took the whole hood down. Even The Pub, our neighborhood bar, got raided and subsequently its doors were padlocked indefinitely. That was a shame because that place had been around since my mother's generation – it was basically a Queensbridge landmark. I guess I wasn't the only one sniffing coke in the bathroom. Apparently, there was a whole underground drug trade going on in there.

Nothing good lasts forever, I suppose, because all of the real money makers in the projects got infiltrated like Nino at The Carter. The only ones left out there were the hand to hand smugglers and of course the ones who were doing all the snitching to begin with. However, even they weren't taking any chances because the blocks were completely deserted. Normally, people were sitting on the benches, blasting their radios and sipping Cognac from five cents plastic cups. Now, it felt like I was walking through unchartered territory. Queensbridge just didn't feel the same to me anymore.

Dana's intercom wasn't working, there was no surprise there. Since I had no idea where her window was, I ended up standing in front of her building impatiently waiting for somebody to open the door. After about ten minutes or so, some lady finally came out. She was acting like she didn't want to let me in the building until I yanked the door handle and bogarded my way inside.

"Well, damn. Thanks a lot," I snapped once I finally entered.

She didn't respond which was a good thing. I wasn't in the mood to be brawling in nobody's hallway.

Dana lived on the second floor and I could hear her music from the front door. I knew it had to be coming from her house because they were blasting Anita Baker which was one of Dana's go-to songs whenever she was drunk. I shook make my head with a smile. Glad some things had stayed the same.

Since she only lived one flight up, I didn't bother taking the elevator. Actually, I couldn't stand people who took the elevator to the second floor. I mean really, there was nothing lazier than that stupid shit.

As I got to her door and went to grab the knocker, I froze after hearing my name.

"But I'm saying, she got on those old ass New Balance sneakers. Who's still wearing those?" Carmen's words were quickly followed by an outburst of laughter.

I looked down at my feet. She was right. My kicks were pretty outdated. Maybe I could've at least washed the dingy shoestrings to make them appear a little whiter or something. But then again, I didn't think anybody was going to be looking that close either.

"My thing is this." Now it was Dana's turn to add her two-cents. "Why you gotta lie and say you working in Philly? Like, how you end up all the way over there anyway? Yeah, aight, now you working and shit. Chaka, please. She got on them expensive jeans and probably don't even got no money in her pocket."

Well, she had a point there. I didn't have a job but damn, was it that hard to believe that I could get one? And well, I did have on some pretty pricey Seven for All Mankind jeans but why the fuck was she worried about what was in my pockets? If she was so caked up herself, she shouldn't have been wearing that GUESS t-shirt. Rhinestone logos been played out.

Staying as mute as a church mouse, I put my ear to the door

so that I didn't miss a word. That's when I heard Ta-Ta's voice.

"Little Miss Military is right back here with us – the same people she left. Anyway, Dana, I told you she wasn't coming. Thinking she's better than everybody else. You already know how she gets down."

Where'd that one come from? I never thought I was better than anybody else. Well, at least not them. I left because it was the only option I had. Why would I stay there if I had an opportunity to do something better with myself? Even if it failed, why were they knocking that?

Listening to the way they were talking about me had me questioning my own damn self even though I knew I had made all the right decisions. My own clique wasn't even giving me credit for at least making an attempt to do something better.

"That bitch ain't better than nobody."

Carmen's fake accent had somehow disappeared because she was now fluent in Ebonics.

"Even if she do got a job, my ring cost more than she make in a year. Bet that."

Knowing my friends were throwing dirt on me while I was down only added fuel to my fire. At first, I wanted to kick on the door and curse every last one of them out. Then, I remembered something my mother always told me, "Keep your enemies close so that you will always know their next move."

Although it broke my heart to consider them full-on enemies, there was nothing worse than a fake friend. At least with an upfront rival, you know how they feel straight off the rip. There's no wondering or second guessing. They don't like you so they don't fuck with you. That was the shit I respected. But this artificial love? Nah, I wasn't bred that way so I couldn't respect it not even a little bit. But I sure knew how to play along. Pretending was always my forte anyway. With that notion, I finally knocked on the door.

"Damn, about time," Dana yelled as I entered the apartment.

Like crickets, they all got quiet and Carmen threw Ta-Ta a side eye that she thought I didn't peep. I only caught it because I went in there with all my guards up. As always, I was one step ahead of them.

Dana's apartment was somewhat bare. Her mismatched living room set consisted of a vinyl couch and a microsuede recliner. The stereo speakers looked like the most expensive thing in the crib. Leave it to Dana, if nothing else, she was going to make sure her music was right. White lace curtains, which looked like doilies hanging from a rod, aligned the windows in every room. There was a wooden table in the dining room where they were all seated. Everyone had a glass in front of them and there was an unfamiliar odor circulating in the air. It wasn't weed and it wasn't cigarettes. Whatever it was, I walked into a heavy cloud of it as I ventured further into her apartment.

"Here, let me pour you a drink."

Dana went to the kitchen while I sat at the table across from Carmen. Ta-Ta was sitting to my right and hadn't even looked up from her glass.

"We ain't think you were coming, Mami."

Alas, Carmen was Spanish again.

"Nah, I had to help my mother with the kids." I turned toward Ta-Ta. "She said you came over to check on her the other day. Thank you."

Fuck it, we were all sitting together, I might as well address the purple elephant in the room.

"It's cool. I ain't like you. I always make sure my people are good."

Finally we would get to the root of this shit. Dana and Carmen said nothing. It was like they weren't even there. Ta-Ta and I needed this moment of clarity. It had been a long time coming – too long, if you ask me.

"Yo, what the fuck is your problem with me all of a sudden?"

"My problem with you? Come on Chaka, you really got the nerve to be asking me that?"

As I peered into her eyes, which started tearing up, I noticed the scar right above her cheek. Part of me never realized she'd walk around with that reminder for the rest of her life. It was one of the seventeen stab wounds she received during the night of her attack. Seeing it brought me back to the moment when I found her face down in a pool of blood. The memory made me begin to cry right along with her. I couldn't even fix my mouth to say anything in response.

"You wanna know what my problem is? This is my fucking problem."

She stood up and lifted her red Polo shirt over her head. Chills went up my spine at the sight of the scars. Puncture wounds were spread out from her stomach all the way up to her collarbone.

It was as if Malik just went on a cutting spree. Though they had healed, some were keloid while others were darkened spots that made her look like a leper. The more I looked at her, the more I realized that could've been me instead.

"Ta-Ta that wasn't my fault. How the fuck was I supposed to know he was gonna do that? You think I wanted this to happen to you? Come on, how could you even think that?"

"See, that's where you got it all fucked up." She was yelling at the top of her lungs and her big Double-D breasts were flopping all over the place as if they were going to pop out of that cheap Dollar Store bra at any moment.

"I'm not mad at you because this happened. You, of all people, couldn't control Malik."

"Then what the fuck? What is it?"

"How the fuck you gonna just leave me like that?"

"I didn't just leave. What was I supposed to do? Manny said..."

She interrupted. "Fuck what that sazón punk said. I could deal with all that. My issue is this." She banged her hand on the table with every word she uttered. "How you just gonna leave me to deal with Malik over some shit you and him had going on? After everything he did to your stupid ass, you just skip town and not even try to get back at him? Now I gotta be the one watching my back and waiting for him to pop up again? 'Cuz believe me, when he do, he gon' get dealt with when I see his bitch ass. But this is your fight, not mine. You shoulda been the one to handle it, not me. But nah, you went and ran off like a little punk."

Wait, that was it? That's the reason she wasn't speaking to me?

I almost wanted to scream, "Do you know what I did to him on the strength of you?"

Of course, I couldn't touch on any of that. Nobody would ever know what went on in that Bronx warehouse except me, Manny and two homicidal Presa Canarios. That night was going to the grave with me. If I didn't know anything else, I knew how to keep my mouth shut. Even if it meant losing a friend in the process, I would never speak on that situation.

I thought long and hard about my next move and how I would play this out. There had to be a way for me to convince her that Malik was never coming around without dry snitching on my involvement in his disappearance. So I bit my tongue and backed down. I'd just have to humble myself.

"I'm sorry, Tashanique."

I resorted to calling her by her government. She hated that name and quite honestly, I too would've been mad if that shit appeared on my birth certificate. But if my emotional plea was going to work, I had to go beyond the nicknames and street rhetoric.

"I'm sorry. I'm genuinely sorry and there's nothing more I can say. I fucked up. I panicked and I ran. I'll always hate the fact this happened to you. But I'm sorry. If I could do it all over again, I would. Only this time, it would have been me instead of you. I'm here now and I swear I'll never leave your side again. All I can say is that I'm sorry. And all you can do is believe that and forgive me."

Though my version of events was untrue, the emotions behind my tears were as real as they could get. I missed my best friend. Truth be told, I missed all my friends. Rather, I missed the friendships we once shared. Mostly though, I wanted that bond back. I needed my Thelma and from the look of sadness in her eyes, she needed her Louise as well.

"Come here." I got out of my chair and wrapped my arms around here. "I'm sorry. Ok?"

Sobbing loudly, her body flinched in my arms. When it was all said and done, Ta-Ta was all bark and no bite. Her heart was full of love that was normally hidden behind a loud mouth and a street persona. But I knew the real her and that was the friend for whom I would travel to the ends of the Earth. Fuck the gangsta circus act she put on for the people around her. Our bond was unbreakable and I knew if I could get beyond her wall, which I was managing to do at that very moment, we would be all right.

"Well, I'm glad that's all over with because y'all are fucking up my high." Dana finally broke up the soap opera drama with some much needed laughter.

"I love you Louise," Ta-Ta whispered in my ear while I was still bent down in our embrace.

"I love you too Thelma. Always."

After that, I didn't even think about the little shit talking they were doing before I got there. In all reality, that's just how girlfriends get down. Believe it or not, your supposed best friend is probably somewhere talking about you right now. It doesn't mean that she won't slide down a razor blade pole into a pool full of alcohol to save your ass if you were drowning. It just means that chics love to gossip. It's what we do. Whenever you have a group of females, there's bound to be some form of cattiness. Accept it and move on. Well, that's what I chose to do anyway.

As I took the first sip of my drink, Carmen opened the cocaine-lined dollar bill. The sparkling crystal in it meant there was hardly any cut and it was pure as snow. My stomach immediately began to bubble up like I had to go to the bathroom or something. Cocaine has a tendency to do that to people. Even though you don't really have to take a shit, your body just starts to react because you're about to ingest some foreign object that doesn't belong there in the first place. It had been a while since I got high and Lord knows I needed a bump or two. So many thoughts were clouding my mind especially as I started thinking about Malik. My brain needed to go numb for a minute and that white girl was the perfect remedy.

"Who got a straw?" I asked to nobody in particular. There was a high probability of them all having a sniffing apparatus in their possession.

"Wait, she's about to make a cigarette," Dana replied as she passed Carmen a Newport from the box.

This was a new twist for me. How the hell do you make a cigarette? They looked pretty well put together already.

Carmen emptied about half of the tobacco out on the table. Then, she turned the cigarette upside down, dipped the straw into the cocaine bill, scooped up some powder and poured it into the opening of the cigarette. She did this about three times, each followed by a shaking of the Newport to make sure the coke got all the way to the bottom, near the filter. After that, she twisted the end of the cigarette together so that nothing would fall out of it once she turned it back right-side up. With her teeth, she pulled out the cotton filter and ripped it in half, from top to bottom. She then stuck one half of the filter back into it so the cigarette was partially open at the top. Once she lit it, the paper burned quickly at first. It was a lot faster than a normal cigarette. And there was that smell again. It was the one I inhaled once I got there.

She passed the fast burning cig around the table and when it finally got to me, I took a long pull causing it to burn even faster.

"Don't pull on it so hard," Dana said.

From the rush I felt, I sure as hell didn't need to inhale any stronger. The smoke was sweet and numbed my tongue. Even my lips started feeling like they were frozen. Soon, Carmen was mixing up another one and my heart was racing for it to make its way around the table again. I loved the high because it instantly made me forget all the shit that had been rummaging through my brain.

There was a whole pack of cigarettes on the table and more than half a bottle of liquor left. I was right back with my clique and we were in for a long night ahead.

"Oh well," I said. "Inhale the good shit. Exhale the bull shit."

With that, we all laughed. And for a second there, it was like old times again. The Sexy Six, minus two of course, were back at it.

Eventually, I would come to realize two very important things about friends in general. The first thing: the hate is so real. The second thing: the love is so fake.

I should've listened to Taylor. I should have been more careful.

Chapter 13

I didn't leave Dana's house until about seven in the morning. By the time I walked out of her building, the sun was already shining and the birds were chirping. Creeping through the hood, with my eyes still bugged out of their sockets, I'm sure I smelled like one big ashtray. I was stuck. Heart beating a mile a minute. Mouth twitching uncontrollably. Usually, I had dominion over the cocaine and knew how to make myself come down when it was time to call it a night. But that cigarette shit had me looking like a fiend.

Once I got to my mother's house, I laid in bed for another two hours. I felt bad when she entered the bedroom and struggled to gather up the kids while I pretended to be asleep. The right thing for me to do would've been to help. Then again, I wasn't in my right frame of mind and my mother was the last person I wanted to see while in that condition. With just one look, she'd know that I was on something a lot stronger than some damn weed.

By the time I actually did wake up, my head was pulsating. It was five in the evening and the house was empty. On the dining room table was a note from my mom telling me they went out shopping and would probably stop somewhere for dinner. She said they tried to wait around but I was sleeping for too long so they went about their business without me.

A pang of guilt tugged at my heart. My poor niece had probably tried to wake me up a few times but I was on crash mode and dead to the world. Not that I could have joined them anyway. I already had plans to meet Salerno for drinks at eight o'clock. Lucky thing I woke up when I did, it was going to take me at least two hours to get myself together.

I made an internal vow to never smoke that shit again. Like any functional addict, I swore to myself that the first time would be my last. That fake promise made me a little less disappointed when I looked at my reflection in the mirror.

I laid out my outfit for the night. Pairing a beige off-the-shoulder peasant top and some skintight Miss Sixty jeans with Piper's red Stuart Weitzman pumps, gave me a supermodel's swagger. Hell, I was a size two, I could make anything work. Salerno said he was taking me somewhere in the city so I wanted to look my best. Once I got dressed, I fidgeted with my hair because I sure didn't have enough money for a wash and set. Thank God I wasn't bald-headed and was able to effortlessly pull it all up, put it in a high bun and brush my little baby hairs down. With a smidgen of lip gloss and some silver hoops, I was ready. Glancing in the full-length mirror behind my bedroom door, I was pleased with what I saw. No matter what, I always cleaned up nicely.

I left out of the building and used my last few bucks to catch a cab to Manhattan. The ride was a quick hop and a jump over the 59th Street Bridge but the cabbie almost charged me twenty dollars. That's what happens when you ride in unmarked gypsy cabs. Those illegal immigrant drivers are highway robbers in every literal sense of the word. A metered yellow taxi would have only cost me half of what I paid but they seldom ever stopped for anybody in the hood and I sure as hell didn't feel like waiting.

We pulled up to the address Salerno gave me and it was a quaint picturesque restaurant with dim lights and an outside patio. As soon as I walked in, I spotted him. He was sitting in a corner booth looking as good as he did the first time I ever laid eyes on him. Instead of the cop gear I had grown accustomed to him wearing, he was exquisitely dressed like a movie star on the cover of the latest issue of VOGUE. His jet black hair glistened as the candle burned in front of him. The lilac buttoned down shirt he wore, popped against his olive complexion. As the hostess brought me to his table, the diamonds in his gold watch flickered in the flame's shadow. The New York City Police Department must have been giving out some serious raises because this dude was looking like a bag of money.

"Miss Adams is here."

The hostess announced me as I reached the table. Salerno

finally looked up and our eyes locked. His gaze hypnotized me as I stood there in a trance. It wasn't until he smiled, actually more of a smirk, just wide enough to flash his pearly whites, that I finally spoke.

"Detective Salerno."

I was in awe. Here he was, my Knight in Shining Armor, so close within my reach. He stood up, his physique was still solid. I'm about five-eleven with shoes on and we stood eye to eye. As he hugged me, I felt his muscles tighten around my shoulder frame. My pussy creamed at his touch.

"Sit down." He pulled my chair out like a gentleman. That was a first. Nobody had ever done that before. "Please call me Paul. Hell, call me Salerno if you want. But by all means, drop the Detective."

"Oh, I forgot." I made imaginary quotation marks in the air. "We're on a date."

He chuckled. "No, it's not that. I'm no longer with the force, Chaka. I'm kind of..." He paused. "I'm kinda retired, so to say."

"Retired? How can you be retired? Wait a minute, how old are you?"

My questions formed out of both curiosity and nervousness. I was used to Red Lobster and Jackson Hole diners. Contrarily, we were in a place with white linen napkins and long stemmed wine glasses. I had to do or say something instead of sitting there twiddling my thumbs. Honestly, I didn't know how to act.

"You're still full of questions, aren't you? Here, why don't you have a drink first? What would you like?"

"Let me get some Henny."

His expression didn't look too agreeable. So, I tried giving it a more sophisticated sound. "Well, I mean, I'll have some Hennessey on the rocks."

I definitely thought I scored with my classy choice of drinks. 'On the rocks' sounded way better than, 'put some ice in my cup'. Or at least in my opinion, it did.

He shook his head, slightly raised his finger and summoned the server to our table.

"No, why don't you try something else. I'll order for you." He turned toward the waitress while I sunk in my seat, slightly embarrassed. "We'll have a bottle of Château Pétrus, 1978."

She nodded and whisked away. In seconds she returned with a bottle and a corkscrew.

Well, why didn't he just say he wanted some wine? Trying to be all fancy about it.

"Are you ready for your entrée?"

Homegirl didn't even look at me while she asked for our order. Apparently, she realized I was way out of my league.

"Yes. She'll have the filet mignon, medium rare. And for me, I'll do the elk tenderloin. Same way."

"Sure thing, Mr. Salerno. If there's anything else you need, I'll be right here."

Her voice was a little too flirtatious for my liking. If this was Red Lobster, I would have been checked her for getting a little too comfortable. But I wasn't in my environment so I had to act appropriately. After all, she was probably going the extra distance to get a bigger tip. This place looked like the patrons could afford to leave more than five dollars on the bill. Really though, I didn't mind her little charm. She was a pretty chocolate girl with a shoulder length bob and a slim shape. Her features were exotic, like a young Iman with a Naomi Campbell body. I'll give props where props are due and shorty was bad. I could tell from her accent that whatever she was, it sure wasn't American. Oh well, I guess the classier the restaurant, the classier the waitresses because the skanks at Red Lobster looked like they just got off the block and decided to stroll into work.

Once we were alone again, I finally found the nerve to speak up.

"I don't like steak."

"It's really good here. You'll love it." He reached over the table and held my hand.

I wasn't used to men ordering for me but it was actually a good thing that he did because I could barely pronounce some of the food on that menu. Admittedly, I was smitten by his take-charge bravado. Who knew he could be so suave? I wasn't expecting that at all. My impressionable ass was digging every minute of it.

After my second glass of wine, I felt more relaxed. Salerno made sure I was comfortable and gave me a sense of actually belonging in a crowd full of rich looking White people. From that point on, my confidence took over. Slowly, I started to come out of my shell. At last, I was free to be myself. Well, the self I had hidden from everybody for so long. I didn't have to act hard or pretend to be street smart. Although I was a little rusty, I was actually in my element. Seldom was I given a chance to have decent conversations with men besides the regular shit them illiterate project bums were spitting.

"Yo, I'm saying though."

"Damn, you gorgeous. Wassup?"

"Fuck that Ma, when you gonna let me rip?"

Seriously, that's how those fools spoke and had the nerve to wonder why a woman like me would never give them any play. Yes, I was a stuck up snobby bitch who thought the world revolved around me but I would have given at least a few of them some action had they stepped to the plate with some class. But Salerno was different. He made me feel like I was on top of the world. We talked for hours about everything from politics to classic Mafia movies. He made me use my brain and I hadn't done that for years. In no time, I was head over heels.

During our conversation he revealed that he left the Police Department around the same time that I went to the Navy. Oddly enough he was still able to send me care packages full of money, even though according to his timeline, he was unemployed by then. I didn't mention it but it was a point that struck a chord with me. Unfortunately for my nosy ass, he didn't go into details on why he quit so I chose to table that question until we got to know each other better.

Likewise, I wasn't completely upfront about my Navy fiasco either. I fed him the same story that I had told everybody else. It was the one where the military threw me out for having flat feet. Although that was a real reason for getting the boot, as stupid as that shit sounds, it wasn't my truth. He didn't need to know all that though so I gave him my version of events and I stuck to it. He seemed to believe me or maybe he just didn't care because he didn't press the issue. Either way, were both so deeply engaged that we hadn't realized the entire restaurant was empty until the waitress arrived at our table with the check. Salerno beckoned her with his finger. As she bent over and he whispered in her ear, she threw me a seductive smile. I blushed and looked away. No woman had ever made me pink in the cheeks before.

He paid in cash, then we made our way to the front door as employees were busy wiping down tables and sweeping the floor. We literally shut the place down.

More and more, I felt like Cinderella who hated to end a night of enchantment. Why would I want to return to my mother's day bed with my niece lying next to me after being swept off my feet by a real life Prince Charming?

Valet pulled a silver BMW 740i up to the front of the restaurant. Since I spent my last few dollars getting over there, I silently prayed for Salerno to offer me a ride home. Once he opened the passenger door, I let out a sigh of relief. I was just happy I wouldn't have to hop the train back to Queensbridge. As I sat down, the waitress stepped out of the restaurant and walked toward us. She was no longer wearing her white shirt and black slacks uniform. Instead, she had a hippie vibe going on with a yellow crop top tee, low-rise blue jeans that were ripped at the knees and white flip-flops. Naturally chic is how I'd describe her look. It was different than the extra efforts us hood girls made to look good. Her style was totally unforced.

"She's coming with us. Ok?"

Salerno waited for me to respond but I was too confused to say anything. Here I thought he was feeling me but this motherfucker was about to drop me off and end his night with the help. Fuck this prim and proper shit, I was ready to go flip-mode squad on both of their asses.

Sensing my disgust at what I deemed was his utter lack of respect, he leaned into the car. With his lips so close to mine that I could almost taste them, he whispered, "I bought her for you."

My jaw dropped. What did he mean by that? Before I could ask any questions, the waitress hopped in the backseat.

"Hi, I'm Ava." She softly slid her finger down my cheek.

Salerno firmly placed his right hand on my thigh and rubbed my leg all the way up to my zipper as his foot slammed on the gas. With that, we were off to our next destination for the night. Despite what Jack, Chrissy or Janet thought, three wasn't just company. It was more like a ménage.

Chapter 14

We drove into an indoor parking lot beneath one of Manhattan's new sky scrapers. It looked like some fancy hotel and was located not too far away from the restaurant. Salerno pulled into a reserved spot, then we walked to the stairwell where he used a key card to open the door. I threw him a side-eye. It was pretty bold of him to rent a room before I even agreed to slide off for the night. Usually, dudes would ask if I was down for a short stay at a local motel before they went through the extra trouble of wasting money on a reservation. Salerno must have been pretty confident about getting some floozy in his bed, whether it was me or somebody else.

We stepped out of the stairway and into a beautiful marble floored hallway with crystal chandeliers and gold plated elevators. The hotel's décor was way more impressive than any Motel 6 that I had ever been in. At least I would feel like a high class jump-off. Really, what other word would I have used to describe myself? He wasn't my man. After all, this was our first official date and I was already giving up the pussy. Well, at least I wasn't being treated like a low-class tramp. Salerno was going all out to get a taste of my cookie.

I made small chit-chat with Ava until the elevator arrived on the twenty-third floor. All the while, Salerno kept his eyes locked on me. He was penetrating me way before anything got physical. My panties were soaked.

Once we entered the room, my eyes lit up like a kid on Christmas.

"Damn, this hotel is like a full-size apartment." I blurted out loud, too impressed with the mammoth sized room to maintain my composure.

He looked amused by my outburst. "Hotel? I live here, Chaka. You're in my apartment."

I felt stupid, especially since he corrected me in front of the waitress of all people. Immediately, I got defensive. "Your apartment? Well, I didn't know a cop's pension could afford all of this. Excuse me."

He wasn't disturbed by my little attitude. Instead, he grabbed my hand and said, "There are a lot of things you don't know about me."

He then called out to Ava and told her to get us something to drink. Before he completed his sentence, she was already in the kitchen.

The windows went from the floor all the way up to the ceiling. Salerno pressed a button on the wall and the mesh blinds seemed to evaporate. The flashing lights pulled me closer. Only a sliver of glass separated me from the sky.

"Wow, you can see the whole city from here." I thought I was speaking to myself but once I heard the sound of my own voice, I realized I had said it out loud.

The hustle and bustle of New York was all around me as I took in the apartment's panoramic view. Instinctively, I walked toward the window facing Queens. The chimneys appeared as clear as day. No matter where I was, I could always find Queensbridge by locating Con Edison's three red smoke stacks that hovered over the projects and pumped mysterious gray smoke clouds into the hood all day every day. As always, the city never gave a fuck about us. An energy plant right next to a residential area where more than half the children suffer from severe asthma? Oh well, as long as they had Medicaid, nobody ever complained.

The projects, which had been my whole world at one time, looked so small and insignificant from my view. As a little girl, I would gaze over the river and daydream about being in one of these high class buildings. And here I was. Only this time, it wasn't my imagination. I was actually living a reality that Chiggy had only fantasized about.

Drifting off in my thoughts, I flinched when Salerno touched my arm. "There's more. Come see everything."

Interlocking his fingers with mine, he led me on a tour. The couches were milky white leather and butter soft. It felt like I was walking through a museum with all the paintings on the walls. They were encased in brass frames which were a far cry from the bullshit plastic ones I used to buy at the little five and dime furniture stores. With the hardwood floors, granite counter tops and stainless steel appliances surrounding me, I felt like I was Elvira in a scene from *Scarface*. Taking it all in at once left me speechless. I could definitely get used to living like that.

Salerno led me down the long mirrored hallway into the bedroom. My heart nearly stopped when I saw the size of his bed. It was like two king-sized mattresses put together. The headboard was taller than me.

"This is beautiful." I finally revealed, not caring if I sounded like an out-of-place hoodrat or not.

"This is nothing. I'm gonna show you the world."

Before I could ask him how he intended to do that, I felt a small hand reach from behind and caress my breasts. Moving slowly, she started to press against my back while Salerno leaned in, passionately thrusting his tongue into my opened mouth. As he unzipped my jeans, Ava slid them down my hips. We moved to the bed, not once losing the groove of each other's bodies. I tried to lean down toward his dick which felt like a rock about to explode as it pressed against my thigh. To my surprise, he pulled my head away and laid me on my back. Reaching into the nightstand drawer, he pulled out an oval shaped mirror. On it, was a mound of white powder. He placed a long line of it on my torso, leading from my navel to the opening of my pussy lips. Ava glided across my body, licking all the cocaine off, until she reached my clitoris.

"Ugh," I moaned.

I had never felt like that before. My body started grinding against her mouth as I held her head between my legs. Salerno put the silver spoon full of coke to my nose and I inhaled deeply.

"You like that don't you?" He asked while nibbling the nape of my neck.

All I could do was nod as I bit my lower lip. My mouth opened wide once Ava began fucking my wet pussy with her tongue. By that time, Salerno had my nipples between his teeth. His bites were rough but felt so sensual causing every nerve in my body to stand on edge. I almost lost it when I watched Ava lick her finger before gently sliding it into my anus. The louder my moans got, the deeper she thrust her finger inside of me.

From the corner of my eye, I saw Salerno's hand sliding up and down his dick. He dispelled every rumor I ever heard about White men having small packages. It grew bigger as he listened to Ava's slurping sounds while she sucked my pussy before moving her tongue to my ass.

"Agh," I yelled.

In my mind, I had become Charlie again; the insatiable courtesan who wanted to behave badly and rock it until waterfalls. Every erotic film I ever watched flashed in front of me in real time. I was the star. Finally, I was given my stage.

Groans turned into screams of ecstasy as I couldn't hold them in any longer. My back arched and my hips rose from the bed. I humped against Ava's mouth harder while my hands pulled at her hair.

Then, every muscle in my body tightened and made me feel like I was having convulsions. I released Ava from my grasp and cried out, "Wait, wait, something's wrong."

I thought the cocaine was giving me a heart attack because my body had never felt like that before. Neither one of them listened to my pleas to stop. If anything, it made both of them even more ferocious.

"Oh, my God. Wait. No. Oh, my God. Oh, my God. Oh, my. Agggghhh."

An electric vibe went through my body and a rush of hot liquid squirted from my pussy. I couldn't stop it as it flowed heavily, spraying wildly all over the bed. Ava's hair and face were drenched in my juices. Tears rolled down my eyes and my body went limp as I gasped for air.

Salerno softly kissed my forehead. I was too embarrassed to look at him. How could I? I just pissed all over his bed.

"I'm sorry. I don't know. I don't know what happened."

I wanted to give some sort of explanation or excuse for what just happened but I couldn't find the words. I was so disoriented.

"It's ok. You never came before?"

I don't know if I was just basking in the afterglow or what but his voice seemed so smooth and comforting.

"Is that what that was? I don't, I mean, I never felt like this. I mean, I don't..." A residual tremble went through my body causing my back to arch while I let out another moan. "Aggghhh."

Ava rose from the bed and walked toward the bathroom. The shower water turned on.

"I'm sorry. I hope your girlfriend isn't mad that I messed up your bed."

The soft cotton sheets were soaked all the way through to the mattress.

"My girlfriend? She's not my girlfriend." He chuckled and ran his finger through my hair which somehow managed to come out of its bun. "I told you, I bought her for you."

"You mean you *brought* her here to fuck me. I know that."

"No, I bought her for you. I know the difference between the words. She's bought. As in, 'paid for'. As in, 'everything has a price'. She's yours for the night. Make her earn every dime."

Ava emerged with a plush white terrycloth robe and announced, "Your bath is ready, sweetie."

My eyes darted back to Salerno and I couldn't help but laugh. If I had died and gone to heaven, I couldn't have imagined it feeling this good.

"What are you trying to do to me here?"

I had to ask. I mean, he was going pretty far for a one-night stand.

"I told you. I'm gonna give you the world and everything in it." His words careened through my head and made their way to my heart.

Before lazily strolling to the bathroom, I took in my new surroundings. Salerno's motives confused me but I figured I'd ride it out just as long as I felt as good as I did at that very moment. The truth was, I had never been more alive in my life. Until that point, I thought I was living. But my hood notoriety and drug money were nothing compared to what Salerno was bringing to the table. With him I quickly learned that project life and real life were two completely different things. Now, if those worlds ever collided, there would be hell to pay. Unbeknownst to me, I was on a crash course to the fiery pits. And wouldn't you know it? I couldn't even afford to pay the toll.

Chapter 15

Sunlight pierced through the bedroom window, waking me from what felt like the best sleep I ever had. According to the clock on the wall, it was already two in the afternoon and there I was with cold still in my eyes. From beneath a mound of down-feathered pillows and a fluffy white duvet cover, I stretched my body so much that it felt like my arm could touch the ceiling. Finally, I turned to Salerno's side of the bed and it was empty. Vivid scenes from the night before played out in front of me. All I could do was shake my head. Charlie was on her absolute worst behavior but the thought of it made my pussy throb. By far, it was the most mind-blowing sex I had ever experienced. And I wanted more.

The television was playing in the living room so I grabbed my robe from off of the bedside chaise and headed toward the sound. I started to feel bad that it was so late in the afternoon and I was just getting up. There's nothing worse than a bimbo who overstays her welcome. Salerno was probably out there counting down the minutes until I left. Hopefully he'd give me a ride home because even after that romp, I remembered, I was still broke as hell.

"Hey, you."

The sight of him made me blush. He looked even better in the daylight as he sat at the dining room table reading a newspaper.

"Hey there, good morning," he said while looking down at his gold Rolex.

His lighthearted sarcasm made me smile even more.

"Well, it's your fault for keeping me up all night. You freak." I taunted him before leaning over and kissing his lips. I couldn't resist it. They were calling out to me. "I'm sorry but that bed felt way too good to get up."

There were shopping bags sprawled around the floor of the otherwise immaculate living room. I had never heard of some of the stores – Henri Bendel, Bergdorf Goodman, Barneys. Those were definitely not the type of shopping bags I was used to seeing.

"Sit down and eat."

He motioned toward the empty chair in front of him where an assortment of fruits, pastries and cheese were laid out on a silver platter on top of the large glass table. There was nothing small about Salerno. Everything he did was larger than life but I sure as hell wasn't in the mood for a damn continental breakfast.

Didn't he know I needed something a little more filling after a night full of liquor, drugs and sex? Where the hell was the bacon, home fries, toast and Schweppes Ginger Ale?

"Umm, no thank you. I'm not hungry," I lied, trying to suppress the grumbling sounds coming from my stomach. "I was actually looking for my clothes so I can head home."

Things had gotten so heated that I couldn't remember where I tossed them after they undressed me.

"I threw them away."

"You did what?"

It took every ounce of self-control to stop me from ripping that newspaper out of his hand. Especially once I realized how cavalier he was being about it. I knew this shit was too good to be true. What kind of Knight in Shining Armor would send me home in a damn robe?

Salerno never raised an eyebrow to respond which made me even more agitated.

"Hello!!! I ain't speaking to myself over here. Why would you throw my clothes away?"

"That's what you call clothes?"

Oh hell no, that little snide ass remark pushed me off the deep end. Fuck being polite, I was screaming at the top of my lungs now.

"What? Yeah, you fucking asshole, clothes. It might not be as fancy as your little slut bag waitress friend. But no, fuck that. Who the fuck you think you are?"

I grabbed the newspaper out of his hand and threw it to the floor. He was going to pay me some damn attention if it was the last thing he did.

Unbothered, he stood up and walked toward the shopping bags.

"Little firecracker," he said as he returned to where I was standing with my hand on my hip, ready to go ballistic. "That's what I like about you. You don't hold any punches. Keep that honesty and we'll be fine."

He dropped the bag at my tapping foot.

"Fuck this." I slightly kicked it away from me. "What am I supposed to do with a fucking shopping bag?"

"I don't know. Why don't you look in it and find out?"

Curiosity got the best of me. Although I was furious, I also wanted to know what was in the bags. So, I bent down and took a peek. I couldn't believe my eyes.

He chuckled, picked his newspaper up from the floor and said, "Now, those are clothes."

Piece by piece, I pulled out garments that I could barely pronounce – like the silk Badgley Mischka blouse, followed by a Diane Von Furstenberg wrap dress and a pair of Yves Saint Laurent gladiator sandals. If I hadn't read the labels on the inside, I would have never known the brands. Anytime I ever saw people rocking expensive shit, it was usually covered in logos. Authenticity, in my eyes, had to be proven with a double GG or a light brown LV against a dark brown canvas. Neither appeared in my bag. Instead, there was a hint of sophistication in every piece of clothing I pulled out. Compared to this wardrobe, I suppose my clothes did belong in the trash.

It wasn't until I opened a bag with bras and panties from some place called La Perla that I thought I finally had one up on Salerno. I smiled at his lack of knowledge. Didn't he know Victoria's Secret had the best, top-of-the-line lingerie? Just as I was about to start bragging about already owning some pricey Vicky's, I noticed the tags. The bra was $240 and the matching thong was $95. Both were way more than what I spent on my five for $25 PINK collection. My mother's words echoed through my head, "A person won't know what you don't know until you open your mouth and prove to them that you have no idea."

With that in mind, I just shut the fuck up and kept digging through the bags. I was more excited than a faggot in Boy's Town but instead of doing cartwheels and handstands at the thought of my impressive come up, I tried to act like I deserved everything Salerno was dishing out.

Purposely trying to hide my enthusiasm, I asked with little emotion, "Why are you doing this?"

A score this big was beyond my wildest dreams. Having been used to hi-top Reeboks and Levi's, Salerno's gifts were completely out of the ordinary for a girl like me. Of course every street chick envisions being scooped up by some Captain Save-a-Hoe but the fantasy usually ends once she's wifed by a project drug dealer. The fairy tale never goes to this extreme.

"I need you, Chaka. I've wanted you since the first time I saw you. You can help me. Well, we can help each other."

"Help you how?"

Looking around the room and soaking in his extravagant lifestyle, I couldn't imagine one thing I could do to help him. From where I was standing, he was on top. How the hell do you help a person who already has it all?

"I need a girl like you. Somebody who knows the game and can play it. This can be yours and so much more. But you have to trust me. And you have to leave that Henny in a cup ghetto girl behind you."

"What do you mean? What can be mine?"

He wasn't making any sense to me. I was a minute away from barking on him for that whole ghetto girl comment but I really wanted to know where he was going with this, so for once, I kept my inner rebel locked away.

"I can put you in all the right places with a look and demeanor that will attract all the money we need."

Money? Wait a minute, he just said the magic word. If I didn't know anything else, I knew how much I liked the sound of that. Ca-ching.

"I don't understand."

Really, I didn't. What the fuck was he talking about? Put me in the right places? I kept my responses short and instead of running off at the mouth, like I normally did, I listened.

"You have to be ready to play a part in something that will change your life. I have connections that will cash out for heavy weight. I need you to find that for me. For us."

He continued to go more in-depth. While he spoke, I just kept seeing dollar signs. It was simple, really. Using what I got to get what I want – I had done that my whole life. Salerno's plan was just a whole hell of a lot more profitable, assuming it was as easy as he explained. With a little flirtatious smile and my gift of gab, I just needed to land some of the top players in New York's drug game. Once I did that, it was on me to get close enough to gain their trust. Salerno didn't care what methods I used to do it, just as long as I delivered.

You see, when a man gets comfortable, he'll reveal all his business. Pillow talk is deadly, especially when your sex is good enough to make a guy think you really love him. By the third cum, he'll scream out the combination to his safety deposit box while you're on your knees sucking out that fourth nut. A man's weakness comes when he listens to the head between his legs. A woman's strength comes when she uses the one on her shoulders.

I was picking up everything he was throwing down but it still made me wonder, why me? There were about a million get-money girls running around the streets of New York who could have easily pulled this con off. He'd undoubtedly have his pick of the litter.

"You could get any girl to do this. What's so special about me?"

"Let me show you something."

Salerno grabbed my hand and led me to a small room that I had somehow missed when I got there.

The four walls surrounding me resembled a shrine. If I hadn't looked closer, I would have thought it was full of pictures of me. The little girl in each of them looked like Chiggy and the woman in the snapshots was the spitting image of Chaka. The childhood flicks were from the early 70's. I could tell by the bell bottomed dungarees and the View-Master hanging from the little girl's hand. The more recent pictures looked more like an 80's Harlem chick with bamboo earrings, a leather bomber and slicked down baby hair. Of course I knew it wasn't me in the pictures but the resemblance was uncanny.

"Who's she?" I walked toward the marbled credenza and picked up a silver frame. The girl's face smiled back at mine. She was beautiful.

Salerno took the photo from my hand and looked at it. His eyes drifted off to a place beyond my reach.

"That's my sister."

"Your sister?"

"Nina. Well, that was her name."

"Was?"

The sadness in his voice made my heart break. Anybody who referred to another person as a 'was', had clearly experienced a loss. I didn't know what to say.

"You remember when I told you that you reminded me of my sister, right?" His focus remained on the picture – as if I wasn't in the same room. "Well, this is her."

"But." I stared back down at the pretty caramel complexioned face and then back up at him. "She's not White."

"Different fathers, Chaka. But this is her."

"Well, what happened to her?"

I wanted to be a little more sensitive but for the life of me, I couldn't understand why he brought me into a room full of old pictures. Because I was dealing with the shit with Camille, I knew the hurt of losing a sister to the street. But at that moment, all I wanted to do was play dress up with my new clothes. This emotional shit was rocking me.

"I couldn't save her. Nobody could. She loved the fast life more than anything else. The first time I saw you, you reminded me of her so much. I realized I had a second chance."

Like Déjà vu, I recalled having this conversation with him. It was during his spiel about me going to the Navy. I blew it off though. Why would I care about his sister in the midst of everything I was going through at that time? It was just a bunch of talk to me but now I realized it meant so much more to him.

His vulnerable posture, as he leaned on the wall and clasped the frame, exposed a side of him that I had never seen. In one night, he went from being a cop to being a sexual encounter, to being so much more. It happened that quickly. Yes, in one swift second, it's quite possible for a person to draw you all the way in and that's what occurred right there in my Manhattan mirage. Regardless of the wall that I managed to build around me, it only took a peek into someone's heart to crumble my fortress. Whether it was Malik's tears after kicking my ass or Salerno's misty-eyed memories of his sister – I was a sucker for love. It was my weakness. Actually, it still is.

Slowly, I walked closer toward him. I wanted to console him or hold him or something. I'd do just about anything to erase that saddened look on his face.

"Where is she now?"

He reached into the credenza drawer and pulled out a black

photo album. As he passed it to me, I had no idea what to expect. Nausea settled into the pits of my stomach once I opened it. Page after page was filled with macabre images. Blood. Yellow tape. More blood. Then, once I got to the last picture, I nearly dropped the album altogether. It was a sight that would forever be embedded in my memory. Salerno, dressed in a Beat Walker's uniform, was knelt down with his sister's lifeless corpse in his hand. Her head was nearly severed and the slice across her neck practically exposed her spine.

"She's gone." His presence was distant as though he was reliving the event. "That was my first homicide call with the department. They had no idea she was my sister."

I was at a loss for words. What the fuck could I say in response?

"She got involved with the wrong people and in the end, she paid the ultimate price."

"I'm...I'm sorry." Of all the things I could have said, that was the only thing that came to mind.

With a sympathetic ear, I listened intently while he described, in detail, the story behind every picture. She was dating some drug dealer and got caught up in that world. It was the same one that I had continuously pursued – money, notoriety, hood fame. At nineteen, she met a hood dude who introduced her to the big time and she soaked up every minute of it. She left home, moved in with him and helped to build his empire. When a rival gang couldn't get next to her man, they caught up to her instead. It was probably a petty drug dispute, Salerno explained, but it took the only thing that ever mattered to him.

"Those bums are the scum of the Earth and I'll do anything possible to fuck over every last one of them."

His tone wasn't apologetic at all. Instead, his voice was cold and vengeful. The sound of it made me uneasy. I closed the book and placed it back in the drawer. Hopefully, I'd never have to see those pictures again. In fact, it confused the fuck out of me that he'd still have them lying around after all these years. What sane person would want to keep looking at that nightmare? This, of course, should have been my first warning. But I blocked it out. Ignoring my intuition always led me to trouble but obviously, I hadn't yet learned my lesson. In time, I would. And it would be one that I'd never forget.

Chapter 16

When I say I dove straight in, head first, I'm not exaggerating. Usually one to pick up on things quickly and camouflage into any surrounding, I slithered with the precision of a snake. Whether posted up in VIP sections at all the top clubs or simply walking across the court at Harlem's famed Rucker Park, I carried myself like money which inevitably attracted the same. Thanks in part to Salerno's wardrobe allowance, I looked and felt like a million bucks. Believe me, you can't expect to be noticed by a King Pin if you're dressed in spandex and a pair of Jordans. That's like having an Ace of Spades champagne taste on a Svedka vodka budget. It'll never work.

Some marks were hard to land but others were easier than taking candy from a baby. Like always, I reinvented myself to take on a whole new persona – there were so many different personalities living in my crazy ass head that I didn't have to go very far to find this one. My new name was London and I was a college girl attending classes at NYU. Remembering how much I loved the Huxtables growing up, I pretended that I came from an upper-class background. My mother was a doctor and my father was a lawyer. Yeah, I know, Cliff and Claire were the opposite but I didn't want to seem too obvious. Purposely, I never used street slang or discussed any of my personal life, with the exception of the shit I made up. To the dudes I met, I was a good girl with an impeccable pedigree who would be their perfect trophy. And every street guy, whether he admits or not, wants one of those. With her, he feels like he finally made it. So, they were quick at trying to impress me by flashing their money and reminding me of their status in the drug game. I milked every word and never missed a beat.

My first score was Sharif. He was from Brooklyn and I met him at a club one Sunday night. It was the perfect spot to land a baller because the place was wall-to-wall packed with them. From his Audemars Piguet watch and canary diamond pinky ring, I knew he was about 'that life'. Salerno had already taught me the difference between a brilliant cut stone and that cheap clustered shit that came from the local pawn shops. So, when I caught wind of Sharif's jewels, I knew he would be the ultimate target.

Never the loud and obnoxious type, I played the little innocent sweet girl role with him. Making my way to the bar, I *accidentally* spilled my drink and apologized as sympathetically as possible even going so far as grabbing napkins to pat down his Armani Exchange t-shirt. He appreciated the extra effort, coupled with my effervescent charm, because we exchanged numbers and then one thing led to another. After a few dinner dates, I was butt naked in his bed.

Since his dick was about the size of a pencil eraser, all he wanted to do was eat my pussy. Of course, I obliged. What girl wouldn't want a warm tongue giving her that neck back love? Especially when it meant that afterwards I could bask in my post-orgasmic glow while eavesdropping on a very important phone call. From his conversation, I knew his connect was dropping off a few bundles at four o'clock the next afternoon. That little tidbit of information was all I needed to know and helped me to quickly forget the degradation I had just encountered to get it.

Once I left his crib, I reported back to Salerno who rewarded my hustle with everything my money-hungry heart desired. He in turn, would then show up at the drop off with his expired police badge and cop's rhetoric. Next thing you know, Sharif's package was in custody. Well, pretend custody because Salerno wasn't really an officer anymore. But Sharif didn't know that. And really, what was he going to do? Call the police and tell them he just got robbed...by the police? I think not.

Salerno would then sell what he got to the highest bidder without fronting a dime of his own money. There was no return on investment to calculate. Hell, we never invested anything. Everything was a profit. It was the perfect crime. And I was clear to move on to the next victim.

One after the other, I set more players up than Chuck Woolery in *The Love Connection*. Months flew by and I was getting better and better at it. Slowly but surely, I stopped feeling guilty about my sexcapades. As long as I was able to extract everything I needed to know, Salerno kept my pockets fat, my wardrobe exquisite and my nose full of the purest cocaine that he scored from the many heists I implemented. I was high off the lifestyle and numb to the damage I was doing to myself. But really, I had been damaged goods for so long, this was nothing new to me.

Ever since the day Mister Danny put his hands on me, I always felt the only way to a man's heart was through the treasure between my legs. Looking back on it now, I think somewhere in my sick twisted mind, I never knew how to enjoy sex without some level of perversion or danger associated with it. Whether it's a golden shower here or a blowjob in the backseat of a taxicab there, despite carrying myself with the utmost level of class in public, I've always required a smut experience to get me off behind closed doors. Childhood molestation affects even the most mature women in one way or another. If nothing else, my pussy was my weapon and I used it to my advantage. Fuck it. If that's all a man ever wanted from me, then why not make it profitable?

Of course, I had Ta-Ta by my side. After the day at Dana's house, when we finally talked it out, we were inseparable again. Thelma and Louise to the fullest. We needed each other actually. When I returned for the first time, I could tell her financial situation had taken a downward turn. It was obvious – her hair wasn't done, nails bitten down to nubs, sneakers leaning to the side. And fuck that, I wasn't about to let my best friend walk around looking dull while I was shining. I've never been that type of chick. When I eat, we all eat. Loyalty was my motto and I kept it one hundred with my right hand. She always had my back and I always had her front. No amount of money would have ever changed that.

Besides, in order for my con to work, I was forced to bring in reinforcements. It would have looked crazy if I kept popping up in all these places by myself. So, although Salerno warned me to keep our business in the strictest confidence, I had to bring a passenger along for the ride. Actually, I brought along two – Piper and Ta-Ta. Together, we were the new Wolf Pack.

Usually, I got half of every dollar Salerno made and that was more than enough to break bread with my girls. At first, I was hesitant about introducing Piper and Ta-Ta to each other. They were both two loud mouths who were always ready to pop off on somebody. However, when Piper came to visit me in New York, they meshed. All three of us were laughing and joking the whole night. You would have thought we were all childhood friends. It was cool to see my two besties getting along. Unfortunately, I couldn't say the same for my other friends.

Dana would have been perfect for this hustle. She was cute enough and when she wanted to, could out-dress all of us. However, she was pretty heavy handed when it came to the liquor. There was no way I could have portrayed my good girl role with her slurring her words and acting all drunk like she normally did. Her behavior would have been more of a liability than an asset. So, unless we were sitting on the block having drinks or in her crib getting fucked up, she was seldom in my circle.

As for Carmen, I couldn't trust that dingbat further than I could throw her so she wasn't even considered. Truthfully, I only kept her around so she could have a first class seat to witness my come up. It gave me extra delight to watch her lips turn up when she saw Ta-Ta strolling around in thousand dollar shoes. Carmen was the type who wanted people around her as long as she was doing better than them. Knowing that my best friend didn't need her little hundred dollars for a bottle anymore was the icing on the cake.

My wit combined with Ta-Ta's street smarts and Piper's hustle, made us unstoppable. They'd even bag their own marks and report back to me so that I could then tell Salerno. We had quite the enterprise going and not near one of us had a need because the money kept piling in. We'd take trips to Miami for the weekend or spend a day at the Elizabeth Arden Red Door Spa. Like a sponge, I soaked up everything Salerno taught me about the finer things in life and shared those experiences with my friends. Like I said, I've always been open with sharing my wealth; whether it was financial or knowledge-based.

Now, I've never been one who easily puts my trust in somebody. I'm a Cancer and true to a crab's fashion, I'm secretive and remain in my shell. But there are a few people who I depend on. Piper and Ta-Ta were the only ones I confided in completely. At least for the most part anyway. They knew the game. They knew the way it worked. They even knew I was living it up with some White sugar daddy on the Upper East Side. But they never knew who he was or that he was the mastermind behind the scenes. Salerno was like my Derek Foreal from that movie, *Blow*. He was the connect I'd never name. That was my big Joker and if you've ever played Spades, you know, people hold on to that card until it has to be played by force. Had I told another broad who he was, she might have tried to slide in and cut my throat. Friend or no friend, chicks get scandalous over money.

Yet and still, I somehow I managed to keep my worlds separated. Although I was living with Salerno, my mother thought I still lived in Philadelphia with Piper. I'd go to Queensbridge every weekend and help her with the kids by doing the laundry, braiding my niece's hair, cleaning the apartment, cooking a week's worth of dinner. It was crazy how I'd go from Charlie the Sexpot to London the Good Girl to Molly the Maid in the blink of an eye. But I made it work.

If nothing else, my mother needed me. Watching her health deteriorate was like a scalpel scraping my heart. Normally, she was a hands-on, independent woman. You couldn't tell her shit. I admired everything about her strong will and determination. When it came down to handling her business, no matter how fucked up we were, she always made sure things got done. If we didn't have food, she somehow scrambled up enough money to buy two dollars worth of chicken legs from the local bodega and miraculously stretch that shit like it was Thanksgiving dinner. Whether we were knocking on the doors of Saint Mary's Catholic Charities or cashing in cans and bottles for five cents, she was always the caregiver and we never went without.

Now, I had to sit back and watch the Multiple Sclerosis strip her of everything. She needed my assistance to do things that I thought were so simple like unbuttoning her pants to use the bathroom or lacing up her sneakers. The medicine wasn't helping despite the fact that the doctors kept increasing her dosage. They had her on all types of shit I had never even heard of: Prednisone, Oxycontin, Neurontin, Dilantin – she was taking every drug imaginable and still nothing helped. Her nights were long and full of pain while she tried her hardest to put on a brave face during the day. In all honesty, I think it was the depressive effects of the disease that made her sicker. Who could be happy when you barely have enough control of your muscles to form a smile?

As for me, I felt every ounce of my mother's pain. Empathy is both a gift and a curse. In order to block it out, I just got high and made sure I never came down. The more cocaine I ingested, the less I had to feel. When I woke up, I took a bump or two and every time I started to see her condition, with clear eyes, I'd take another. Simply put, I couldn't accept the fact that she wasn't getting any better. But when I was zooted, it didn't affect me. So, I stayed as coked out as possible for as long as I could. Sobriety forced me to face reality and like always, I just didn't have the heart for all that.

From the outside looking in, it seemed like I had it all together. I was making money. I was helping my mother. I had some good friends on my team. My jewels were iced out. My shoes were Italian. My bags were foreign. My home address was exclusive. To top it all off, I had Salerno who was spoiling me rotten with gifts, funds, date nights and the kinkiest sex you could ever imagine. Basically, my attitude was fuck it. I was up and nothing else mattered.

As luck would have it, I was so high that I had forgotten the biggest lesson I ever learned. In Science class, they teach you about gravity. I never realized how it would eventually apply to my life. Had I paid more attention to Sir Isaac Newton and his law of universal gravitation, I would've known that what goes up will eventually come right back down. It's just the way things happen. My descent was right around the corner and I was either too blind or just too stupid to see it coming. Nevertheless, it was on its way. And when it came, that shit caught me off guard like a motherfucker.

Chapter 17

I should have known that day was going to be fucked up by the way it started. Maybe if I would have listened to my gut instincts, I'd have never gotten out of bed. But hindsight is always twenty-twenty because I swear, even in my wildest dreams, I could've never predicted it ending the way it did.

Just the day before, everything was rosy. Salerno surprised me with dinner on a private yacht that sailed the Long Island Sound. That was the first time I had ever been on a boat, except for the Staten Island Ferry or the yearly school field trips aboard the Circle Line. Being with my Caucasian Persuasion, as I'd refer to him, was full of firsts for me. He introduced me to things I only dreamt about as a child growing up in the projects.

I can't front, I loved the way he treated me. Despite how I got down, he always made me feel like a princess. We never discussed the dudes I fucked with besides the information he absolutely needed to know such as their physical descriptions, drop-off locations, car make and model, as well as their temperaments so he'd know how to handle them during his bogus traffic stops. Other than that, he never wanted any additional details, which was a good thing for me because most of them were so sordid that I tried my hardest to wipe them from my memory even before the morning after. Regardless of all that, Salerno made me feel worshipped and for a self-centered chick like me, that was all he ever needed to do.

One thing's for certain, I learned everything I know from being with him. He exposed me to a touch of class and culture. I was never really a ghetto type of bird but I did have a lot of hoodrat tendencies like being loud in public and asking restaurant waiters for a cup of boiling water to soak my utensils in before using them. But with Salerno, I always had to bring my A-game. From learning which wines complemented foods the best to knowing how the Dow was moving on Wall Street, I altered myself as best as I could in order to fit into his world.

Weirdly, when I went back to Queensbridge, people couldn't understand how this new sophistication emerged. Most of them just labeled me as a stuck up or plain old bougie. Unbeknownst to them, I had always been this way. Ironically, it was the street persona that was a hoax. I just acted like that in order to fit in with them. Since I no longer had to dumb myself down to make people accept me, motherfuckers were forced to step their games up if they wanted to be anywhere close to my level. My confidence bred more hate than I had previously known. As long as you're in the same barrel with the other crabs, everybody shows you love. But when you start doing some high class shit, people start treating you differently. I didn't give a fuck though. I was living.

Despite finding my Prince Charming, I still felt empty inside. I mean, I had love for him but I wasn't in love with him. Sure, my heart melted every time I gazed into his hypnotic eyes but my brain resented him for introducing me to this lifestyle. Salerno was my oxymoron in the flesh. Similar to my relationship with Malik, this one was also a love/hate *situationship* from which I couldn't escape. I don't even think I wanted to get out of it. At that age, I thought the perfect love story was cliché anyway. Somehow, I always ended up right back at the bottom of love's totem pole. Stupidly, I willingly accepted it as my lot in life. I hadn't yet realized my worth.

But as far as that night went, I felt loved. We ended our whimsical evening with the type of debauchery that made God set Sodom and Gomorrah ablaze. Salerno's gentleman ways disappeared behind closed doors. He was an uninhibited freak who liked bondages and whips. Some real S&M shit which I thought only appealed to White people who hung out in swingers clubs. Once I got beyond my sadomasochistic phobia, I actually loved every minute of it. From the leash and collar to the locked handcuffs, his deviance stimulated every nerve in my body. Salerno's pipe game was much more fulfilling than the typical yet boring sex I used to have: missionary, doggy-style and if I really felt like a night of depravity, the reverse cowgirl.

None of those elementary positions could compare to my new sexual prowess.

So, by the time my head hit the pillow that night, I was still somewhere up on cloud nine. But as soon as I opened my eyes that next morning, I had this indescribable feeling that my bubble was about to burst.

Then, it all came crumbling down.

Chapter 18

Beep. **Beep. Beep.** Alas, a quiet pause before it started back up again. **Beep. Beep. Beep.**

"What the fuck?" I yelled as I reached over to wake Salerno. The alarm clock was on his side of the bed and he'd usually turn it off by the second alert. I patted the pillow beside me. It was empty.

Beep. Beep. Beeeee...

Rolling over and slamming the snooze button as hard as I could, I laid there for a second hoping the throbbing in my head would go away. Too much red wine and cocaine lines the night before always resulted in a killer hangover the next morning. I swore every time would be my last time, especially when I woke up feeling like death warmed over. But after an Advil and some coffee, I was usually right back at it again.

Luckily, my eyes were hidden from the sunlight piercing through the opened blinds. I've never been a heavy dozer so I depended on a black satin sleep mask, which I wore religiously, to protect me from even the slightest glimmer of light. In my self-imposed darkness, I wondered where Salerno was and why the hell he had left so early in the damn morning. If the alarm was going off, that meant it was only seven o'clock and as usual, it was time for me to call my mother. I had it set for the same time every day.

Even though she was out on disability, my mom still woke up early as if she had to get ready for work. Consequently, she would then be reminded that she was homebound and too frail to walk down the stairs. This realization would depress her even further and she'd sit on the couch, in one spot, unmoved but crying for hours on end. So, I made it my business to call her every morning with a cheerful word or just some sort of something to brighten her otherwise bleak day.

Pulling the mask from my eyes and resting it on my forehead, I squinted as I tried to block the sun from blinding me. I felt like a vampire and probably looked like one too, but my mother relied on our phone calls so no matter how fucked up I got the night before, I forced myself to pull it together. It wasn't like I had a typical nine-to-five so I'd be able to go right back to sleep once our brief fifteen minute chat was over. With that to look forward to, I grabbed my cell phone from under the pillow and dialed her number.

Surprisingly, my father answered. Normally, he'd be getting ready for work or heading out the door at this hour. The last thing he'd be doing was picking up the phone. Seemingly, I was shocked to hear his voice.

"Daddy? What are you doing home?"

"Oh, hey Chiggy. I live here, remember?"

On any given day, my father's upbeat personality could be felt even through the phone. But while he was speaking, I couldn't sense any of that.

"Yeah, yeah, yeah. I meant to say, why aren't you at work?"

"Nah, I'm not going today."

"Oooooh, you're playing hooky."

I chanted melodically, like a school girl teasing one of her classmates. Laughing was always the best form of communication with my dad so I tried to slide in a little joke. It didn't work. I could tell from his response, there wasn't anything funny.

"I wish I was Chig. But nope. Debra's not doing too well today. She had a bad night."

His serious tone caused me to sit up in bed. If my father was missing a day of work then I knew my mother must've been in really bad shape. He never called out. In fact, his job used to force him to take vacation days because he'd accrue months worth of time off. So, the fact that he took a personal day was a big deal.

"Is she ok? Where are the kids?"

"Taylor came down and got them last night. She's bringing them to daycare this morning. My job is having a banquet tonight so I don't know how I'm gonna do this."

He still hadn't told me how my mother was doing which

prompted me to ask him again.

"Is Mommy ok?"

"I don't know, Chig. She's in a lot of pain. I called her doctor and he said to bring her in if it gets worse. I'm just playing it by ear."

Worry. Fear. Uncertainty. Normally, these were all emotions my father never displayed. He'd always been like a superhero to me so hearing his vulnerability come through the phone, was uncomfortable. I had to give him some reassurance.

"Well, I'll be home tomorrow. It'll be ok, Daddy. For real, watch."

"I was about to see if you can come home tonight. I'm going to this event for my job and Taylor said she's heading out of town. I need somebody to sit with Debra while I'm gone."

I sighed heavily and rolled my eyes to the back of my head. Usually, I went home on the weekends. Here it was, a Thursday and my father needed me there. This was completely fucking up my schedule. On top of that, I had a date that night to meet up with a potential cash cow who I had been courting for nearly a month. I was certain that he'd finally break and give me the information I needed in order to get Salerno to make a move on him. Timing was everything and this monkey wrench being thrown at the last minute, wasn't part of my plans.

On the other hand, I knew my brothers were both attending college in Upstate New York which was nearly eight hours away. My other sister, Olivia, lived all the way in Long Island with three young toddlers of her own so there was no way she could be there. As for Camille, she was somewhere getting high and had no intentions of mothering her own children. After it was all said and done, that only left me. What other option was there?

"Ok, Daddy. I'll catch a bus in a little while. I should be there like six."

Since my parents thought I still lived in Philadelphia, I had to play it smart and allow enough time for me to make this imaginary two hour trek to the city.

"My girl." His mood immediately lifted. "I'll see you later then. Hell, I'll even make you some dinner."

"Daddy, you only know how to cook franks."

"I'm saying, that's food, ain't it?"

He laughed heartily and I was happy to hear that sound.

We hung up before I had a chance to speak to my mom.

Daddy said she wasn't up to talking anyway. With the way my attitude was going, it was probably best. My mother and I had a bomb ass relationship when we were both in a good mood but if we weren't, that bomb quickly tick-tocked before exploding. On those rare occasions, we butted heads like crazy. So, in a way, it was a good thing she didn't come to the phone. We probably would have ended that call with some choice words for each other.

I could already sense it was going to be a long ass day and the shit had only just begun. Reaching into the nightstand, I pulled out my bejeweled round pill box full of cocaine and took a quick bump. Long gone were my days of creased dollar bills.

After realizing I wouldn't be able to go back to sleep, I finally got out of bed. My mother's situation was weighing heavily on my brain so I was happy when I heard Salerno's keys opening the front door. I needed some type of company to stop me from over-thinking.

I made my way toward the living room wearing a yellow silk camisole and my hair pinned up in a high bun. He hated it when I wore scarves and t-shirts to bed so I always made sure that I was just as pretty on the wake-up as I was when I was stepping out. Not too many women know this little secret. Sexy pajamas and a dab of Chanel No. 5 behind your ears can go a long way. There's no man on Earth who finds it attractive to sleep next to a chick who looks like she just came from a Zumba class at her local gym. Salerno was adamant that I carry myself like a lady, twenty-four hours a day.

"Good Morning there gorgeous. I could look at that face all day."

Greeting me like a ray of sunshine and seeming too exuberant for a Thursday morning, he kissed my forehead before rushing toward the kitchen counter with an arm full of Gristedes shopping bags. The high end grocery chain was a far cry from Pathmark and the local bodegas of my past but it was the only place he shopped.

"Why did you leave so early?" I asked while he pulled out a long French baguette from his bag.

Sometimes, I just wanted a bowl of buttery grits and fried whiting, especially after waking up all hung-over. But breakfast with Salerno meant bruschetta or bagel and lox. I didn't mind. Slowly, I was acquiring a taste for the finer things in life.

"Today's your special day. You know I always make you breakfast on this day." He looked up at me from the groceries that were laid out on the kitchen island as he playfully reached in and tapped my nose with his index finger. "But since you're awake, you can help me like you used to. Here, dice this up."

He threw a ripe tomato in my direction. Thankfully, it landed in my hand instead of being splattered across the granite counter top. Completely ignoring his request, I placed the freshly picked produce to the side and hopped up on the high barstool directly across from him. I hated cooking so I knew for a fact that I never helped him before and I damn sure wasn't about to start. Anyway, what was so special about today of all days? To me, it was supposed to be just another day of hustling. In the past, these types of days never made him want to go out at the butt-crack of dawn to get the freshest bread for breakfast. I had no idea what he was talking about and the way my concentration was set up, I wasn't even trying to figure it out. I had serious things on my mind that didn't include a fucking baguette.

In front of me, was a metal bowl full of green seedless grapes that were calling out my name. I popped a few in my mouth before explaining the details of my morning.

"Oh, about today, change of plans. I have to go home so I can't meet that guy tonight."

Salerno, who was in the midst of slicing through a red onion on a wood cutting board, looked up at me. His piercing eyes seemed colder than the stainless steel knife in his hand. His smile vanished.

"I thought you only go to that shit hole on the weekends."

A look of disgust flashed across his face.

"Shit hole?" I asked with attitude. "It wasn't all that when you met me there."

"Yes, it was. That's why I don't know why you keep running back."

"In case you forgot, my mother's sick. I have to go home."

Explaining myself to him was ticking me off. We seldom argued, except for when it came time for me to go back to Queensbridge. Then, all of a sudden, his niceness would disappear and he'd transform into a condescending creep. By the tone of his voice, we were currently going down that path.

"Your mother's sick every day. What difference will changing the schedule make?"

"Fucking dick," I murmured under my breath.

Any other chick would have hauled off and knocked the shit out of him for that blatant show of disrespect. But I had learned to ignore his rants at times like this. He never had a real family so he couldn't understand what I was going through. According to his stories, his mother was a schizophrenic alcoholic and he never knew his father. He practically raised his little sister on his own. When she died, his mother went completely berserk and ended up in Bellevue's psychiatric ward where she eventually hanged herself during one of his visits. I couldn't blame him for his lack of sympathy. Shit, he never had a mother to love so he couldn't fully respect the lengths to which I would go for mine.

To make matters worse, he knew about my plans to meet a major connect later on. That cash cow I had been working for so long, finally asked me to accompany him to some industry party where I'd undoubtedly get a chance to meet his boss. From the start, I knew dude was minor league so I had to butter him up long enough to get a formal introduction to the real money-maker. Word on the street was that homeboy was bringing in some serious weight from Atlanta that he'd get straight from Mexico for dirt cheap. Hell, prior to that, I thought all cocaine was imported from Columbia. Who knew them dirty ass Esses were getting it too?

Rightfully, I was looking forward to some face time with the man behind the scenes. The workers never excited me. I wasn't prone to fucking with the help. With a little smile and a nonchalant flirt here or there, I had worked my way up to meeting the runner's boss. The way people were describing his money, this score would be enough to set me straight for a minute. My ass needed a break anyway. Constantly looking over my shoulder and lying up with random men was taking a toll on me. If I set this up the right way, I could put some money to the side and live a little. Believe me, I was pissed off that I had to change my plans that night but I was stuck between a rock and a hard place. The least Salerno could have done was show a smidgen of compassion. Was that too much to ask?

"You're going to that meeting tonight."

His words were final as the sound of his crisp knife chopping against the cutting board got louder.

"How am I supposed to do that?"

"How you do it, doesn't concern me. It never did. But I have people expecting this package and unlike you, I don't fail to deliver."

He didn't need a knife because he cut right through me without one. I hated for people to say I failed at anything, no matter how menial the task. He was aware of this and he knew just what to say to piss me off.

"Fail? Oh, now I'm a failure all of a sudden?"

"Your words, not mine. But if the shoe fits, you have some pretty expensive ones in that closet over there." He pointed the glimmering knife toward the bedroom. "Remember? I bought them. Or you could go back to wearing the hand-me-downs you had on when I saved you from that skid row of a home you keep running back to every chance you get. Your choice. Until then, you will be going to that meeting tonight. Your mother's about to die anyway. End of discussion."

These were the moments when I hated him. Usually, I'd just walk away but he picked the wrong day to fuck with me. My nerves were already on edge.

"You know what? Fuck you."

I flung the bowl of grapes across the counter, nearly missing his head as he swerved to the side. Before I had a chance to blink, he was running up on me with the knife in his hand. I swirled my barstool around but couldn't get my feet to the floor fast enough. In a matter of seconds, his hand was wrapped around my neck. My arms flailed rapidly as I gasped for what little air I could get down my throat.

"Do you have any idea what today is? Do you?"

I couldn't answer. His thumb was indented so firmly against my esophagus that I couldn't breathe much less get a word out. Like a fish out of water, I was steadily panting for survival. Trying to pry his fingers from my slender neck was useless until he loosened his grip just a little.

"Breathe," he ordered while still pinning me against the counter top.

It was just enough for me to inhale but too tight for me to move. I filled my lungs with as much oxygen as I could before he squeezed my airways shut again. This time, he slid the cold steel of the knife down my cheek. The aroma of the onion he had been cutting burned my eyes. Tears formed as I held my breath. Who knew when he'd let me breathe again.

"You're lucky you're worth more to me alive. I've already

invested too much in to you. Breathe."

I did as he said, feeling like I was drowning and had momentarily reached the top of the water before going back beneath its surface.

"It's always about you, isn't it? Today is your birthday, Nina. We always spent it together. Now, you want to run off to the gutter like you always do instead of enjoying this life I made for you. You make me sick. You know that, Nina? You don't appreciate anything. You never did."

Clearly, the lack of oxygen going to my brain must've caused me to mishear him calling me by his sister's name. That was my initial thought until I looked into his eyes and saw the same look he had when he first showed me her pictures. Suddenly, I realized, there was no mistake about it.

"I gave my life to you but it was never enough. Was it, Nina?"

At that very moment, he was gone. Somewhere beyond reality and definitely in another time and place. Glancing to my right, I saw the glass vase a few inches from my reach. If only I could somehow move a little closer, I'd be able to grab it.

"Answer me."

He choked me tighter as I squirmed toward the direction of the vase which unfortunately was still beyond my grasp. Since I needed to distract him long enough for me to inch my way to the one thing that could save me, I nodded my head yes. If he thought I was Nina, fuck it, I was Nina.

"Look at you." He stroked the knife up and down the side of my face similar to how a person would pet a puppy or a kitten. "You could have the world. You keep settling for the slums. Why, Nina? Why?"

His grip tightened while staring into my eyes, which I could feel were bulging out of their sockets. With every ounce of self control, I tried my hardest not to fight back. Ever since my days with Malik, I swore I'd never be another man's punching bag. But this episode with Salerno was far from anything I had ever encountered.

"I'm sorry."

I managed to whisper a dry apology as I moved closer to the vase. Never once did I look away. My eyes were locked on his.

"Don't leave, Nina. Don't leave me again."

He leaned in to kiss me and that's when I decided to make my move.

As his soft side slowly materialized, I broke away. Pouncing off of the barstool, I grabbed the vase with my right hand and turned toward him. With it lifted above my head, I firmly planted my legs in order to position myself in the right angle to connect with his skull. Still dizzy from the sporadic asphyxiation, I stood there until I could regain my balance. He was defenseless. Although he still held the knife, the chance of him getting to me before I got to him was slim to none. He was defeated and he knew it. After dropping the knife to the side, he threw his hands in the air. All I saw was a white flag being waved. This was his surrender, so I thought he'd be apologetic. I thought wrong.

"I should've just let that spic kill you when you lost those three kilos."

Instantly, I was brought back to that night. Actually, I had never forgotten it. That was the night my whole life changed. Trust and believe, that's some shit I'd remember. Nobody ever knew how much cocaine Ta-Ta and I had in the house that night except me, her, Manny and presumably Malik. After all, he was the one who stole it so of course he'd know. Then I remembered how I came to that assumption. It was Salerno who put that bug in my ear. While I was in the hospital, still drenched in my best friend's blood, he came there and told me Malik was trying to get rid of some heavy shit. I believed him. I mean, why wouldn't I have trusted him? He was the police. It was his job to protect and serve. Wasn't that their motto? I never gave it a second thought. Especially not after telling Manny that Malik robbed us. Then, the bone-chilling incidents at the warehouse occurred and I thought it was over. Still, a part of me never felt vindicated. There was still something missing from this puzzle. So, I kept my mouth shut and I knew for damn sure Ta-Ta did the same. We never told anyone how much shit we had that night.

We lost exactly three kilos. There was only one way Salerno could've known the approximate amount. He was the same bastard who was always lurking around, always popping up unexpectedly. Then, it hit me like a ton of bricks. I wasn't a hustler after all. This motherfucker had been hustling me from the very start. It was him. He was there that night. Lo and behold, I was the mark. Blindly, I just couldn't see it.

Engulfed in rage, all I could see was red. Like a bull, I charged toward him. The ding of the vase cracking against his head as the glass shattered to pieces, echoed throughout the apartment.

His body crashed to the hardwood floor with a loud thud.

Frantically, I ran to the bedroom, threw on a pair of jeans and a white wife-beater. With no time to put on a bra, my brown nipples poked through my shirt. The blow was just enough to knock him out but not enough to cause any serious damage. Time was of the essence. I had to get the fuck out of there.

Grabbing the pill box from the nightstand, my cell phone from under the pillow and an overnight bag which was already packed for the weekend, I quickly threw some flip-flops on and sprinted back to the living room. Salerno's wallet was on the table and I grabbed whatever cash I could before heading out the door. As I exited, I heard him groaning. Slowly, he was regaining consciousness. It would only be a matter of time before he'd fully awake but I'd be long gone by then.

Repeatedly, I pressed the elevator button.

"Come on. Come on," I said while watching, with anticipation, as the numbers illuminated on the overhead panel.

Finally, it arrived on the twenty-third floor. Continuously, I pressed the lobby button before backing into the corner as the doors closed. When they did, I heard Salerno cry out, "Nina."

I knew it wouldn't be the last time I saw him. My life consisted of constantly running. I ran from my past. I hid from my shame. Salerno was no different. But this time, I was determined to close the doors of my life before I opened any new ones. If he wanted Nina, I was going to bring her right to him. However, it would be on my terms. Unfortunately for him, it wasn't going to be the joyous reunion he expected.

Chapter 19

"**J**ust go," I yelled to the cab driver as I jumped in the yellow taxi parked outside of Salerno's building.

"Where are you going, Miss?"

Urgently I banged on the bullet proof partition separating me from him while constantly peeking out the window to make sure Salerno hadn't made his way downstairs.

"Right over the 59th Street Bridge. Just go ahead. Go."

Nobody had time to explain my destination to this Harold and Kumar sounding driver so I stuffed a fifty dollar bill in the money slot before yelling again, "JUST GO."

All he had to do was see dollars signs because as soon as he grabbed the money, his feet were on the gas and we were heading toward the bridge. Relief only hit me once we had gotten so far away, that I could no longer see the building.

"Oh my God," I said aloud as I raised my hands to my head and rubbed both temples.

My thoughts were racing. This fucking black cloud that always follows me was right back above my head. I was stuck beneath it with no umbrella, no raincoat and a pair of flip-flops. How the hell did I always manage to get caught up in some shit? It never failed.

Bending down far enough so the driver couldn't see me through his rear view mirror, I inhaled a spoonful of coke. The rush of it, mixed with my adrenaline pumped body, caused me to shake from my shoulders down to my feet. Quickly, I got my involuntary tremors under control and sat upright. Paranoia got the best of me because I kept looking over my shoulder to make sure I wasn't being followed. Realistically, there was no way

in hell Salerno could pop up like a scene from one of Stephen
King's stories and say, *"Thanks for the ride, Lady"*. Still, I kept
picturing his face, with blood dripping from his forehead while
he sped alongside the cab taunting me. The vision scared me to
my core so I pulled out a Newport to help relieve my anxiety.

"No smoking in here, Miss."

Ignoring the cabbie as he spoke, I stuck another twenty
dollars in the money slot and lit a match.

"Listen, Habib." No, that wasn't his name but it fit his Hindu
looking ass so I just ran with it. "I need to smoke. Just take me
to Vernon Boulevard and 40th Avenue. I'll open the windows.
Really, don't aggravate me. Not right now."

The extra tip must've reminded him that he could easily spray
some air freshener after I got out because he never said another
word about it. In fact, nobody would even be able to smell my
cigarette smoke over the funk of his armpits. He should've been
thankful. I was actually improving the quality of air inside the
car.

As I inhaled my Newport, my thoughts jumped from one to
the other. Had I known it was Salerno's sister's birthday, maybe
I would've been a little more subdued. Perhaps I wouldn't have
popped off and threw a metal bowl at his head. Then again, if
I hadn't, he would have never let his guard down long enough
to reveal his little secret. The thought of it made me sick to my
stomach. All this time, I had been blaming Malik for stealing
Manny's shit only to discover it was my Knight in Shining Armor
who had his hands in the cookie jar.

"Motherfucker."

The cab driver peeked through his mirror at me while I spoke
to myself. He probably thought I was some crazed lunatic. If so,
he wasn't too far from the truth. I was stark raven mad.

As I leaned back in my seat, I took another bump and let out
a chuckle. I'll give credit where it's due and Salerno was one
brilliant bastard. He played me like a pawn on a chessboard
and managed to walk away with three kilos while Malik paid for
them with his life. My head was plotting for vengeance but my
heart was filled with remorse. Without question, Malik was the
one who attacked Ta-Ta. She saw him with her own two eyes.
However, she was nearly unconscious by the seventeenth stab
so she could never say, with certainty, if Malik was the one who
took the drugs. Automatically I assumed, as did everyone else,

that it was the same person who attacked her. With that mind, I thought I was doing the right thing by telling Manny. Now, I had second thoughts. Although Malik got everything he rightfully deserved for his bitch ass actions, he wasn't the only one who should've felt the wrath of Manny's revenge. Salerno should have been tied up to a chair right beside him. My dumbass, with my naïve little heart, brought death to the wrong man's doorstep. Surely, karma caught that grave mistake.

I was so deep in thought that I hadn't realized the cab was already stopped in front of Ta-Ta's building. Because I was supposed to be living in Philadelphia, I couldn't just appear at my mother's house. I had to kill some time. Luckily, Ta-Ta's building door was propped wide open because I wasn't in the mood to stand there for however long it would take for someone to come open it. I jetted to her apartment on the third floor, took a long deep breath to calm my nerves and entered without knocking. Her mother never locked the door, at least not in the day time. There were so many people coming in and out of there, it was really no need to go through the trouble.

Since her mother had custody of nieces, nephews, cousins and the random runaway teenager, Housing had given her a double apartment. Well, that's the way they described it but in reality it was just two side-by-side cribs that had the dividing wall knocked down. Even with five bedrooms, there was still somebody balled up on the couch when I entered. Ta-Ta's mom was like that though. With a heart of gold, she'd take in just about anybody and put a roof over their head and food in their stomach. Of course I'd find her in the kitchen. She was always cooking. With all those mouths to feed, she barely had time to do anything else.

"Hey Lorraine."

I practically had to bend all the way down to kiss her cheek. She was a petite little lady with a lot of mouth. If it wasn't for Ta-Ta's gigantic boobs and dark complexion, they could have been twins. Lorraine was honey coated with bright red hair that was naturally curly as if she had Indian in her family. A no-frills type of woman, she could hustle a nun out of her virginity if she wanted it. However, after a few stints in jail, she retired from the street life and became the hood's quote-unquote godmother. Yet and still, she never lost that hustler's spunk.

"Hey baby. What you doing out here?"

Her voice was raspy, presumably from too many years of smoking. She was stirring a large pitcher of cherry Kool-Aid with one hand while pouring nearly an entire bag of sugar into it with the other.

"Nothing," I replied. "Just stopping by for a little bit before I go see my mother. Where's Ta-Ta?"

"Oh, she ain't here. Damn, you just missed her too. She went to Steinway. She's coming right back though."

I had forgotten all about the neighborhood shopping hub. It had been forever since I bought anything from Steinway Street. Shit, I didn't even know what stores they had up there anymore. Since she had just left, I figured Ta-Ta could be up there for hours so I sat on the loveseat and made myself comfortable.

For some reason, the kitchen table was in the living room and the loveseat was in the dining room overlooking the kitchen. It was the weirdest thing but somehow it felt like that's how all furniture should have been laid out. With Lorraine spending most of her time cooking, I guess she wanted to be able to entertain her guests while she was in there. The set-up was ass backwards but hey, if they liked it – I loved it.

"How is your mother doing anyway? Tell her I said hi."

"Umm, she's fine. I'll tell her."

I lied because I hated explaining to people just how bad my mother had gotten. I thought if I didn't speak it into existence, then it wouldn't be so.

"That's good." She placed the mixing spoon to her mouth for a taste of Kool-Aid. By the bitter expression on her face, I could tell it needed another round of sugar. Sure enough, she started pouring more into the blue plastic pitcher.

"What's wrong with you? Why you looking like that?"

Clearly my attempts at hiding my emotions weren't working. Either that or Lorraine knew me well enough to know something was wrong. Finally, I couldn't hold it in any longer.

"I'm just sick of this shit."

Lying back on the loveseat, I placed one arm across my forehead as the other dangled off to the side. Immediately, the tears rolled down my face. Lorraine stopped stirring and slammed her hand against the kitchen counter.

"Nah-ah. Suck that shit up, Jack. You ain't gonna play no damn victim around me."

Her voice was blunt. If I was looking for a sympathetic coddle,

I had surely come to the wrong house. She always kept it gully and this time was no different than all the others.

"I'm not a victim. I'm just saying, why does this always happen to me?"

The question was rhetorical but she wouldn't have been Lorraine if she didn't have an answer.

"Why the fuck it happens to you? The same reason it happens to every other motherfucker in the game." She pointed her finger directly at me as she spoke. Like her daughter, she also neglected to ever find her inside voice which just so happened to get louder. "You ain't special. What you think? Life is gonna treat you fair because you's a good person? Shit, that's like thinking a lion ain't gonna eat yo' ass because you ain't eat him."

It took a minute for me to relate to her metaphor. Usually, I was witty enough to find the hidden meaning in what people said but the massive amount of cocaine I had been sniffing all day seemed to slow down my thought process. Once I caught on, I realized what she was saying and it did make sense. Still, I rolled my eyes at the fact that she had to spit it in some Triple O.G. Bobby Johnson lingo that initially went over my head. This conversation was fucking up my high so I lit a cigarette in hopes that it would bring me back up.

"Let me get one."

Lorraine took the Newport I gave her and turned on the stove. It ticked until the burner sparked. With the cigarette perched on the side of her mouth, she bent down, stuck it in the fire and inhaled. Once she could take a full pull, she turned the stove off and continued with her rant.

"I keep telling y'all to get the fuck out of here. Y'all making money now. Shit, leave while you on top. You see what happened the last time y'all got greedy."

I grunted as she brought that night back up. Another reminder of it wasn't necessary. It haunted me every single day. Salerno's trip over the cuckoo's nest brought it back, front and center. After leaving his apartment, the whole thing was on a looped replay.

Lorraine made it all sound so easy to get up and leave. In reality though, where the fuck was I supposed to go? I couldn't leave my mother in her condition. Besides, the last time I left resulted in an utter disaster and proved to me that I was a fuck up. Queensbridge, which from an aerial view looked more and more like the devil's labyrinth, was all I knew. I wanted to get away, really I did. When I was a little girl, I never dreamt of being a project chick. My goals didn't consist of drugs, sex, jewelry and money. Scratch that, I always wanted to be rich. But as a child, with big dreams, I pictured myself attaining wealth as a high-priced lawyer or a bestselling author. Hell, I thought I was going to be a famous movie star until Mister Danny stole that vision from me.

The person I saw in the mirror everyday wasn't the woman I ever thought I'd be. I wanted to be like Claire Huxtable, wearing a two-piece suit and carrying a black leather briefcase with gold handles. Actually, I would've even settled for being Denise where the biggest issue I'd face was learning how to handle an annoying Southern Belle like Whitley Gilbert. In reality, those images existed in a different world and were only seen on my television screen. My everyday role models wore doorknocker earrings and leather 8-Ball jackets. For the life of me, I couldn't even recall one Queensbridge chick who graduated from high school, much less attended college. None of that shit really happened for girls like me.

My real life wasn't a sitcom or some tear-jerker interview on Oprah. My future was staring me in the face as I gazed out of my project window. Fuck the Huxtables. Those motherfuckers never loved us anyway. I related more to the Evans family even though I hadn't seen too many good times throughout my short lived life.

"Lorraine, you act like this shit is easy. You just don't know."

Heavily blowing the smoke from her mouth, she sat next to me, placing her hand on my knee. This was about the most emotion I'd ever witness coming from her so I sat up and looked her square in the eye.

"I know Chaka, I know. But easy come and easy go. If shit is easy then it ain't worth it. That's the shit that could be gone in a New York minute. There's a big ass world out there. Y'all ain't got no records. Never been arrested. It's a clean slate. Go get yourself a job and live life before these streets take whatever little bit of life you got left."

Her Doctor Do-Good speech, although truthful, was going in one ear and right out of the other. Get a job? Been there, done that and ended up shaking my ass on a stage in front of a room full of perverts. Still, she continued on. After fifteen minutes or so, she began to sound like every other talking head with a whole bunch of good advice but no practical suggestions on how to achieve any of the stuff she was yapping about. She had a motor mouth just like Ta-Ta and could go on for hours. The only difference between the two of them was that Lorraine would say something and then extend her hand for you to slap her five on some old school shit. If you did it once, she was high-fiving, low-fiving and blackhand-siding all day. Amongst ourselves we called her the Dap Queen. Not only did I have to listen to her nonstop babble, I also had to slap fives about a hundred times during her spiel. Once Ta-Ta finally walked through the door, it was like a breath of fresh air. Good thing too, because my arm was getting tired of all that fiving.

"Louise," Ta-Ta yelled.

Jovially, she entered with her hands full of bags. I couldn't help but notice the rolling suitcase she had alongside her. Apparently it was new because the tags were still attached.

"Well, there goes your Thelma," Lorraine said as she made her way to the back of the apartment. "Remember what I said, Chaka. I love both y'all but you need to get the hell out of here too."

"Girrrrrlllllll, where have you been? I got some serious shit to tell you."

I thought long and hard about giving Ta-Ta the full scoop on Malik, Salerno and the missing drugs. Hell, I was even planning to divulge details about the warehouse incident for the first time ever. After all, she had a right to know what really went down that night and with Salerno flipping out, I wanted her to be one hundred percent on point. In all honesty, I probably needed to let the cat out of the bag in order to allow myself to heal from it. Bottling that shit in for so long was constantly eating away at me piece by piece, consuming every aspect of my life. I was ready to get it out.

Luckily, I had a best friend like Ta-Ta. She'd hold me down no matter what just like I had always done for her. Regardless of what happened in our lives, we always had each other's backs.

As I prepared to come clean, I felt an immediate sense of relief. For once, I'd be completely honest and release the thing that gnawed at the very core of my being. I opened my mouth to speak but before I could get a word out, she interrupted.

"Well, I got something to tell you too."

She reached into her bag and pulled out an envelope. I recognized the red and blue writing on it but I couldn't figure out why she was handing it to me.

"What's this?" I asked.

"Go ahead, open it. It's my ticket. Bestie, I'm leaving. I'm finally leaving."

Her words struck me with the force of a wrecking ball. Pulling the Greyhound ticket from the envelope, I scanned it over and over again; New York City, New York to Charlotte, North Carolina. *ONE WAY* was written in bold letters along the right hand corner.

"Wait, what? When are you? I mean, what the... What?"

Baffled, I looked at the ticket, then back up at her, then back down at the suitcase before I looked back up at her again. This happened a few times before I even noticed the date on the ticket. She was leaving tonight.

"I was gonna tell you face to face. I ain't wanna just leave like that but my aunt been telling me to move down there with her and last night we had a long talk and..."

"So you're moving? Like, you're leaving for good? Just like that?"

I couldn't care less about what she had to say. It was unfathomable to me that she, of all people, would be leaving. Ta-Ta was as hood as they come. How the fuck could she possibly make it out before me?

"Yeah, Bestie. I can't take this shit no more. Living in my mom's crib. Seeing the same fucking people, day in and day out. I need more."

Obviously, her aunt had really gotten in her ear because she had never expressed a desire to move away. She wasn't like me. She didn't know shit about life outside the hood. Hell, she'd never even been on a plane until I took her to Miami. Now, she was talking about getting out of here all of a sudden? Envy shot through my blood. Although she was optimistic, I couldn't help but throw a little bit of salt in her plan.

"Well, how do you plan on living out there without a job?"

At that point, I'd say anything to deter her. Selfishly, I needed her there with me.

Unzipping her suitcase and stuffing it with the new items she pulled from her shopping bags, she said, "There's a McDonald's up the street from her house. She knows the manager and they said they can hire me as soon as I get out there."

"McDonald's? Wait a minute, let me get this straight. You're leaving New York to go flip burgers for five dollars an hour? Come on, what type of come up is that?"

She stopped packing and snatched the envelope from my hand.

"Everything ain't about a come up, Chaka," she yelled. "Do you know I almost died? You don't think that shit be fucking with me every day? Now I'm right back in this bitch doing the same thing all over again? Nah, that shit ain't for me no more."

"But what about me?" As always, I somehow managed to make it all about myself again. "You flipped because I left and now you're doing the same exact thing to me."

"It ain't about you. You don't gotta be here. You wanna be here. I ain't got the same choices as you do. Ain't nobody taking me on boat rides or putting me up in Manhattan apartments and shit. You always thinking about yourself. You don't think I want a life too? I gotta take shit as it comes. This is a chance for me to do better. Fuck, I thought you was gonna be happy for me."

When I looked at her, familiarity sparkled in her eyes. I saw the same sought after approval I had in mine whenever I longed for somebody to be proud of me for something. Despite the fact that we were only a couple of years apart, she looked up to me and there I was acting like a spoiled brat. Instinctively, I dug deep within my soul to find some happiness to share with her. At least one of us was making it out. Albeit the last one anybody on God's green Earth would've expected to take the first step. Still, she was my friend. No, fuck that, she was my BFF and although I felt somewhat deserted, I had to support her decision. Even if it was a minimum wage fast food job and a spot on her aunt's couch, she undoubtedly had the courage to walk by faith and not by sight. Her actions were a lot more than I could say for myself. She was making it happen while I just complained about things that happened around me. Quickly, our roles switched and she took the lead. For all the times she spent in my shadow, the moment had come for her to shine. And for that, she deserved all the applause and accolades. She was right, it wasn't about me anymore. A supporting role in someone else's life was new for me. But for my Thelma, I'd gracefully bow out and let her have the main stage. It was her turn.

"I'm gonna miss you."

My tears flowed as I accepted the fact that whether I liked it or not, she was moving on.

"Oh, Bestie, I'm gonna miss you too."

Finally, she received the response she had anticipated from me and we embraced. It was all a part of growing up, really. Seldom do friends remain in the same place throughout their lives. The secret behind sisterhood is actually being happy that your road dog is moving on to bigger and better things. If you have a friend who doesn't want you to take chances in life or feels threatened by your opportunities to succeed, then you should sink that ship. That bitch is a hater and she'll never want anything good for you.

During the next hours or so, I helped her pack. Decidedly, I kept the events of the day to myself. She didn't need to share in my misery. Had I said anything, it might have altered her decision to leave. In my heart, I knew it was the best thing she could have ever done. There wasn't shit left in Queensbridge besides a bunch of broken dreams. And well, we all know what happens to those once they're deferred – they shrivel up like raisins in the sun. Ta-Ta was about to blossom and she didn't need my drama holding her back.

Within a day, I lost everything that mattered to me. My man. My best friend. Both would eventually become distant memories. But I still had one constant rock on which I could lean. My mother. She'd always be there.

Soon enough, I would realize that she was gone too. I'd be lying if I said this wasn't the worst day of my life. Honestly, it only went downhill from here. The bottom was even closer than I thought. Actually, I was already there. I just didn't know it yet.

Chapter 20

"I promise. I'll be back before then."

With a bittersweet smile, I hugged Ta-Ta on my way out the door. Her bus was leaving at midnight and she made me swear to ride with her to the Greyhound station. Since my prior plans for the night were now non-existent, especially with Salerno going all Redrum on me, I figured I might as well accompany her. All I had to do was get to my mother's house, sit with her until my father came home and then I'd head right back out. It sounded simple enough but things in my life were never as easy as they appeared.

Thankfully, Ta-Ta and I hadn't finished all the coke I had in my pill box as we listened to music and I helped her pack. Our stroll down memory lane provided a momentary, yet much needed, break from reality. Now that it was over, I had to face my hardest realism yet and that was being around my mother while she was in her condition. Luckily, I was high enough to lessen the pain but I still had a little white magic in my pocket just in case it became too much to bear.

As I walked through the block, I checked my cell phone to see what time it was. I forgot that I even had it with me because it never rang while I was at Ta-Ta's. Once I pulled it out of my pocket, I realized why. The battery was completely dead. Well, no wonder Salerno hadn't been blowing me up; my goddamn phone was off. I wasn't pressed about charging it back up though. Talking to him would only piss me off even further and I couldn't deal with that just yet. His time was coming but for now, I needed a clear head. Or at least as clear as I could get it.

"Sit down."

I heard my mother yelling through the door. Usually soft spoken and meek, her whole personality changed when she felt overwhelmed. Her loud delivery meant she was nearing her breaking point. I shook my head. Hopefully, she wouldn't start picking at me too. Patience wasn't one of my strongest virtues.

"Auntie," my niece yelled as she ran toward me.

Her innocent smile could brighten even my gloomiest days.

Not far behind her was my nephew. His speech wasn't advanced as hers so he just grunted and giggled while waddling to my side. I was happy to see him making some sort of emotional progress. Whenever I visited, I made sure to spend a little extra time reading to him and teaching him new words. Raising two toddlers was hard work. Understandably, this was putting a lot of pressure on my mother which subsequently rolled down on me.

"Hey Mommy."

I spoke softly, feeling like I was walking on egg shells. I didn't know what type of mood she was in so I proceeded with caution.

"Hi Chaka."

Her greeting was dry and she barely looked at me while saying it. When she didn't call me Chiggy, like she always did, I automatically knew that she wasn't feeling like herself.

"I said, sit down," she yelled at the kids who were both climbing all over me.

"It's all right Ma. I got them. Chill out, ok?"

The last thing I wanted to do was be stuck in that house with her feeling like that. Because of the Multiple Sclerosis and all the medication she was on, her mood swings were severe. One minute she'd be happy, then in the blink of an eye, she'd start crying out of nowhere before going into a maddened frenzy. Quietly, I counted to ten. Arguing with her wasn't going to help the situation but shit, I was at my boiling point too.

"Come on guys, come sit down and eat."

There were two bowls of half-eaten ravioli sitting on the plastic children's table in the middle of the living room. The kids both sat in their small matching chairs and dug in.

I heard the shower running in the bathroom so my timing was perfect. Daddy was getting ready for his banquet. My niece and nephew were having dinner. And my mom, despite her attitude, didn't seem like she was in that much pain. Maybe, this wouldn't be so hard after all.

"Somebody keeps calling here from a blocked number and hanging up. They called like twenty times already," my mother announced.

Immediately, I knew who was calling. Since he couldn't get me on my cell phone, Salerno had resorted to harassing my mother's line. Still, I wasn't ready to deal with him.

"Mommy, can I make you something to eat?"

She was agitated so I wanted to make her as comfortable as I possibly could.

"I'm not hungry," she snarled.

Every attempt I made to be nice was shot down. If she only knew the type of day I was having, she'd understand that at that very moment, I just needed my mother's support. Little did I know, she needed mine as well.

"Hey Chiggy."

My father walked out of the bedroom looking sharp in his navy blue suit. He always knew how to turn on the charm and was quite dapper for an old man. From my peripheral, I caught my mother cut her eyes at him. When she was healthy, they'd both step out together, hand in hand. Now, she seldom changed out of her sweats or even combed her hair. It had to hurt to watch the world go on living without you.

"Owww, Mr. GQ," I teased.

"Yeah, yeah, I know. They love my style."

Daddy did a little two step while popping his collar. I think he just wanted to lighten the mood in the house or maybe he was genuinely happy to be getting out. Depression could easily jump from one person's spirit to another's. I had only been there for all of fifteen minutes and the buoyant effects of the cocaine had already subsided.

"Whatever, Freddy," my mother snapped. "I hope you put my medicine out because I know Chaka won't know how much to give me."

"Already done, Deb," my father said as he passed me a plastic case full of pills. Each were in their own compartments with a time stamp on them. He pointed to the different tablets while continuing on with his instructions. "Here, Chiggy. She gotta take these in ten minutes. Give her the rest of them at the time it says right there."

They were acting like this was new to me. I'd been giving my mother medication ever since I was a little girl. Back then, it was the methadone bottles she had stored in the refrigerator. As a recovering addict, her drug program would send her home with a week's supply of the heroin alternative so that she wouldn't have to keep going in every day. The little vials were stocked in the fridge and I'd bring her a daily dose every morning to help her wake up. She used to always say they were filled with orange juice. Although, in my opinion, it looked more like TANG because the liquid inside the bottles was bright red-orange and thick as hell. Every time I asked for a sip, she'd flat out refuse. I knew it wasn't really OJ though. I was just testing her. Like always, she'd pretend and I would too. It was the way we dealt with things in our family. I was used to it.

So, administering her medicine was a simple task. I had done it for so long that I could've probably passed Harvard Medical School had I tried.

"I know Daddy, I got it."

He kissed my mom and headed out the door. As he did, the phone rang again. My mother answered it before I could tell her to ignore it. Finally, whoever it was on the other line spoke up and she passed the phone to me. Because it was old-fashioned, with the cord attached, I had to take the call right in front of her. Privacy wasn't in her vocabulary. Instead, her eyes were glued to my mouth. She was making sure she didn't miss a beat.

I knew it was Salerno before he even said anything. Nobody else ever called my parents' house looking for me besides him.

"Do you know what I will do to you?"

"Umm." I paused. I had to choose my words wisely especially with my mother all up in the business. "Can I call you right back?"

"No, no don't hang up. Listen to me, whatever happened in the past is over. That piece of shit got what was coming to him."

"Of course." I tried to smile and even added a jolly ring to my voice.

"I saved you from him. He would've brought you down right along with him. Don't you know that? Look at what he did to your friend."

"Oh, ok. That sounds good."

I wanted to reach through the phone and rip his heart out. My blood was boiling. Still, I tried to keep my composure as my mother looked on.

"Just come home. We'll talk about this later. But I need you to go to that meeting tonight. Don't fuck this up."

Again, his voice was firm.

"Ok, call you later. Bye."

I hung up before he could say anything else.

"Who was that?"

My mom didn't waste any time. She went dodging for answers.

"Oh, nothing. Just a friend."

"Hmmm."

Her lips turned up. Obviously, she needed more than that.

"Hmmm, what?" The animosity I held back over the phone, was creeping out. "Ma, leave it alone."

"Well, tell him to stop calling here and hanging up then. This is still my house. I ain't dead yet."

"What are you talking about, dead? Why would you say that?"

More and more frequently, she'd go into these spells where she'd talk about dying. It infuriated me. Death was imminent for all of us so I couldn't fathom why she'd always want to talk about hers. With every word she spewed, I was pushed a little closer to the edge.

My nephew, who probably sensed the tension in the room, started to cry. He was already sensitive to loud noises so the fact that I started raising my voice, set him off. Like a domino effect, my niece started whining right along with him. Surrounded by two temper tantrum having babies, my mother's pessimism and Salerno's malicious threats, I felt like the lady in the Calgon commercial. I just needed to be taken away.

"Come on, come on, come on. Get it together." I clapped my hands as I walked toward the kids' table. "Y'all tired. Let's go to bed."

"It's not their bed time yet. If you put them to sleep now, they're going to wake right back up."

"Then, I'll put them back to sleep again. But right now, they need to go to bed."

I snatched my nephew up by his arm and my niece followed.

As soon as I got them cool, calm and collected, my mother called out, "It's time for my medicine."

Damn, I knew she saw me trying to lay them down. Why the hell did she have to start yelling like that?

"Auntie, I'm not tired," my niece cried.

"Just lay down Kyla. Here, take Maximus."

While passing her my old teddy bear, a vivid picture ran through my head of him sitting on Mister Danny's lap. Disgusted by the memory, I tossed him to the side and gave her one of the dolls instead.

"Nooo, nooo, Auntie. I want Maximus. Gimme Maximus."

She started screaming at the top of her lungs.

"Chaka, I need my medicine," my mother barked again.

All the commotion caused my nephew to wail furiously. I had just gotten him to close his eyes and now he was with the crying shit again. Seriously, I never suffered from postpartum depression or knew anyone who has but if those women had to live everyday lives similar to the few hours I was being forced to endure, then I couldn't blame them for snapping. I felt like a short fuse burning at both ends. It was only a matter of seconds before I'd explode.

"Listen, Kyla, just take the stupid teddy bear. Here."

I threw him on the bed and nearly took her eye out as he landed across her face. She didn't seem to mind. Innocently, she hugged him tight and curled on her side.

By that time, I found my nephew's pacifier and practically shoved it down his throat. I would have dipped it in Hennessey if it would've knocked his ass out faster.

All I wanted was a little peace and quiet. Serious changes were in order and I had to formulate a plan. There was no way in hell I could do that with the commotion going on around me. I knew I should've never come here. Not in this state of mind.

Before my mom started yelling again, I turned the light off in the kids' bedroom and went to get her medicine.

"Here, Mommy."

After handing her the pills, I poured a large glass of water from the jug in the refrigerator.

"You know I like my water from the sink," she snapped.

Nothing I did was good enough. She was in a funk and I despised her when she was like that. I emptied the cup and poured another one straight from the tap. The faucet didn't have a filter so the water was all cloudy and murky looking. She didn't seem to be bothered by it because she gulped it down along with her dose of pain medication.

We sat on the couch for a couple of hours. Neither one of us did much talking. She was watching old episodes of *In the Heat of the Night*, which was one of my least favorite shows of all time. But as long as it kept her entertained, I didn't make a fuss about it. Finally, I could get some rest. As I closed my eyes, it dawned on me that I had been awake since seven in the morning. A little shut eye would do me good. Zoning out, while watching over my mother, brought back memories. I recalled the first time she got sick. As it seems, I've been on watch ever since.

CHIGGY

"Freddy, Freddy."
My mother's screams woke the whole house up.
"Freddy, my eyes. My eyes."
My bedroom was right next to my parents' and was shared by Camille, my two brothers and my other sister, Olivia. She only stayed over on rare occasions. Because she was my father's biological daughter and not my mother's, she had another family outside of ours. Still, my mom loved her like her own so she always had a spot at our house.

On this morning in particular, it was just me and my brothers in the bedroom. I'm not sure where Camille was. She was old enough to have boyfriends by then so she could've been anywhere. Our small bedroom had a bunk bed, where my brothers slept and a twin-size bed off to the side that I shared with my sister. We usually slept with one at the foot and the other at the head. When she didn't come home, it was a privilege because I got to have the whole bed to myself.

Although that morning, I wished my big sister was there. I didn't know what was going on in the next room but the piercing shrieks scared the heck out of me.

My brother Khalid, who was only a few months older than me, was the first one up. Leaping to my bed with the quickness, he shook my shoulders and yelled, "Chiggy get up. Mommy's crying."

Kareem, our youngest brother, jumped down from the top bunk and scurried toward me as well. He was only five years old so he was just following suit.

"Go see what happened. Go."

Although I was just as frightened as them, Khalid persisted. He always pushed me to go ahead and test the waters regardless of what we were getting ourselves into. With the curiosity of a cat and the heart of a lion, I was always the first to step out into the unknown. This time though, I was more hesitant than usual. Unsure of what awaited beyond our closed door.

"Debra, calm down. Calm down. Let me see."

Holding my finger up to my lips to keep my brothers hushed, I pressed my ear against the door for a better listen to what my father was saying. Daddy's feet scuffled around as my mother continued to bellow.

"Just go out there and see," Khalid ordered with a hard shove.

"Shut up. Don't be pushing me."

I turned and swung at him. He dodged out of the way and my slap landed on Kareem's forehead instead. He started hollering on impact.

"See what you made me do, stupid?"

Khalid nudged my shoulder again and said, "You stupid."

He was taller than me but that didn't mean I couldn't take him. Growing up, I was a tomboy and caught wreck with the best of them. However, there were more important things to worry about right now besides getting my licks off. Hurriedly, I covered my little brother's mouth with my hand.

"Be quiet. I'm sorry. It's all right. Stop crying," I gently whispered in his ear.

Kareem never made a big fuss so once I gave him a little attention, he calmed down.

"Go 'head."

Khalid pulled Kareem from my arms and again demanded that I go find out what was happening.

"All right. Shoot, don't rush me. I'ma go see."

Slowly, I turned the doorknob and opened it. With just my head peeking out, I looked to the left and then to the right. For some reason, I thought there'd be blood all over the place or something. For as long as I could remember, the sight of it made me nauseas. Luckily, there was none, at least as far as I could see. As I stepped out of my room, my brother shoved me one more time. It was a rough push so I almost landed, face first, on the floor. Once I regained my balance, I tried to go back in the room but I couldn't open the door. He must've been pressing his whole body against it because it wouldn't budge.

With nowhere else to go, I took a deep breath and turned the corner. My mother's door was wide open and she was sitting up on the bed. As if she was playing a game of Peek-a-Boo, she kept covering and uncovering her eyes with her hands. Daddy was bent over in front her with a doctor's flashlight shining in her face. Surely, that was a prop he'd stolen from a doctor somewhere. My house was like a bootleg medical supply store. Stethoscopes, gauze pads, blood pressure pumps – Daddy took his foray into the medical world very seriously.

"Mommy?"

Both my voice and my steps were soft as I approached her side.

"Chiggy, don't come in here. Don't see me like this."

Obviously, she didn't realize I was already standing right next to her. I placed my hand on her knee to let her know I was closer than she thought. I was right there.

"Daddy, what's wrong with Mommy?"

"I don't know Chiggy. I don't know."

Placing the flashlight down on the side of the bed, he ran to the wooden bookshelf right outside their door. He slid his finger across the row of hard-covered Encyclopedias until he found the one he needed. Then, he returned with it propped open.

"Chiggy, hold my hand."

My mother gripped my little fingers so tight, there was barely any circulation going down my arm. I didn't complain. The tighter she squeezed, the less she cried. As the tears slid down her face, I took the sleeve of my pink flannel *Jem and the Holograms* nightgown and wiped her face. We might have gone outside with holes in our sneakers but my mother always made sure we slept in decent pajamas.

"It's ok, Mommy. Don't cry."

I didn't know what else to say as my eyes misted up too. She was normally the one consoling me but there I was, all of eight years old and I was making sure she was ok.

"Freddy, take me to the hospital. Let's just go."

My mother took a step and banged into the dresser that was right in front of her. That's when I realized, she couldn't see. Daddy grabbed her arm and led her to the living room.

"Go get the boys and y'all put some clothes on. Hurry up," Daddy said.

I darted to my room and my brothers were already getting dressed. They must've been eavesdropping.

"Come on. Y'all moving too slow. We gotta go get Mommy

some eyes," I shouted, before tucking my floor-length nightgown into a pair of corduroys and slipping on some raggedy pumpkin seed sneakers.

Kareem was moving like molasses but I couldn't blame him. He never dressed himself before so I had to help him like I always did.

"She ain't got no eyes?" Khalid asked. His face was full of horror.

"Ain't ain't a word, stupid. But no, she don't have them anymore. Her eyes are gone. They just disappeared."

I didn't literally mean she had two empty sockets in her head but I didn't know how else to explain that she was blind. I thought if we just got her to the hospital, like she wanted, they could give her some new eyes.

After I tied Kareem's sneakers, I stood him up and gave him a once over. His dingy green pants were high-waters and stopped all the way above his ankle. However, his skin wasn't exposed because I never took his He-Man onesie off. It was January and I had to make sure he stayed warm. With no time for lotion, his face was chalkboard ashy. So, I licked my fingertips and tried to wipe away the white crust around the corners of his mouth. My mother would have never approved of us going out of the house looking like some homeless orphans but I took my chances anyway. Drastic times called for drastic measures.

"Come on. Y'all too slow."

Khalid marched out of the room like a little soldier going to war. With Kareem in tow, I followed his lead. Mission 'Save Mommy's Eyes' was in full effect. We were ready for battle.

In a matter of seconds, we were heading to New York Hospital. During the ride to Manhattan, I held my mother's hand the whole way. Repeatedly, I told her everything would be all right. Everything would be all right. Khalid continued staring at her, checking to see if she still had eyes or not. He was waving his hands in front of her face but she didn't acknowledge him. Every time I caught him doing that, I'd silently call him stupid and then he'd stop.

Surprisingly, the emergency room was empty and they took my mother right in to see the doctor. Because we were so young, we had to stay in the waiting room and couldn't go in the back. Daddy kept checking on us every so often but it still felt like a lifetime of waiting. We were so hungry that when the nurse offered us some nasty hospital food, we chomped down every little bit like we hadn't eaten in years.

After a while, Daddy came back and announced it was time to go home. I looked behind him, expecting to see my mother. She wasn't there.

"Where's Mommy?" Khalid asked.

I was glad he had the heart to say something because I was too afraid to say anything. Our eyes opened wide in anticipation of what my father was about to tell us.

"Come here, y'all."

We followed Daddy to the sitting area. He put Kareem on his lap while Khalid and I sat on opposite sides.

"Your mother is gonna stay here for a couple days."

On cue, we all started crying. What did he mean she was staying? We had never gone a day without her, much less a couple of them.

"They don't have no eyes for her?"

Khalid spoke up again with snot running down from his nose and into his mouth. Despite his crybaby antics, he was like our spokesperson with all the right questions.

My father gently placed a hand on his shoulder and in a reassuring voice, said, "They're gonna make her eyes work again. That's why she can't come home right now."

How was I supposed to survive without her? Mothers were meant to be home. I lost it and started bawling out of control.

"MOMMY. I WANT MY MOMMY."

During my meltdown, Khalid put his little arm around me and tried to mask his own sorrow. At the end of the day, I was his little sister and his need to protect me was evident, even at that age. Sometimes, he could be an ideal big brother when he wasn't making my life a living hell.

"It's all right, Chiggy," he said. "She just gotta wait 'til they order her some new eyes. It's ok, don't cry."

Even Kareem jumped off of Daddy's lap and started patting my head. Nothing worked. I couldn't stop the loud sobs as they ripped through the tranquil hospital. All I could do was picture her back there all alone. What if she walked into a wall and I wasn't there to guide her? I felt helpless which made me cry even more.

"Chiggy, you wanna see her before we leave?"

My father knew his little girl better than anyone else did.

Seeing my mother would be the only thing that might have put me at ease. Amid my hysterics, I lifted my head from between my legs and nodded yes. With that, Daddy walked to the nurse and said something. She looked skeptical at first but then he returned and led me to the back, beyond the double doors. My brothers sat in the waiting room. They were trying their hardest to hold in tears. That was fine by me. I had enough for all of us.

Lines of beds were placed in rows. My mom was lying in one toward the back of the room. Breaking away from Daddy, I ran to her as fast as I could.

"Mommy. Mommy. I'm here."

I intertwined my fingers with hers.

"Chiggy, it's ok, baby. Mommy's ok."

Her voice was less frantic than it was when we were home. She almost sounded like she was half asleep. I looked at the needle in her arm. It was attached to a bag of water that hung from a silver pole above her bed.

"Mommy, when is you coming home?"

"When *are* you coming home?" She was well enough to correct my grammar. "I'll be home soon. Don't worry, ok?"

I nodded and then I remembered she couldn't see me. "I was saying ok with my head, Mommy."

She smiled. "You listen to your father and help him with your brothers, ok?"

Again, I nodded – forgetting she had no idea that I was responding. "I mean, yes."

"Do your homework and you can even write me a letter every day until I come home. Would you like that?"

Even then, she knew how much writing meant to me.

"I will Mommy. I promise."

"Now go ahead and I'll be home soon. Gimme a kiss."

She puckered her lips up but couldn't find me. So, I leaned in and kissed her as she raised her hand and softly ran the back of it across my cheek.

"Are you crying, Chiggy? Don't cry."

Tears began to form in her eyes. I felt bad that my show of emotion made her sad so I came up with a quick lie.

"I'm not crying. It's just raining outside."

Of course, it wasn't raining and we hadn't been outside for hours. But it was then that I realized she needed me to be strong. My tears weren't going to help her, if anything, they only made her condition worse. At that point, at the tender age of eight, I learned a valuable lesson. Sometimes you have to hide your pain on the inside, especially if letting it out would only hurt somebody else.

"I love you Chiggy."

"I love you too Mommy."

After giving her one more kiss, Daddy led me back to the waiting room. As the doors were closing behind me, I took another peek at my mother who looked weak on that hospital bed. Unfortunately, that would become an all too familiar sight throughout the years that followed.

"Chaka. Chaka." She nudged my elbow. "I think it's time for my other medicine."

"What? Huh? What time is it?"

Sleep-eyed, I squinted hard to make out the numbers on the clock above the entertainment center. It was already ten o'clock. I didn't realize I slept that long. Aches shot through my neck and shoulder. Sleeping on a hard couch always did that to me.

"My medicine, Chiggy. It's time."

Her reference to my nickname didn't go unnoticed. It meant the medication I gave her earlier had kicked in. She was herself again, which was a good thing.

"Oh, I'll get it Ma."

I practically yawned through my response. That little bit of sleep was everything. My father should have been walking through the door any minute now. If he was on time, I would still be able to meet up with Ta-Ta.

"I've been thinking." My mother pulled her thumb out of her mouth and started talking. Yes, she still sucked her thumb. Yes, she was a grown ass woman. It was kind of cute though. It's not like she did it in public. Only those with whom she was most comfortable would see her childhood habit in full effect.

She continued, "Maybe tomorrow we can go to the park or something. Just me and you."

These rare glimpses into my old mom struck a chord in my heart. She hadn't been out of the house in over a month and even then, it was only to go to the hospital. Her rediscovered enthusiasm for life caused me to smile from ear to ear. This happiness only lasted for a second because I then remembered there wasn't shit for me to be smiling about.

"Really?"

My reply lacked any compassion. It was a little too late for all that. Either I woke up on the wrong side of the couch or I had realized my situation was still as fucked up as it was when I closed my eyes. Part of me hoped it was all a dream. Maybe even a beautiful nightmare. But when I woke up, it was quite the opposite. I was right back where I started – in a fucked up predicament.

"Really. I'm sorry, baby. I just get so mad. I hate being like this. I don't mean to take it out on you. You know what? I'm not gonna be mad anymore. I'm putting this in God's hands now."

She threw me a thumbs-up. I brushed it off. Easy for her to say, I was still angry as hell. Infuriated by what my life had become. Nah, she might not have been mad anymore but I woke up and I was still pissed the fuck off.

Without even cracking a smile, I handed her the next dose of medicine along with a cup of water. This time it was straight from the sink. I didn't want to set her off again.

The minute hand slowly made its way around the clock. The longer I sat, the more I thought about Salerno and inevitably Malik. I had no more places left to hide. The memories finally caught up to me.

Overwhelmed and over-thinking always led me to take the coward's way out. There was only one way to move my worries to the back of my head so that I could clear some space to see the bigger picture.

"I'm getting in the shower, Ma. I'll be right out."

As my mother continued talking about her newfound zest for life, I closed the door and turned the water to the hottest degree. The showerhead was set on pulsate and I positioned it so that it was pointing directly toward the crook in my neck. Turning around, I let it beat against my back. Immediately, I felt a little more relaxed. Hot showers were underrated. They did more for me than any anxiety pill ever did.

With a towel wrapped around my body, I walked to my parents' room where I got dressed. Their queen-size bed was too big to be inside of that little ass room. It was barely enough space to stand up. Primping in Salerno's walk-in closet had spoiled me. Now, everything else seemed so minuscule.

Fortunately, I packed my overnight bag before the shit hit the fan. I pulled out a pair of skin-tight Roberto Cavalli jeans and topped it off with a plain white wife-beater and a Christian Dior belt that had a large CD on the buckle. It was some plain shit but I still looked better than about half of these other chicks even on their best days. My yellow Chanel sandals and matching purse provided the perfect pop of color. Besides my 3-carat diamond studs and my watch, I didn't have a chance to grab any other jewelry. Still, I was shining without it. Once I put on a dab of lip gloss and a squirt of Hanae Mori perfume, I was almost ready to hit the streets. The last thing I needed to complete my look wasn't actually anything materialistic but it was mandatory if I wanted to be the least bit functional.

Looking around my mother's room, I found a CD case lying on top of her dresser. It was some old Hezekiah Walker gospel music but it would work for what I had to do. Pulling the small pill box from my bag, I scooped out the last little bit and made two lines on the back of the case. As I shook the leftover residue from the bottle onto my tongue, I let it sit there for a minute before rubbing my lips together. The cocaine was potent enough to make my whole mouth numb within seconds. Placing the straw to my right nostril, while holding down the left one with my index finger, I bent over and with one long inhale, the first line disappeared.

"Wooh."

My heart beat quickened as the rush gave me a much needed boost of energy. Habitually, I dug my finger in my nose to wipe my nostril clean before then sliding that very same finger across my gums to soak up any residual powder. Switching nostrils, I hovered back down to finish the other line. Midway through, the worst possible thing that could have ever happened, did. Without knocking on the door, my mother charged into the room.

"Chiggy, why don't you bake some coo..."

Her lower lip fell to the floor. It all happened so suddenly, I didn't have time to hide it or clean my nose. An awkward silence arose and we both stood there in utter shock.

"What are you doing in here? What are you...?" She yelled so violently that she could barely get the words out.

Instantly, I got defensive. A grown woman would have handled getting caught with a little more tact. Looking back on it now, my reaction proved the fact that although I was doing grown up shit, I was still a little girl mentally.

"Why you bursting in here like that anyway?" I screamed right back at her.

I offered no apologies. No explanations. There I was, acting like she did something wrong to me.

"Gimme that. Gimme."

She reached for the CD case but I knocked it off the dresser and the remaining powder spilled on the floor.

"Mind your business. Nobody told you to come in here like that."

She was standing in the doorway so I had to bump her to the side in order to get out. Her walking cane helped her stay balanced as she hobbled behind me.

"I can bust in anywhere I want. This is my house. Chaka, please, talk to me. Why are you doing that?"

"Just leave me alone. Stop following me all around the house. Just go sit down."

I stormed into the kitchen, turned around and she was right there all up in my face again.

"No, I'm not leaving you alone. Drugs, Chaka? I raised you better than that."

She had me cornered as she blocked the entryway. Like a trapped rat, I went for the jugular.

"What?" I roared at the top of my lungs. "You raised me? You raised me? No, I'm the one who always took care of you! I'm tired of you always in my business. All the fucking time, damn."

That was the first time I cursed at my mother. She knew I had a foul mouth but it was never directed at her. For some reason, I couldn't control myself. So many emotions came over me all at once and they were filled with an untamable rage. After being on edge all day, my inner grenade had finally exploded. This incident opened the flood gates, allowing the fury I'd been suppressing to come to a head. Too bad, it was all aimed at the wrong person. None of this was her fault but when you're hurting for as long as I was, sometimes the closest one to you gets caught up in your wrath. Especially, when it all comes unearthed and brought to the surface.

"I should have never come here. I hate this fucking house. All you do is sit there and feel sorry for yourself. You think I want to be here taking care of you? I got my own life."

Hysterically, I kept raising my voice higher and higher while slapping my hand against my chest. "Everybody always has to change their whole lives around to take care of you. Why can't you just be like other mothers? I swear I fucking hate you sometimes."

Her head dropped to her chest. If there was any will to live left inside of her, I just sucked it dry. It wasn't until I, myself, heard the words come out of my mouth that I realized I actually said them. If I could've taken them back, I would have, but the damage was already done.

Dejected, she turned away and slowly walked back to the couch. I should've apologized, right then and there, but no amount of sorry's would have helped. She was already broken.

From where I was standing, I couldn't see her but I could hear her cries. She tried to muffle the sound but it rang through my ears and burned a hole in my heart. Just as I was about to console her, my father walked in. There was no way I could face the both of them. Not after what I had done. He didn't see me standing in the kitchen and walked right over to my mother.

"Deb, what's wrong? What happened?"

She was speechless.

Before my father had a chance to say anything to me, I grabbed my keys off the table and jetted toward the door.

"Chiggy, what happened? What's wrong with her?" My father asked.

Ignoring his question, I kept heading out of the apartment. As I did, I caught a glimpse of my mother. Her forehead rested against the palm of her hand. Her posture, normally upright, was slouched over. She was defeated. Her body flinched with each tear. I had never seen her look so desolate. My words did more damage than Multiple Sclerosis ever did.

"I'm sorry," I said aloud – too ashamed to face what I had done any longer. "I'm so sorry."

As the door slammed behind me, I could still hear her. Had I known then what I know now, I would have turned around and begged for her forgiveness. On bended knee, I would've prayed for her to look beyond my venomous tongue and see the love in my heart. Above all, I would have kept repeating how sorry I was. But that's what a good daughter would have done. Unfortunately, I didn't do any of that. Instead, I ran.

As my luck would have it, that was the last conversation I ever had with my mother in 40-05 12th Street, Apartment 4A. Regrettably, this memory continues to haunt me every day of my life.

Chapter 21

Bidding Ta-Ta farewell was completely out of the question. There was no way I could handle another emotional situation. Instead, I figured it was still early enough to make the meeting with my cash cow so that I could possibly get an introduction to his connect. Attention from the opposite sex, accompanied by a few drinks would definitely take my mind off of what happened with my mother. Drained by this point, I needed to engage in something less intense and more enticing. Not to mention the fact that I still had to find me another sponsor. My relationship with Salerno was all but done. After what he revealed to me about Malik, he couldn't pay me enough to stay with him. Yes, I was a money hungry wrench at times but he straight violated. There was no going back from there.

My only chance for survival was to add a new sponsor under my belt. With a little luck, I could bag the big fish and live happily ever after. It was a long shot but one I was willing to take. Financially, I couldn't fend for myself. Fuck that, I needed to secure my next source of income. I just hoped he was somewhat attractive with an heir of swagger. Who was I kidding? Even if he was an ugly gorilla looking motherfucker, I wouldn't have cared. Money was what attracted me the most and from what I heard on the streets, that dude had lots of it.

As usual, I caught a cab to the city. I swear, it would have been cheaper for me to buy a car instead of paying so much money on taxis but I didn't have a license and I sure as hell didn't know how to drive. My cousins, who lived down south, were always bragging about getting their first cars at the age of sixteen. In New York though, all you need is a MetroCard or cab fare. Maybe one out of every twenty hood chicks actually has a license. Being self-sufficient wasn't on our list of things to do.

Looking down at my Presidential Rolex, one of Salerno's generous gifts, I realized I was actually making decent time. Originally, I was supposed to meet up with him at nine. Since it was only eleven o'clock, I'd still be able to catch him although I'd be making a fashionably late appearance. Actually, he probably expected that. I was never punctual. My clock was on CPT, Chaka's Personal Time and that shit was at least an hour behind the rest of the world.

When I arrived at the bar in Manhattan's trendy Meat Packing District, the scene was packed. Industry parties were known for bringing out all the people you wanted to see and those desperate motherfuckers who were longing to be seen. In one corner were the groupies vying for attention and hoping to get saved. I gave them a once over. Their skirts were too short. Weaves were too long. Makeup was too colorful. The thirst was real.

Thankfully, I had never been forced to play that role. Even in kicks and sweats, I could still pull a hottie or two.

Then, there were the drug dealers who invested the occasional dollar in studio sessions and amateur video shoots for unknown yet aspiring rappers. They also suffered from some level of thirst because they'd usually find a random project nobody, who was decent on the mic and put all their money behind him in hopes that he'd make it big enough to take care of them in the long run. As quiet as it's kept, that's just how the top money-makers in Queensbridge developed Nas, who is now one of the most prolific rappers in history. He used to be a quiet kid with a dredlocked high top and an undeniable talent. His early years were funded by a scholarship from the street. But once he made it, he seldom came back to the hood. Who could blame him though? With all the conniving haters begging for hand-outs and record deals, I would've stayed gone too.

As I looked across the small dance floor, I spotted my friend sitting at a table with a bunch of guys. I pulled a MAC C-thru lip gloss from my Chanel bag and added another coat of shine. Nude colors always looked good on me. They added a natural looking enhancement to my DSL's. You know, those Dick Sucking Lips. Way before girls were taking duck faced selfies, we depended on that good old MAC to give us a sexy pout.

Prior to walking over to my crowd, I stopped at the bar for a drink. My mind was still weighed down heavily with thoughts of my mother. Wondering if she was still upset had plagued my conscience ever since I stormed out of the apartment. A shot of Tequila would help put my mind at ease.

The bartender poured my drink and I quickly downed it before asking for another. It had been one hell of a day and I didn't have any coke left so liquor was the only way I could deal with it all. Since I was basically in work-mode, I had to stay in character. There was no way I could ask the dude I was meeting to hit me off with a bag of powder. To him, I was London − the good College girl who seldom hung around drug dealers and never partook in anything remotely associated with the streets. *Yeah right, if he only knew the half.* But it was a role I played well. Because I did, it always resulted in being able to hustle a man without him even knowing it. Of course, this was the reason he invited me to meet his connect. He thought he was using me to impress the next man, when in actuality, I was using his gullible ass to get close enough to fuck with that man. Life is funny like that. Everybody has a role to play.

"Let me get another one," I shouted to the bartender as I placed a twenty dollar bill on the counter.

I took it straight to the head. Slamming my glass down, I shut my eyes and swallowed hard. The liquor burnt my chest but gave me a little extra oomph. Armed with some liquid confidence, I began to sashay my way through the crowd.

"This is VIP," the bouncer announced as I approached the red velvet rope.

I batted my eyes and flashed a full smile before saying, "I'm with them."

Clearly, I was with the right crowd. As soon as I pointed to my friend, the bouncer was quick to pull the rope back and let me in. He knew exactly who they were and apparently could tell that I belonged right with them.

As I walked toward my friend, he spotted me immediately and threw a head nod in my direction. There were other girls sitting in their little section but they didn't hold a candle to me. With my nose all up in the air, I put on my best catwalk. There's only one chance to make a first impression and I was determined to catch his connect's eye at any cost. Whoever he was, no matter what he looked like, he was my target for the night so I had to put my best foot forward.

"London, what's up Ma?"

Before I could even get all the way to their table, ol' dude was shouting me out. Like a little boy with a new toy, he couldn't wait to show me off. Playfully, I waved and acted equally as excited to see him. After all, I was in full character – a bad girl gone good.

Once I got closer, the connect finally turned around. My heart stopped when I saw his face. Actually, my feet came to a halt for a second as well. The look of surprise was written all over him as he squinted his eyes to make sure he was seeing things correctly. I took a deep breath but couldn't seem to close my lower lip which had practically fallen to the floor. All of a sudden, everything around me vanished. The music went mute. The only sound I could hear was the thumping of my tell-tale heart. ***Bomp, bomp. Bomp, bomp.*** Our eyes locked and for a moment, it was just us despite being in a room full of people.

It can't be. I forced my legs, which felt like concrete pillars, to continue walking.

"What's good Bae?"

My friend spoke but I couldn't respond. Although my mouth was agape, the words just wouldn't flow. I was stuck in a trance.

He continued, "Let me introduce you to my man from Atlanta. London, this is Jamere. Jamere, this is my lady, London."

There was no need for introductions. Jamere, the only man who ever truly loved me, knew just who I was. However, he had no clue as to who I had become.

Chapter 22

If I could've turned around and ran in the opposite direction, I would have sprinted away like Lolo Jones. Seeing him, after all this time, was the last thing I expected. With over eight million people in New York City alone, how slim were the chances of bumping into Jamere? The last I heard, he was in Atlanta and running a successful, yet legitimate, business. Come to find out, this motherfucker was actually the connect with pockets that ran as deep as the abyss. Luckily, he didn't blow my cover.

"Hi, umm, what's your name again? London, right? Nice to meet you." He extended his hand in my direction.

Without saying a word, my eyes begged for him to follow along. I couldn't afford to be exposed – not here, not now. He nodded his head at me as if to let me know he wasn't going to blow me up. I felt a tiny bit of relief. The average man wouldn't have been smart enough to play along. He'd probably say some dumb shit like, "What's up Chaka?"

Jamere was anything but average. Between hustlers, there's a code of ethics. The unspoken rule goes something like this, "When you know what's up, be smart and play dumb". Thankfully, that's just what he did.

For the next hour, we pretended like we didn't know each other. He continued talking amongst the fellas and I sat over to the side by myself. After all, I was only brought to the meeting for the sole purpose of providing some eye candy. I didn't give a fuck. I played my position like a quarterback.

Occasionally, Jamere and I would catch ourselves staring at each other. During those brief moments, every happy memory

I ever had of him came rushing to the forefront. I had to force myself to look away. If I stared too long, there's no telling what I'd do. In my heart, I just wanted to run to him and feel the warmth of his body next to mine. But in my mind, I knew I had work to do. Realizing Jamere was actually the connect had changed my whole game plan which left me right back where I started – ground zero and looking for a come up.

After awhile, all I wanted to do was get the fuck out of there. Mixing my personal life into this hustle was the last thing I wanted. Up until then, I managed to stay a step ahead. Both worlds co-existed without overlapping. Bumping into Jamere, fucked that all up for me. I didn't know if I was Chaka, London, or Charlie's freak ass. Slowly, I was coming apart at the seams. Forcing myself to sit there and pretend like everything was gravy only added to my mental anguish. My life was unraveling right before my very eyes and I didn't have a contingency plan. Once I acknowledged that hard truth, I felt a sudden urge to scream. I'm not sure if it was my lack of cocaine or not but for the first time, in a long time, my heart felt an unquenchable pain. I needed to break free.

"Hey, I'm going to head out of here. I've got a class in the morning so I really need to go, ok?"

I whispered to ol' dude, who was so busy trying to floss that he practically paid me no mind.

"All right Ma. Call me tomorrow," he said before continuing on with his conversation.

Like a hawk, Jamere watched my every move from the moment I got up to leave until the second I past the velvet rope. When I felt he could no longer see me, I dipped into the Ladies Room.

"Agghhh," I screamed from the stall.

It was crowded but I didn't care. If they knew how my day was going, they would have been screaming right along with me. In the past, I'd always break out into these dopefiend-looking anxiety attacks where I'd start breathing all heavy and sweating profusely. This accidental meeting with Jamere caused it to happen all over again. My heart was beating a mile a minute and my mouth was as dry as the Sahara Desert.

In through the nose, out through the mouth. In through the nose, out through the mouth.

Repeating this to myself was the only way I could stop from

hyperventilating. The walls were closing in around me. Being locked inside of a two-by-five box only intensified that feeling. Quickly, I burst out of the stall and ran to the sink. Splashing cold water on my face, I said to myself, "Get it together Chaka. Get it together."

Feeling the curious stares of the other women in the bathroom, I pulled a rough brown paper towel from the dispenser above the sink and dried my face. Looking in the mirror, I slicked down my ponytail's loose strands with the palms of my wet hands, added a fresh coat of lip gloss and dabbed the emerging sweat beads from my forehead. The last thing I was going to do was let another woman see me crumble. I lifted my head and walked out with what little bit of dignity I still had left.

I didn't get a full two steps away from the bathroom before I heard Jamere's voice.

"London? You couldn't come up with a better name than that?"

I bit down on my lower lip to keep myself from having an emotional outburst. With a hint of sarcasm, that he knew so well, I responded, "I was gonna use Jamereiqua but I thought that would sound too ghetto."

He laughed and suddenly it felt like old times. Besides a few extra pounds plus the fact that his salt and pepper goatee was now more salt than pepper, he still looked good as fuck. I couldn't help but wonder how much better my life would have turned out had I gotten with him instead of Malik. Boy, did I know how to pick them or what? I sure fucked that one up.

So many things had transpired in my life since I last saw him. I was a different person back then. He knew the good me; the one who still believed in love. She was long gone though and I thought she'd never resurface. That was, until I saw his face. Every happy memory I ever shared with him flashed across my eyes from sitting on the bench for hours and laughing at each other's jokes to the day I barged into the bathroom while the python between his legs stood at attention. He was still the love of my life.

"What's going on with you?"

His lightheartedness, that I loved so much, disappeared. I was expecting him to be judgmental or disapproving but he wasn't. His genuine concern shocked me. I forgot what that felt like. With Jamere, I wasn't an object or a conquest. He saw beyond my exterior and beneath my many masks. As ugly as I felt on the inside, he still managed to find the beauty within. Besides him, no other man had ever done that. He was the only one who knew the real me.

Unable to speak, I just shook my head. This wasn't the time or the place. Anybody could've been watching, especially ol' dude. Talking to Jamere would have appeared suspect.

He got a little closer, not so much so that it looked like we were all on top of each other, but just enough for me to hear him clearly.

"Go to the corner and wait for me. Right outside of here on Ninth Avenue. I'll be right there."

He didn't wait for my response. Instead, he walked off and never bothered looking back. He knew I'd be there waiting. Jamere and I had this intense attraction that kept pulling us together. Neither time nor distance could change that.

I wasn't standing there long before a black Range Rover pulled up. The heavy tints made it impossible to see inside. As the window rolled down, I could hear his voice before I saw his face.

"Hey, Lady. How much for the night?"

With my middle finger up, I walked toward the truck and teased, "Believe me, you couldn't afford it. Not even with your senior citizen discount."

"Yeah, I got your senior citizen," he said with a chuckle. "Get in this damn car."

Without giving me a chance to put my seatbelt on, he leaned toward me. Grabbing my face with both hands, he kissed my lips. At first, it was soft but then grew passionately. As our tongues danced, tears quietly fell from my eyes. Life had brought me full circle and right back into his arms.

He pulled away from me and gently wiped my cheek. There was so much to say but I didn't know where to begin.

"Chaka, you know you gotta tell me what's going on," he said while turning down the radio.

I knew this conversation was coming and although I had so many lies rehearsed, at that moment, I drew a blank.

"I mean, you just get up and leave like that? You don't tell nobody? Not even me?"

I looked out the window, too afraid to look in his eyes and tell him the truth.

"I just didn't want anybody to know."

"You ain't want nobody to know? You leave your homegirl in the hospital and then the next thing I hear, you in the Navy some damn where. I come here to meet this wangsta ass clown and now you pop up out the blue."

"What was I supposed to do?"

"Why didn't you call me, Chaka? Damn, your mother told me you broke out but that was only after I called her like ten times looking for you. What the fuck happened that night?"

"Oh, you ain't hear about it?" I asked, knowing full well everybody in the hood knew what happened to Ta-Ta.

"Yo, I don't know what the fuck really popped off. The hood is gonna talk, you already know that. They said Malik robbed y'all and stabbed Ta-Ta the fuck up. Now he's on the run and nobody heard from him. Then, you get up and disappear."

Though he said more, the only thing that kept replaying in my head was the fact that he really thought Malik was on the run. The only reason I never contacted him was because I thought he would look at me and know the truth. He could see through my lies any other time and simply put, I didn't want to get him involved in my mess. At the end of the day, Malik was his friend just as I was. I wasn't sure where his loyalty would lie. However, it appeared that he believed the story on the streets. Instantly, the burden was lifted. Jamere had no idea what really happened that night so I was just going to ride with the scenario he believed. My world of pretend always came in handy.

"I was scared. I didn't want Malik to find me," I cried, finally turning from the window and looking at him with tears streaming down my face.

With his left arm still holding the top of the steering wheel he raised his right hand to wipe my face with his thumb. He threw me a moment's glance before turning back to the road but never dropping his hand from my cheek.

"You don't gotta be scared no more, Chaka. He'll never hurt you again."

It almost made me feel guilty to go along with this story. I wanted to tell him everything and I knew he deserved to know the truth. He was re-entering my life and at the same time was completely blindsided by my bullshit. But I couldn't tell him just yet.

"I know. I'm not scared anymore," I said, while tightly

holding his hand.

It was true. Malik would never hurt me again. Right?

We drove through the city where the street lights gave me a burst of life and energy. When you're down to nothing, God always send you an angel to guide you to the next step. Jamere was present throughout all my trying times. When all else failed, he was right there to pick me up. Maybe, he was actually my Knight in Shining Armor and I was just too blind to see him for who he really was.

As we pulled into a parking spot overlooking the East River, we sat in silence for a few minutes before he asked, "Why don't you leave from here?"

Here we go again. Another person making it seem like it was so easy to get up and move. I was sick of having this conversation already. It was like a scratched record that kept repeating itself over and over and over again.

"I can't leave, Ja. Where am I supposed to go? And anyway, I can't leave my mother."

My mother. For a second there, I was feeling so good to be in Jamere's company that I nearly forgot all about our argument. A strong sense of urgency came over me. I needed to go home and make things right with her.

"You don't think your mother would want you to leave?"

I hadn't thought about that. Of course she hated me being in Queensbridge. Her biggest fear was that I'd end up there for the rest of my life. In fact, she didn't want any of her children to raise another generation within those six blocks. We were supposed to break the cycle. Not keep that shit revolving.

"I don't know. I mean, where am I supposed to go? People are always talking about leaving but then what? Leave and do what?"

"Well for one thing, you can go somewhere and stop being somebody you're not. London? What was that shit about anyway?"

I didn't know how to respond. There was no way I was telling Jamere about my little hustle. If he didn't think the worst of me before, he'd definitely hate my guts for doing all the things I did for money. He could never know about that. He just wouldn't understand.

"Oh, that was nothing. Just some dude I met and didn't want to give him my real name. It wasn't all that."

"Well, you can forget about him now. I'm deading that. Matter of fact, why don't you come with me."

His words were firm. There was no uncertainty or shakiness in his offer.

"To Atlanta?"

I heard about the southern city that was on the rise but I had never actually been there. If the rumors about Jamere's status in the drug game were true, it was definitely a place to kick back and enjoy the good life.

"Yeah, Atlanta. Look, I wasn't there for you like I shoulda been but I'm here now. People don't know you like I know you. We spent hours on the bench, day in and day out. The funny thing is that I used to come outside and actually wait for you to come around. Like clockwork, you were always there with something crazy to say with your little smart ass mouth. Talking to you made me think different. It's just something about you. You light up a room and you don't even realize it."

As he spoke, I became overcome with a mixture of happiness and fulfillment.

"I can't imagine my life without you in it. I don't wanna be friends no more. I love you Chaka. Do you even know that?"

For the first time ever, I heard the words and I genuinely believed them. Somebody loved me. With all my flaws and every shameful secret, somebody still loved me. I didn't think that was possible until he said it.

Reaching across the arm rest, I hugged him for dear life. He pulled my little lightweight ass over and I plopped on his lap. Coddled like a baby, he held me close. I buried my head in his chest and listened to his heart. It was beating for me and that feeling was better than any high I ever experienced.

"I love you too, Jamere."

We sat there and watched the city's lights twinkle along the surface of the river. Neither one of us said much of anything else. We didn't have a need for words anymore. Our bond was emotional and what's understood doesn't have to be explained.

I planned on going home and talking to my mother about moving to Atlanta. Knowing her, she'd be overjoyed. Maybe one day, when her disease went into remission, she could come visit me at my big house in the country. Overjoyed with an optimistic eye into my future, my thoughts were all over the place.

What should I pack?

How will I like it there?

What do people in the sticks do for fun?

I fell asleep in his arms and finally understood the true meaning of the phrase, "Peace be still."

That peaceful high would soon collapse and I'd plunge, head first, into my worst nightmare. Too bad for Jamere. I was bringing him down right along with me.

Chapter 23

The first thing I noticed when Jamere dropped me off in front of my building was the sirens. Their red and blue lights continuously flashed. As always, there was a crowd of people standing around, being nosy, trying to see who the ambulance was coming to get. As I walked closer to the building, a few of them pointed in my direction before covering their mouths to whisper to their equally meddlesome counterparts. The fucking Bench Dwellers were always the first ones on the scene.

My building door was propped open and I saw a paramedic leaning over a gurney in the hallway. I couldn't see who was stretched out but whoever it was, it didn't seem like they were in the best of shape. From my vantage point, I could only make out the paramedic pumping his arms up and down like they do in the movies when it's a Code Blue.

"What happened?" I asked some lady who was watching from a distance.

She usually knew all the gossip, even before the shit actually happened, so I could depend on her to give me a full account.

"Umm, I don't, umm, I don't know," she said and then hurried away from me like I had the bubonic plague or something.

Well damn, I thought. *That bum ass had the 411 every other time.*

I stood on my tippy toes to get a better look. It wasn't helpful. I still couldn't see shit but the back of a bunch of heads. The first thing I was going to do was run right up to Taylor's house. If anybody knew what was going on, I knew she did.

When my father came out of the building, it didn't automatically click. I thought he was just leaving out and had gotten caught up in the mayhem. But the look on his face told a different story.

Inching my way toward him, I started to get a better view. Especially once the paramedics exited behind him.

"Mommy," I yelled as I ran toward them, pushing people out of my way just to get there.

She was laid out with a white sheet draped across her body. There was a tube sticking down her throat. It was attached to a bag the paramedics kept compressing as they rushed toward the ambulance.

"Daddy, what happened? What happened?"

"Chiggy, come on. Just get in the ambulance."

My father grabbed my arm and we ran behind the gurney. There was barely any room inside the small ambulance especially with the paramedic moving around so frantically. He'd squeeze the bag of air into the tube and then apply pressure to my mother's chest. Her eyes were closed and her limbs dangled from the side of the stretcher.

"Mommy. Wake up."

She was unresponsive.

I tried to lean toward her but Daddy held me back. "Let them work, Chiggy."

Sweat came rolling down my forehead and my chest tightened. Another one of those fucking anxiety attacks was in full swing and I couldn't do anything to stop it. My stomach began to bubble and I tasted the bile piling up in my mouth. Any second now, I would lose it. Consciously, I tried my best to hold it in. With each heave of my body, I felt the throw up get closer and closer to my throat. Reaching over, I grabbed the garbage can that had been used for medical waste and stuck my head inside of it. Vomit filled the bag while my father rubbed my back. He knew how these attacks affected me but this one was by far, the worse.

We arrived at the hospital and the paramedics rushed my mother through the emergency room. Her physician, Dr. Patel, was already there. During the ride over, my dad said he called him the moment he realized how bad she was doing. I didn't bother to ask but the guilt of our argument ate away at me.

Was that the reason she was there? Did my words hurt her that much?

"Chiggy, what happened to her?"

Since Daddy had to ask, I figured she never told him how I treated her. Although I should have been upfront about it, I couldn't bring myself to tell him either. Shame covered me like a black cloak.

"I don't... I don't know. She was just sad all day."

I lied through my teeth, knowing exactly what was wrong with her. After all, I was the one who caused it. She wasn't sad. Well, at least not all day. In fact, she had just turned the corner on her depression until I pushed her back into it. Me and my fucking mouth.

Dr. Patel entered the waiting room. My father and I rushed to his side. He had been my mother's doctor since the early stages of her disease. As one of the leading Multiple Sclerosis physicians in the world, we always trusted him to be blunt and direct when it came to my mother's condition or her chances of recovery. He stood about six feet tall so we had to look up to him as he spoke. But with my mother, he was a gentle giant. As soon as we called, he immediately came to her side.

"We got her stabilized but that's just for the night."

"What does that mean, just for the night?" My father asked.

The look of despair in his eyes was obvious.

"I don't know. I ordered an MRI. I'll know more in the morning. How long was she like this before you brought her in?"

I stayed quiet and let my dad do all the talking.

"Well, remember I called earlier when she was in pain but it wasn't this bad. When I got home, it just got worse from there."

"Stress could be the cause of such a severe attack," Dr. Patel explained. "Was she upset about anything recently?"

My stomach bubbled again. I knew it. I did this to her. Was she upset? Was she upset? Was she upset? The more I heard the question, the more my head spun around in circles.

"Daddy, I need some air."

I couldn't listen anymore. The truth was right there smacking me in my face. Nothing Dr. Patel said would've made a difference. My actions put her in this situation. I knew that. She knew that. God knew that. If something happened to her, I'd never forgive myself.

Feeling as if I was about to pass out, I sat on the curb right outside of the emergency room. So much for moving to Atlanta. There was no way I could leave her. Not now. Not like this. And what about my father? He looked like he could barely stand up straight. This ordeal was taking a toll on him as well.

With Jamere, I was just at the pinnacle of my life. Now, I was right back at the bottom of it. Every time I felt like something good was about to happen for me, it would all go south in a matter of minutes. It was as if there was an omen on my life. Like, I was born to suffer. No matter where I ran, that black cloud always had a way of finding me.

Looking up, I realized why this spot on the corner was so familiar to me. Not too long ago, I was standing in this very place being questioned about Ta-Ta's attack. Suddenly, Salerno appeared in my thoughts. This was where he told me about Malik stealing the drugs. Right here, on this very street. Here I was again, with some more gut-wrenching news. In this movie, that was my life, I felt like I was steady watching the same repeats over and over again. Just when I thought it was a new episode, I was brought right back into an old one. The only way it would change is if I changed. I felt a sudden urge to pray.

"Dear God, if you're listening, this is me, Chaka. I'm sorry for everything I've done. I don't know why I can't do anything right. Believe me God, I try but for some reason, I just can't. I don't come to you all the time because I know you don't listen to me. You never do. But this time, I'm begging you and I hope you hear me. Please don't let her die. I promise if you give her another chance, I'll change. I promise you that. Please don't take her away from me. If you have to take anybody God, please take me. Don't take her. She doesn't deserve this. Please. Please let me know that you hear me. I'll be good if you give her another chance. Please."

Tears poured from my eyes and I just let them run. I'd been bottling up so many emotions that I couldn't hold them in any longer. It had been years since I prayed. For some reason or another, I hated God. My mother changed her whole life and devoted herself to him yet he still struck her with an insufferable disease. How could a God do that to one of his faithful believers? I knew a whole bunch of other people who deserved to suffer. She wasn't one of them. She practically went to church every day whether it was for a service or a support group meeting. Obviously, that wasn't good enough for God because he didn't do anything to stop her pain.

And what about me? I thought he was supposed to protect his children. Well, where was God when Mister Danny was ripping my insides out with his fingers? If there was a God, he must have forgotten all about us. Hopefully he listened to my prayer this time, but then again, he never did.

Hopelessly, I got up and headed back inside the hospital. If God was listening, he'd prove it.

My mother was admitted and brought up to her room. The nurses on the floor knew my family by our first names. Shit, we were in and out of there so much, it almost felt like our second home. Daddy was sitting in a recliner at her bedside. He looked like he hadn't slept in days.

"Daddy, why don't you go home for a little while? I'll stay here with her."

"I guess I should go now and make sure the kids are ok. Taylor came down and got them but I'll pack them some clothes so they can stay with her for the night. I'll bring Debra's pajamas up here too. She hates sleeping in these hospital gowns."

I laughed. Honestly, my mother really did have a thing about pajamas. Whenever she was in the hospital, it was the first thing she requested.

"So you go now and then when you come back, I'll go and get some rest."

Daddy said he called my brothers but they weren't coming home until the next day so it was just me and him on watch for the time being.

"All right, Chig. I'll be back."

Before leaving, he kissed both me and my mother on the cheek. It was a scene that had played out so many times before.

The cold hospital room sent chills up my body and made the hairs on my arms stand up. Why did they have to keep the temperature sub-zero all the time? Luckily, there was a white blanket draped across the chair. I wrapped it around my body, from my head all the way down to my calves. There was a pair of hospital socks in the drawer next to my mother's bed and I put those on as well. After a minute or two, I stopped trembling but I still felt like I was bathing in an ice tub.

"Ugh," my mother moaned.

Quickly, I threw the blanket to the floor and stood next to her. The doctor had removed the tube but she had a tracheotomy in the front of her neck.

"Ugh," she moaned again.

"Mommy, can you hear me?"

I leaned in so close that I almost had her ear in my mouth. "Chiggy?"

Her voice was frail but I could make out everything she said as clear as day.

"Yeah, Mommy. I'm here."

"Chiggy."

My head collapsed on her stomach. God finally answered my prayers.

"Mommy, I'm so sorry. I didn't mean to do this to you."

She ran her hand along the top of my head.

"It's ok, baby. I forgive you."

"Mommy, I don't hate you. I love you more than anybody. If anything happened to you, I wouldn't know what to do with myself."

"Come here Chiggy." She held her arms open and I rested my head along her bosom. "You have to make me," she took a short breath before continuing. "You have to make me a promise."

"Anything Mommy. What is it?" I could tell she was straining to talk so I listened closely.

"Go live your life."

The medication must have been getting to her. Didn't she know I was already living? I thought she was going to make me promise not to do drugs anymore. Instead, she wanted me to promise to do what I was already doing.

"Huh, Mommy? What do you mean? I'm alive right now."

This time she took a longer breath before speaking again.

"There's a difference between being alive and really living. I want you to get away from here. This place isn't good for you. It will only bring you down."

Come on, you too? There was that scratched record again. I wasn't saying anything about moving to Atlanta with Jamere. In fact, I had forgotten all about that option. It was a dream that would never come true. I wasn't about to leave my mother's side.

"All right, I will."

I only agreed in an effort to appease her. I think she knew that because then she really laid it on me.

"You know what's special about you?"

I shrugged my shoulders. For the life of me, I couldn't come up with one thing that mattered. What, I was cute? I used to have potential? I knew how to hustle a man's pockets? I mean, really, she made me think – what was so special about me?

"You were my Lucky Number Seven Baby. You know that, right?"

As my eyes watered, I nodded yes. My mother had recited this story so many times before. Actually, I used to make her tell it to me every night before I went to sleep. Most kids wanted to hear a fairytale. Not me, though. I found the story of my birth even more enchanting.

"Tell me again, Mommy. Please."

Although I knew it like the back of my hand, it felt so much better hearing it come from her mouth.

"Well, I just turned twenty-three on March twenty-third and you came along on June twenty-third. You didn't even cry when you came out because you were so busy sucking your thumb and looking around. You were very alert, especially for a newborn. All the nurses thought you were just too cute with that big red birthmark on your bald head. You were so light. Everybody thought I had me a little White baby."

I laughed, remembering the pictures of me with big bows slipping down the little baby hairs that eventually sprouted out.

"What else?" I asked, eager to hear the rest of the story that I had heard so many times before.

"Well, you were seven pounds, seven ounces, seventeen inches and born at exactly seven o'clock. Right here in New York Hospital. That's why I call you my Lucky Number Seven Baby. I always knew you were special, Chiggy. Don't you ever forget that."

I felt like her little girl again. It had been so long since we had these kinds of moments. With the sickness and raising the kids, along with my affinity for the streets, we hadn't had time to ourselves in forever. Truth be told, I was always a Mommy's girl. If you ask me, I would say I was her favorite. Of course, every child probably feels that way about their mother but in my case, it was true. Well, at least I liked to believe it was anyway.

"I won't forget. Mommy, I'm so sorry. Can you ever forgive me?"

Although she had already accepted my apology, I still couldn't say it enough. The fact that she was still so sweet to me, even after I crushed her with my words, only made me more apologetic.

"I forgive you baby. But you have to release that anger you've been holding in your heart for so long. It's destroying you. One day, you have to forgive yourself for whatever it is that hurts you so much."

Once she said that, I could no longer hold it together. The wave of emotions flowing through my body came gushing out.

"I've always admired you, Chaka. No matter how many times you fall, you always pick yourself up, dust yourself off and you keep going. You've been like that ever since you were a little girl. You never gave up then, so don't start now."

Throughout my entire life, nobody ever told me they admired me. I mean, men lusted after me and friends copied me, but not once, did anyone ever say, they admired me. Armed with that kind of encouragement, I knew I could accomplish anything. Despite what I saw when I looked in the mirror, there was a person out there who still admired little old me.

"I won't give up, Mommy. I promise. I'll keep going."

She smiled and when she did, there was an indescribable glow around her. It radiated from inside, like a burst of light. "That's all I wanted to hear Chiggy. Who loves you baby?"

When I was younger, she'd always ask that question before I went to sleep at night and I'd answer it the same way every time.

"You love me. You're my Sugar Lump Lollipop." I giggled.

"And you're my pretty little Honey Lamb."

She dozed off within minutes of our chat. While she slept, I said another quick prayer.

"Hey God, it's me again. I just want to say thank you for listening. I'm gonna stick to my promise; for real this time."

Finally, I felt God and I had made amends. For all the times he let me down before, he actually showed up when it mattered the most. My mother was still here.

Just as I was praising the Lord for some unforeseen miracle, the machines started beeping. At first, it was a slow beep. In seconds, it got louder.

"Ma," I yelled as her trach made a gurgling sound.

The beeps roared to deafening decibels. Then, red lights started flashing.

"Nurse, Nurse." I jumped off the bed and ran to the nurse's station. "Come quick, come on. Something's happening."

Rushing past me, they headed toward her room with a crash cart on their side. The beeps quickened as did the nurses' movements. Pulling the curtain around her bed, they pushed me outside of it so I couldn't see what was going on.

"Let me in there. Ma." I shouted. "MOMMY."

A male nurse held me back as I struggled to get beyond the curtain. I tried to elbow him away but he was holding me too tight.

"What's happening? MOMMY, CAN YOU HEAR ME? MAAAAAAAA."

The sounds of an electric shock, like sticking a metal pin inside of a wall socket, resonated throughout the small hospital room. Everything went quiet for a second. Then, the sound of another jolt of electricity sparked through the air. All the while, the nurses were speaking in medical terms that I couldn't understand. The room was spinning out of control.

A perpetual beep chimed the loudest of them all.

"Call it," the nurse said.

I didn't need a medical dictionary to understand that. With all my might, I broke free from the male nurse and pushed my way beyond the curtain. I was too late. With one look, I knew she was gone.

"NOOOOOO."

Falling to my knees, I dropped my head in my lap and screamed toward the floor.

"MOMMMMMYYYY. MOMMY."

"Miss Adams, please come with us."

The nurses tried to console me. I couldn't move. My body felt paralyzed. My cries didn't even make a sound. I was there but my heart was yanked from my chest.

They finally left me alone for a second. I couldn't even open my eyes to look at her. I just sat on the cold floor and reached up to hold her lifeless hand. Just moments before, we were laughing together and now she was dead.

She would have never been there if it wasn't for me. She didn't die from Multiple Sclerosis. She died from a broken heart. I should know. I'm the one who killed her.

Fade to black...

Chapter 24

Black. Black suit. Black dress. Black limousine. Black hearse. Black coffin. Why is it that everything at a funeral is always black? Isn't there enough gloom surrounding death without having to see black every time you open your eyes? The only thing that has a little color is the flowers. And even those are a reminder of death. Sitting there, in a pool of black, I looked at them and wondered how long it would take before they dried up and shriveled away?

The week leading up to my mother's funeral was the hardest. No one in my immediate family had ever died, at least nobody I knew, so the fact that my mother was my first encounter with death, made the situation even worse. I didn't know what to expect. How do you choose a casket? The funeral home was pressuring us to buy one that was airtight, waterproof and had stainless steel fixtures. Why the fuck did any of that matter? From selecting a burial plot to dropping off her burial outfit, it all seemed surreal to me. This was my mother and I was burying her. No fancy casket could have changed that.

When I got back from the hospital on the day she died, I pulled all her t-shirts out of her drawer and slept on them. I wanted to smell her all around me. I cried even harder when I wondered how long her scent would last on them. Would it be gone in a month? Or would it be sooner?

I could still hear her bangles jingle as they did when she was alive. She always wore a wrist full and never took them off. Every time I came in late, thinking I was being sneaky, she'd move her arms just enough to make her bangles jingle. This was her way of letting me know that she waited up for me the entire night. Even when I was roaming the streets, I was still her baby.

As I prepared to lay my mother to rest, happiness evaded me. Actually, it still does. When my mother died, she took any chance of me being genuinely happy with her. No matter what I accomplish in life, I'll never have her here with me to share in it. So, I will never truly experience any type of joy ever again. Without her, I'm incomplete.

If it weren't for my friends, I'm not sure how I would have made it through that week. Dana, Carmen, Zakia and Sophie were either at my house or calling my phone every day. In fact, Dana practically moved in with me and wouldn't leave my side. Surprisingly, Ta-Ta didn't show up. Come to think of it, she didn't even call to offer her condolences. That hurt more than anything else. Maybe she was mad that I didn't ride with her to the Greyhound station like I promised. Surely, she could've overlooked that during a time like this. Sometimes though, it takes a real situation to expose fake people. This was one of those times.

Thankfully, I found some comfort in listening to the remaining members of my Sexy Six clique as they shared memories of my mother. They talked about all the Kwanzaa celebrations she threw every year and reminded me about the time she rented a bus to bring us hood chicks to the Million Woman March. Prior to her death, I couldn't grasp how much she meant to so many people.

Her funeral was on a Friday night. The church was jam packed and standing room only. The line of people waiting outside to get in would have made you think you were at a popular nightclub. Ironically, I always wanted to be a Queensbridge celebrity but I didn't realize my mother already had that title. There were folks there who I hadn't seen in years. My godmother Thongo, along with my mom's childhood best friends, Deena, Poochie, Brenda and Yvonne were all in attendance. She grew up with these women but somehow life got in their way. At the end of the day, it didn't matter. They were all there to pay their last respects; even stopping by to see my grandmother and still calling her Ms. Lena as if they were back in their teens. My mother used to rehash happy memories about her old Queensbridge clique all the time, especially the one about them touring the city as part of an African Dance Troupe. I think she was most proud of that memory because she went so far as to teach me their dance moves along with a Yoruba chant that went something like this, *"Fanga Alafia Ashe, Ashe. Fanga Alafia Ashe, Ashe"*.

She would've been ecstatic to see them all together again. But it was too late now.

I stared at the casket. The body inside of it wasn't my mother's. Well, let me rephrase that. The body was hers but her soul wasn't there. I felt no connection to the corpse that was lying in front of me. She wore a peach two-piece skirt suit. It was the same one she bought to wear to my graduation from boot camp. Obviously, she never got a chance to wear it. Well, at least not in her living years.

My grandmother, with her Caribbean heritage, insisted my mom wear white satin gloves. God forbid she entered the pearly gates without some sparkly white gloves. I protested. My mother would have never wanted to wear gloves, especially not those old-fashioned things. But what I could say? The pain of burying your child trumped my opinion of her wardrobe so Nana's tacky accessory appeared on my mom's tiny hands that were folded across her chest. We left her bangles on. At least that was something we could all agree on. They were with her in life so it was only right for them to continue to travel with her on her journey.

Jamere sat directly behind me during the service and touched the small of my back every time it seemed like I was going to lose it. He was scheduled to go back to Atlanta but he postponed his trip in order to be with me. Piper sat right next to me and held my hand as the preacher, who was one of my mother's dearest friends, delivered a heartfelt sermon. She barely knew my mom but that didn't stop Piper from giving me her unwavering support. True friends show their loyalty when it's most needed not when it's most convenient.

As for me, I was so high that I barely knew what was going on around me. Fuck that little promise I made to God. He didn't stick to his part of the bargain, so I didn't either. Besides, I couldn't have made it through the day without numbing the debilitating pain in my heart.

I was in a daze but I was cognizant enough to notice him when he walked through the doors of the church. Dressed in a charcoal gray Armani suit with a black Hermès belt and a pair of silver-framed reflective Ray-Bans, Salerno caused heads to turn. This was the first time he ever showed his face in

Queensbridge since his days as a narcotics officer. I watched in silence as he walked conspicuously toward the casket. Stopping in front of it, he looked down in silence before making the sign of the cross and moving along. That motherfucker had a lot of nerve showing up here. I hadn't spoken to him since the day he spazzed out on me and I had no intentions on ever seeing him again. For the sake of keeping what little bit of sanity I had intact, I decided I was just going to let it go. There was nothing I could do to bring Malik back or change my story regarding the missing drugs. I had every intention of letting Salerno gradually disappear from my life altogether. And there he was, looking like Michael Corleone, during what had to be the worst period of my life.

As customary in a funeral, he made the rounds to pay his respects to my family. We were all seated in the front row. My father stood up and shook his hand while Salerno passed him an envelope. Surely, it was packed with money. Although other people had done the same thing, I could bet their cards weren't as stacked as his.

As he stopped in front of me, I was relieved that he wore shades. His eyes always hypnotized me so it was a good thing I didn't have to look at them. Preoccupied with mentally preparing myself to address him, I didn't pay attention to the change in Piper once he entered. All the color drained from her face as if she saw a ghost. Had I not been so high, I would have felt the tightening in her hand as it clung to mine. But my mind was on other things so I missed all the signs.

Turning my face to the side, I forced his kiss to land on my cheek. I wasn't sure if he was going for my mouth but he was awfully close.

"Thank you," I said, as I did to everyone else who offered some form of compassion.

Before walking away, he whispered in my ear, "Come home or you'll be lying in a casket right next to her."

Just like the old days, Salerno popped up when I least expected it. It's true what they say, "You can't injure a snake". If you do, that slithering motherfucker will eventually recover. Once he does, he'll come right back and attack you. The only way to completely rid yourself of that venomous piece of shit is to chop its fucking head off. Salerno's time was coming.

Chapter 25

My mother's apartment was filled with love. People came through with flower baskets and foil roaster pans full of food. Sitting on the table was a gold frame with her picture in it. Everyone stopped by to gaze into that beautiful face just one more time. Daddy, who was normally the host with corny jokes and conversations about the Black Power Movement, didn't disappoint. He was his usually loud self but I could tell it was his way of hiding and eventually coping with his pain.

Camille sat on the couch. She finally came home once word started circulating about my mother's passing. What kind of person are you if you have to find out your mother died from a fellow crackhead in the middle of a smoke session? The thought of it disgusted me so I kept my distance from her. I did notice that her eyes were swollen but I couldn't tell if they were like that from crying or if she was, in fact, still high. It didn't matter to me. I wasn't even trying to find out.

Nana hummed church hymns while cleaning up after everybody. As long as she was busy, she was ok. Olivia and my brothers were off to themselves; not really mingling with our visitors. They also had their own way of dealing with our loss. Eventually they would break down, but for now, they put on a brave front.

Piper stayed with me but she wasn't herself since leaving the church. There was way too much happening for me to be concerned with any of that. I figured it was just the whole atmosphere getting to her, that's all. Hell, I wouldn't have been jolly either had it not been for the twenty dollar bag I inhaled right after we left the burial site. I was numb again and feeling no pain.

"Hey, I'm gonna walk to the store," Piper said.

"It's right across the street. You want me to come with you?"

"Umm, no. You stay here with your family. I just need some cigarettes."

"Oh, I got some in my bag," I responded as I reached for my pocketbook.

"Yeah, but I umm, I wanna get some beers too. Maybe a six pack or something. I'll be right back."

Pulling the keys from my Prada knapsack, I tossed them to her. "That intercom be acting funny. Take these with you."

Once she left, I felt alone again. Even though I was surrounded by a room full of people, I could have very well been on a deserted island. I sat at the table and away from our guests. My plate was covered with food that reminded me of a Thanksgiving feast. Turkey, roast beef, fried chicken, potato salad, collard greens, candied yams. Despite not wanting to eat, everything looked delicious. Well, everything except that dry ass macaroni and cheese. I couldn't complain though, the neighbor brought it over. It was her one good deed of the day. My mother always told me that she couldn't cook worth a damn. If she was alive, she would've thrown that whole pan in the incinerator. Not because she was ungrateful but simply because she didn't play when it came to her Mac & Cheese. If that shit wasn't made with at least four different types of cheeses, plus some chunks of Velveeta, she wouldn't even waste her time eating it.

Out of all my mother's recipesand she had many, that was the only one I managed to perfect. I was always running the streets and didn't have time to learn how to cook. But her baked macaroni was my favorite. She'd always convince me to sit in the kitchen and grate the cheese while she prepared it. Salted butter. Evaporated milk. Five eggs. Gulden's Spicy Brown Mustard. Salt. Pepper. Little did I know, she was making sure I watched everything she did. She taught me how to make it without realizing I was in the middle of a cooking lesson.

I cracked a smile. No wonder where I got my hustle from.

"Damn, I miss you already."

As I spoke to her picture on the table, a tear strolled down and landed in my plate.

Flicking the food around with my fork, I shook my head knowing full well I couldn't eat. The cocaine suppressed my appetite and even if it hadn't, I wasn't really in the mood for food. Actually, I hadn't had a full meal since my mother died which was a whole week ago.

"Fuck this shit," I muttered under my breath.

I needed something a lot stronger than the beers Piper was going to buy. If I caught her in time, we could go to the liquor store instead.

"Daddy, I'll be right back. I'm going to the store."

He didn't even hear me over the loud laughter. I wanted everybody to get out but since they were keeping him company and lifting his spirits, I didn't make a big stink about it.

I pressed the button for the elevator and impatiently tapped my foot as I waited for it to arrive. After a couple of minutes, I figured it never would. The shit was probably broken just like everything else in that worthless rat trap anyway. So, I decided to take the stairs.

I lived on the fourth floor, which really wasn't that long of a walk to get out of the building, even with the two separate staircase landings between each floor. It wasn't like there was a back stairwell or anything. The stairs led to the next floor with no side doors separating the steps from the apartments. You couldn't just sneak up and down in a Queensbridge building. Besides the elevator, this one staircase was the only way to get to the floor above or below.

By the time I got to the second floor, I heard a familiar voice which stopped me dead in my tracks. Leaning against the wall, so that I couldn't be seen, I craned my neck in the direction of his voice. I didn't want to miss a word.

"You had one job to do and you failed."

There was silence on the other end. Salerno was talking but who the fuck was listening?

"Do you know how much money you cost me?"

I strained harder, trying to hear the other person. They were either mute or using sign language because he, or she, didn't say shit in response.

"It was all set. All you had to do was go to your station and bring the packages back with you to the states. You were untouchable. Five girls. Five. And only three made it through. Then, I find you here. With her."

Five girls? What the hell was he talking about? Furthermore, who the hell was he talking to? What packages? As I stood there, every question ran through my head all at once.

"At least she's paying me back. She's in debt for the rest of her life. But you? You disappeared. No calls. No letters. No nothing. Do you know how much time you would've gotten if I didn't let you go? Only for you to turn around and cross me? I told you before, don't ever cross me."

I heard a slight whimper and held my breath in suspense. Finally, I would hear the other voice in this conversation.

"I," the phantom person whispered.

Just as the voice was getting loud enough for me to hear, the lady from the first floor walked out of her apartment and saw me. Waving my hand side-to-side, with a cut-throat gesture, I tried my hardest to shut her up but it was too late and she was all too loud. If I heard her big ass mouth, I'm sure Salerno did too which meant he knew I had been listening the whole time.

"Chaka, hey honey. I'm still so sorry about Debra. She was a good woman. I was just coming up there to bring y'all this cake," she said with a burnt ass bundt cake in her hand.

Footsteps led out of the building as the front door slammed.

Fucking neighbors, I thought, *now I'll never know who he was talking to down there.*

Then, a light bulb went off in my head. Perhaps I could peek out the door to catch a glimpse of who was exiting with him. Fearful that he might have still been there, off in the cut, I took a deep breath before turning the corner leading to the last stair landing.

My jaw dropped when I saw her standing in front of me. A look of panic was drawn across her face. Bewildered, I wondered, how the fuck did she know him? What the hell was going on here?

"Piper?"

She looked up at me with a sense of urgency.

"Chaka, we need to talk."

Chapter 26

We couldn't go back to my house because there were far too many people there. Instead, we went to Taylor's where we wouldn't be interrupted. This jigsaw puzzle needed my undivided attention if I was ever going to put it all together. Taylor was downstairs with my father, so I had Piper all to myself. I wanted to know everything.

We sat at the kitchen table and she explained.

"Remember when we were in boot camp and I told you about the cop who pulled me over?"

Dropping my head to my chest, I shook it in disbelief.

"Well, I didn't tell you everything." She exhaled a deep breath while tapping the filter of her unlit cigarette on the table to pack the tobacco before putting it to her mouth and lighting it. "The whole Navy thing was fake."

Confused, I hunched my shoulders up. "What?"

How could it have been fake if she was actually enlisted right along with me?

"Not really bogus but more like a cover-up. Chaka, he knows people all over. Once we got to our stations, he would give us an overseas connect and we'd bring the stuff back for him on the ship. It ain't the airport. We actually worked for the military so we'd never get checked. He was simply cutting out the middleman and getting drugs straight from the suppliers."

"We? What's with all this we shit?"

She looked at me, her eyebrows furrowed. "You didn't know?"

"Didn't know? I don't even know what the fuck you're talking about right now. Connects and packages and overseas. What the fuck is this Frank Lucas shit?"

My hands flailed rapidly as I spoke. Nothing was adding up.

"Come on, you can't be that naïve. What cop is gonna save your ass from a street life and send you to the Navy of all places?"

For once, I was speechless. All along, I thought he was pulling me out of danger and come to find out, all he was doing was changing the scenery.

Piper continued, "I knew there were five of us in boot camp. That much, I did know. But I didn't know you were one of them. Well, until he walked through your mother's funeral. You never told me it was him."

She was right. My tightlipped moves didn't necessarily include making major announcements about my past or my current situations. My whole life had been hidden behind a veil of secrecy and it worked for me. At least I thought it did.

"We have to get away from him Chaka. He's fucking ruthless."

I could see it in her eyes, she was petrified.

Rising from my chair, I walked toward the window. From Taylor's fifth floor apartment I could see the lights of the 59th Street Bridge as they shone down on the project's rooftops. If I ran, I'd be running for the rest of my life. I knew him too well. He would never let us win, let alone, walk away. Unlike everything else in my life that I pushed to the back of my mind, I knew at that moment, I was going to have to face Salerno head-on.

"We can't run, Pipe. We'll be hiding forever. I think I know what to do."

The survivor in me was ready to take on the beast. I did it once before, when I finally stood up to Malik. I was confident in my ability to do it again. Really, there was no other choice. My father just lost his wife and I'd be damned if I was going to let him lose a daughter too. I sat back at the table and looked Piper square in the eye.

"This is what we gotta do..."

Once I was done verbalizing the plan, that had previously seemed so logical in my head, I realized just how much of a risk I was taking if it didn't go through as I envisioned. She must have thought I was out of my rabid ass mind because she was quick to give me her opinion.

"That's the plan? Are you serious? This ain't *New Jack City* and your ass ain't Keisha. Nah, we need to pack our shit and get the fuck out of here," she said matter-of-factly.

"We're getting out of here, all right, but we're doing it on our terms." I yanked the cigarette from her hand as she was just about to put it out and took a long pull. "Trust me."

Chapter 27

"**C**ome back with me," Jamere pleaded.

It had been about a week since my mother's funeral. The visits from neighbors had all but ceased. Daddy's bereavement leave from work was just about over and he was getting ready to return. Camille moved in to help with the kids and according to her, she was clean. She said losing our mother showed her the light. To me, it was a typical line of bullshit said by every crackhead in America. I didn't believe her but I was relieved in knowing somebody would be there with my father. My biggest worry was leaving him alone, especially after my brothers went back to school. But he seemed convinced that my sister would stay on the right track so he gave me his blessings when I announced my plans on moving to Atlanta.

"I will. I'm coming, I promise. I just have to make sure my dad is all right and then I'll be down there."

"Aight, Chaka. I'ma be waiting. Love you."

"Love you too. Always."

I hung up the phone before I said too much. I wanted to tell Jamere everything but I knew he'd try to stop me. If I wanted a life with him, I had to handle some unfinished business first. It's crazy how things happen. A soul-mate ends up with a different personand then another person after that, only to discover everything they're looking for is right in front of them. I wasn't going to lose Jamere again. Not now. Not ever.

The next number I dialed would set off an entire string of events. Deeply I inhaled. I was ready.

"Hello."

"Hi." I paused, trying to make my voice sound pathetically

frail. "I miss you."

Salerno had been calling the house back to back on a daily basis. I avoided his calls. In order for this to work, I had to take a few days away from him to clear my head.

"Where have you been?"

He was softening up a little.

"I've just been thinking. Trying to understand everything."

"Why haven't you answered my calls? I could have explained it all."

"I'm sorry. It's just been a lot for me to deal with, that's all."

"Where's your friend?"

He was referring to Piper. She skipped town and headed back to DC while all this shit blew over.

"She's gone. She lied to me. I have nothing left to say to her."

I had to fake our friendship status. If he thought I was alone throughout this ordeal, he would undoubtedly think I was vulnerable enough to need him.

"I want to see you."

"Yes, me too. Can I come now?"

My tone was soft and sought approval. If anything a control freak likes, it's the feeling of power. I'd stroke his ego just enough to gain his trust, one more time.

"Of course you can. Come on."

The dial tone hummed in my ear as I kept the phone there for a few seconds. Of all the roles I've played in my life, this would be the most important one. It could also be the most dangerous if I didn't play it to perfection.

I hopped in the shower to freshen up for my big scene. Once I got out, the steam from the hot water made the whole bathroom feel like a sauna. Wiping the condensation from the mirror with my forearm, I looked at my reflection long and hard. My eyes were empty. They had lost their sparkle long before Salerno entered the picture. The prettiness that people saw when they looked at me actually covered up an ugly soul. It was something only I could see when I looked in the mirror. For years, I blamed everybody else. "Woe is me", had become my mantra. It was time for me to grow up and stop playing the victim. My life was a reflection of the decisions I made. In short, I was a train wreck just waiting to happen. The only one who could avoid the inevitable crash was the woman looking back at me. This time, I was going to get it right.

Quickly, I got dressed in a denim mini-skirt that stopped a little bit above my mid thigh, a black lace Dolce & Gabbana camisole and a pair of black patent leather Manolo Blahnik pumps. The art of seduction began externally so I had to make sure Salerno liked what he saw. I didn't bother wearing panties. He'd practically nut on himself once he reached under my skirt and realized there was nothing blocking his entry into my body. I doused my neck and the backs of my knees in Chanel No. 5 – his favorite perfume. Once I combed my hair down, added some eyeliner to my upper lids, rolled the mascara brush along my lashes and puckered up with some lip gloss, I was ready.

My father was sitting on the couch in my mother's usual spot. That was the first time anyone sat there since she died. I walked over to him and pecked his cheek.

"Bye, Daddy."

Once he got a good look at what I was wearing, he responded as any father would. "You gonna put some clothes on first?"

"Daddy, this outfit almost cost me a thousand dollars. Believe me, I got on enough clothes."

"See you later Chaka," Camille said.

Raising my upper lip, I snarled, "Yeah, bye."

She'd have to do a lot more than cook an occasional dinner for my father and her own damn kids if she wanted to regain my respect.

The ride to Salerno's apartment normally took fifteen minutes. On this day, it felt more like fifteen hours before I pulled up and walked through the lobby. I stopped and greeted the man behind the front desk.

"Good evening. Would you happen to have the time?"

Without a word in response, he pointed to the large clock behind him. It was in plain sight.

"Oh, I didn't even realize that was there." I giggled. "Thanks. Good night."

Of course I saw that big ass clock. Hell, Ray Charles could have seen that shit. But I had to make sure my presence was acknowledged just in case I didn't make it out of there. Somebody had to know where I was.

Salerno was waiting at the door as soon as I got off the elevator. He must've told the front desk to alert him whenever I arrived. That was a good thing. At least I knew he wasn't going to try anything.

Before fully entering the apartment, his hand was around my neck and my back was pinned against the wall. Forcefully, he shoved his tongue in my mouth as his loose hand reached under my skirt. I lifted my right knee, causing my tiny skirt to rise above my waist.

There were no words to be said. The power of the pussy is a strong weapon and I knew how to armor up when it was time for war.

"Take me," I whispered, while grabbing his bulging dick. "I'm yours."

He growled like a wild animal as he pulled my camisole over my head. I raised my arms, which he then pressed against the wall. My bare breasts stood erect, even more so, once he gnawed at my nipple.

"Chaka," he screamed in ecstasy.

"I'm Nina," I panted. "Call me Nina."

He stopped for a moment and looked up at me. His head cocked to the side as his eyes pierced through mine. With a sinister snarl, he continued. Harshly, he bit down on my nipples. My pussy creamed once he jammed his hardened dick inside.

"I told you I would take care of you, Nina. Didn't I?"

Every time he said her name, he fucked me harder, penetrating deeper and deeper. I came all over his dick one time after another until my own hot liquids trickled down my thigh. I could feel the head of his penis throb as it began to swell and rub against my inner walls. Tightening my pussy muscles for a firm grip around his dick, I squeezed as hard as I could. That always did the trick and this time was no different.

"Arrgggh," he yelled as he pulled my shoulders down so hard, I could feel his balls pound against my ass. Every inch of him was inside of me.

We stayed locked in that position for a couple of minutes before he finally took me by the hand and led me to the bedroom where we continued our romp but with less animalistic rage.

I obliged, simply because I needed him in his most opened and trusting frame of mind. My plan would only work if he found no reason to doubt my love. And since sex was the only way I knew how to prove it, I gave him just what his blackened heart desired.

Once we were done and our bodies had experienced every last bit of pleasure we could handle, I reached into the nightstand and pulled out an already rolled joint. This was our normal routine.

We'd fuck like cannibals and then mellow out on some ganja. I didn't want to switch up the regularly scheduled program.

I laid my upper body across his chest.

"I have a score," I said, in between totes before passing him the joint.

This was the perfect time to lay it on him. At that very moment, he was at his weakest and totally unguarded; just the way I needed him.

"You do? So, you trust me again?"

Leaning over, I sucked the smoke from his mouth as he blew it out. After exhaling it into the dimly lit bedroom, I responded, "I never stopped."

"When's the drop?"

"Tomorrow at eight. Right across the Pulaski Bridge, at the BP gas station on McGuinness Boulevard."

"That's my girl."

He tenderly stroked my hair, obviously happy that I could still deliver.

"We'll be in a black Mercedes S500. He's always carrying. It's usually in the right side of his waistband."

Secretly, I was hoping he'd get his head blown off but I was stretching the truth. The mark never even carried a gun. However, I had to make Salerno believe that I was giving him a full report as I had done for the many set-ups in the past.

"Well, get some rest. You can leave from here in the morning."

Sleep was the furthest thing from my mind. His day was coming and the next few hours were crucial. Every possible scenario played out in my head like I was watching some straight-to-DVD snuff film. The only difference was that I couldn't afford to have any bloopers or deleted scenes. Nobody would be there with a megaphone, calling cut or giving me another take. I only had one opportunity to get this right or it would literally be the very last scene in this Shakespearean tragedy that had become my life.

In addition to my erratic thoughts, Salerno's snores kept me awake. If my plan worked, that would be his last peaceful sleep. Too bad his pussy whipped ass was too blind to see it.

"Paybacks a bitch, motherfucker."

I mouthed the words silently before turning over and finally shutting my eyes.

Rock-a-bye, Baby.

Chapter 28

6:30 AM
Gently, I got out of bed without waking Salerno and tippy-toed to the walk-in closet. I slid on a crisp white Carolina Herrera blouse, black jeans and the same four-inch pumps I wore the day before. My hair was in a sleek ponytail that hung down my back and stopped right below my bra strap. The only piece of jewelry blinging was my studs. Black framed Chanel reading glasses brought it all together. It was very important that I looked professional which was the reason for scheduling the drops so early in the morning. With so many working people on the streets during rush hour, nothing stood out as odd or peculiar. My mark would also be dressed in something other than a backwards fitted, iced out Jesus piece and pants falling off his ass. That dumb shit was an immediate heads-up to the police that somebody was up to no good.

"Ok, I'm gone." I blew Salerno a kiss and walked toward the door.

"See you there," he said. "Be careful."

I wanted to tell him to take his own advice but I kept my smart ass mouth shut and just smiled before exiting.

As soon as I got outside, I hailed a taxi. I was supposed to get picked up at seven and I needed to be standing outside when he arrived. This mark, who called himself Black, had been on my heels for quite some time. He was just the drop off dude and at the bottom of his crew's totem pole. But once I decided to put my plan in motion, I reached out to him. He thought he was getting lucky, when in fact, his stupid ass was auditioning for a role. His part was minor, more like an extra or even a credited walk-on, but still I needed him.

After gassing him up with late night phone chats and a couple of hand jobs, I convinced him to take me along for one of his drops. We then planned to go to Atlantic City afterwards where I'd show him just how much I was feeling him. This motherfucker was so anxious to get in my pants, he would've believed anything. In reality, I hated Atlantic City. That place was for broke ass ballers with absolutely no class. If he really wanted to impress me, he should have flown me out to Vegas. All of this didn't really matter, though. I wouldn't be leaving to go anywhere with him. He was just the pawn I needed to take down the opposing king. Yeah, everybody has a role to play.

I got out of the cab in front of a random post-war hi-rise on 86th Street and Broadway, on the Upper East Side of Manhattan. I never let my marks know where I really lived. In their minds, they were behaving like perfect gentlemen by picking me up from the front door of my deluxe apartment in the sky.

From the payphone on the corner, I dialed the number knowing she'd be waiting for my call. After she picked up on the first ring, I got straight to the business at hand.

"We're good. Make the call," I said. "It has to be at exactly 8:15, Piper. Not a minute later."

"Got it," she replied.

"You remember the car's description, right? It's a black Ford Taurus."

"Chaka, I know what to do. I got it."

"I know you do. I'll see you on the other side, Pipe."

"You sure will. Wolf Pack forever."

"Forever."

I tightly gripped the phone for a second before hanging it up. The ball was in Piper's court now and I was confident she wouldn't drop it. The plan was so simple, there was no way she could have fucked it up even if she tried. I just hoped Salerno stuck to his normal routine from which he seldom varied. Watching him long enough helped me predict his next move. I've always been observant. While most people talk, I sit back and watch.

The black Mercedes S500 pulled up. *Game time.*

"Hey you!" My voice was high-pitched, allowing the Valley Girl inside of me to come out and play her part.

"Wassup London? You ready?"

He undressed me with his big old fish eyes that popped out of his head. The name, Black, suited him because he was so dark he could probably leave fingerprints on charcoal. His lower lip was bright pink and just sat there without touching the upper lip. Ever.

Giggling like a nymph, I responded, "Ready, willing and able! Atlantic City here we come."

We made small talk as we traveled to Brooklyn. I babbled on about how hard my classes were and how much I was looking forward to long walks on the Jersey Boardwalk. I teased him with detailed descriptions of the many ways we would enjoy our romantic weekend together. For good measure, I reached over and played with his dick while he drove. The expectation of good pussy could make a man lose all common sense.

As we crossed the Pulaski Bridge, my heart started pumping even more. I looked down at my blouse to make sure it wasn't protruding out of my chest. Talking was the only thing that kept me focused so I chit-chatted away.

"Once we see this guy, we outta here. Then, you could do all that shit you was saying."

His breath smelled like there was a little man taking a shit inside his mouth. I had to grin and bear it.

Only a little while longer.

On schedule, we pulled into the BP station on McGuinness Boulevard. As we did, the lights from Salerno's car started flashing. He pulled directly behind us. From the rearview mirror, I could see him talking into the fake police scanner as if he was calling in the license plates.

"Fuck!"

Black cursed while banging his hand against the steering wheel. Turning on the waterworks was easy for me so I cried on cue, "Oh my God. Are we getting pulled over?"

Fidgeting in my seat, I acted nervous so he'd have to try to calm me down. If anything, he would remember how scared I was throughout this entire ordeal. My left foot tapped rapidly on the floor of the car.

"Don't do that shit, yo. Just relax, we good. The plates are legit. He don't have no reason to search us."

He put his hand on my kneecap to stop my leg from shaking. Breathing harder, I wasn't holding anything back. He had to feel the fear pumping from my heart.

Salerno approached the car while pulling his badge from under his shirt. It hung on a silver chain around his neck and was now prominently displayed. Black rolled down the window.

"Yes, Officer?"

"Yeah, let me see your license and registration."

Salerno bent over, peeked into the car and looked directly at me. "And let me see your ID too," he demanded.

"For what? Why you pulling us over?"

Black had every right to ask. It wasn't as if he really violated any traffic regulations.

"You didn't use your blinker, buddy."

That had to be the oldest trick in the book. How could Black deny it? Shit, I didn't even remember if he signaled before turning into the gas station or not.

With no other recourse, he did as he was instructed and passed his ID, along with the registration from the glove box, over to Salerno. I took my counterfeit non-driver's license out of my bag and handed it to him as well.

Once he had our stuff, Salerno walked back to his fake radio and pretended to be reading the information to some imaginary dispatcher somewhere. Beads of sweat popped from Black's forehead. He was just as nervous as I was pretending to be. We sat in silence until Salerno returned.

"You know your license is suspended?"

Defiantly, Black answered, "What? No it ain't."

His reaction was reasonable, especially for a person who really had a valid license but just so happened to have five bricks in the trunk.

"I need you to step out of the car, now."

"But officer, my license ain't..."

Abruptly interrupting, Salerno flung the driver's side door open and yelled, "What the fuck did I say? Get out of the car now."

"Yo, this is some bullshit, man. My license is good, yo."

Although he was still running off at the mouth, Black followed directions and stepped onto the gas station's parking lot. The employees were looking through the window but didn't set foot outside to get involved.

We stood in front of the car's hood while Salerno leaned into the front seat and hit the trunk button. Black shook his head.

"Yo, I'ma need you to call my man and tell him what

happened. I'ma make sure he let you go but I know he about to take me in. Remember this number."

Black recited a telephone number to me which I repeated back to him. As soon as the digits rolled off my tongue, they were already forgotten.

Because the trunk was open, it blocked our view through the front windshield. We were unable to get an unobstructed shot of anything behind the opened hatch. Salerno's car was parked so close to the back of Black's that we couldn't see him jump into his driver's seat. Until we heard the screech of the tires, as they peeled out of the gas station, we thought he was still back there. Well, Black must've thought so. I already knew the jook.

"Yo, what the fuck?" Black rushed to his trunk only to find it completely empty except for our travel bags. "MOTHERFUCKER."

I ran to his side and frantically waved my hands.

"What's going on? Oh my God, what's happening?"

Pacing back and forth, Black placed his hands on top of his head and cursed loudly.

"These motherfuckers set me the fuck up."

That was always the reaction. I scheduled it perfectly. Making sure we arrived exactly ten minutes before the scheduled drop-off time was an important detail that couldn't be overlooked. Salerno would appear with his lights blaring and make an obvious scene. By the time the connect showed up, ten minutes after we got pulled over, there was police activity going on. Surely, nobody's going to stop in the middle of that ruckus. Especially not a drug dealer. Transaction aborted. But the mark wouldn't know that. He'd automatically assume the connect didn't show up and sent a decoy to rob him instead. Nobody suspected the pretty little proper speaking good girl to be in on it. That just wasn't her style. And if they ever did, they had no idea who the fuck I was. My name was an alias. My address was falsified. For all intents and purposes, I never existed. London was a mere figment of their imagination.

"I can't get involved with this Black. My parents would kill me."

Like a brat, I whined. It was pretty much in the bag already but I actually enjoyed playing along.

"Yo, fuck your parents, yo. Do you know how much money I fucking lost right now? Yo, I gotta get the fuck outta here. You need to catch a cab or something. I gotta get this shit straight."

"You're just kicking me to the curb?"

I cried even more. Halle Berry had nothing on me. Where the fuck was my Oscar?

"Nah, but I gotta handle this." He pulled a hundred dollar bill from his pocket. "Here, get a cab yo."

Without looking back, he hopped in his car and drove off.

Act I played out as it should have and Salerno drove off in the direction I anticipated. I ran to the corner and took the first cab that drove up.

"I need to get to Queens, right over the Pulaski Bridge. Hurry up," I shouted while the cabbie busted a U-turn and headed in that direction.

The time was exactly 8:15 AM. If my calculations were correct, Act II had just started. I'd be making my way across the bridge right before the final curtain fell.

End Scene. Exit Stage Left.

Chapter 29

I could see the flashing lights before I got all the way across the bridge, which meant Piper pulled it off. However, I wouldn't be satisfied until I saw it with my own two eyes. To tell the truth, I wasn't one hundred percent confident it would work. But I knew it was our only hope. I played the cards I was dealt but I held on to the Joker and used it as my last resort. I replayed that conversation with Piper over and over again in my head.

"He'll be coming over the Pulaski Bridge, heading to the 59th Street Bridge, right around 8:15, Piper. Exactly 8:15."

"How do you know this for sure?" She asked with a tone full of skepticism and what-ifs.

"It's the quickest route from Brooklyn. He'll need to get out of there as fast as possible. There's no telling who could be on the lookout. He won't linger around."

She nodded her head, finally seeing this play out the way I described.

"This is the number to the Narcotics Task Force. Call it from a pay phone. Ask for Detective O'Harry."

Back when I first met Salerno, as I recovered from a botched attack by Malik's Far Rockaway crew, I had the displeasure of meeting Detective O'Harry. He and Salerno were partners at the time and O'Harry was the stereotypical Irish cop with a cocky attitude and a genuine disgust for criminals. Although he was a dickhead to me, he bled NYPD blue to the fullest so I could trust that he'd go all Commando style. He had a penchant for catching the bad guy. I remembered that much about him because he aggressively interrogated me while I still heard the ringing in my ears from being pistol whipped. Compassion was non-existent when it came to him exacting justice and that's just what I needed.

I continued, "Give him a full description of the car, including the license plates."

Looking around Taylor's apartment, I found an envelope and used it to write down all the pertinent information.

"Tell him the car will be coming across the bridge at 8:15 and will be transporting a large amount of raw, uncut cocaine. Say this bust will make him famous. Then, hang up."

"What if he doesn't believe me?"

"He will, Piper. He thinks he's Dirty Harry. He's been waiting for a score like this. Trust that."

Even as I rehashed that moment, I still couldn't believe it actually worked. As I got closer to the flashing lights, it all became a reality.

"Slow down," I shouted to the cabbie.

I had to witness this for myself. Salerno was being handcuffed while an officer pulled the duffle bags full of drugs from his trunk. I could've ridden away, unnoticed, but I wanted him to see me clear as day. As we inched by, I rolled the cab's dark tinted window down just enough so that my eyes peered out. At that very moment, Salerno looked in my direction. Once he spotted me, his steps came to a halt. Even in restraints, his malevolent gaze was still hypnotizing. A chill shivered up my spine as he cracked a sinister grin that would later give me nightmares. In my heart I knew, right then and there, my days of being lured into his twisted world were far from over.

Rolling the window up as I leaned back in my seat, I directed the driver to my final destination.

"40-05 12th Street. Queensbridge."

Checkmate motherfucker.

Chapter 30

9 Months Later

"So, I applied for Housing and guess what? I got approved." Camille sounded like a kid on Christmas morning.

"That's good. Hopefully they'll keep you close to Daddy," I replied.

After leaving New York, I was still skeptical about my sister's sobriety. However, she surprised the hell out of me and actually stayed clean. She even got a job as a front desk clerk at a hotel near LaGuardia Airport. Leaving my dad didn't feel so bad since I knew she had his back.

"Well, I'm about to get the kids from nursery," she said proudly, finally being a mom after all this time. "I'll call you later. Make sure you kiss my niece for me."

"Haha." I laughed. "I will."

Once she hung up, I got back to writing my list of baby shower invites. Hardly anybody from New York was coming, with the exception of my immediate family. Dana and Carmen would probably come too. Despite our catty ways, we still celebrated each other's milestones. At the end of the day, we looked beyond the petty shit when it came to stuff that really mattered. That's just what friends do.

Ta-Ta was supposed to come as well. She and I had reacquainted after I visited her in Charlotte a few times. As a cashier at a local gas station, she was struggling to make ends meet. However, she kept grinding and had no intentions of going back to Queensbridge. I helped her out financially, whenever I could. What type of friend would I have been if I just sat back and watched her go without? Regardless of what we went through, she was still my Thelma. Without going into details about why she didn't come, she was apologetic for missing my mother's funeral. It was all water under the bridge to me. My life had done a full one-eighty and I was tickled pink about the bun in my oven. In fact, I even asked her to be my baby's godmother. Holding grudges was a thing of the past.

With all this planning before the birth, I was getting nervous about life after my baby arrived. Luckily, her other godmother lived about fifteen minutes away from me. I needed all the help I could get. Lord knows, my big ass could barely move. With the size of my bump, you would have thought I was carrying twins.

When Piper decided to move to Atlanta, I was beyond excited. Starting over, in a brand new city, was difficult enough but she and I had done it before so I knew we wouldn't have any issues fitting in with these slow ass country bumpkins. Besides, Jamere was happy I had someone down here other than him. It freed him up to run his business. That was, of course, after he made sure I was finally self-sufficient and could get around on my own.

Atlanta's public transportation system only consisted of two train lines, one going north to south and the other, east to west. The trains were nothing like what I was used to in New York so I had to learn how to drive if I wanted to get around on my own. Their cab system was a joke so hopping in and out of taxis, wasn't even an option.

It didn't take long for me to learn how to handle myself behind the wheel. Jamere was patient and gave me lessons every day leading up to my driver's test. He didn't even flip out when I reversed so hard that we ended up in a ditch. Instead, he laughed and told me I needed to take my time. I wonder how he would have reacted if he knew I got too close to a parked car one day and swiped their mirror completely off. I didn't tell anybody about that little mishap. Once I realized nobody was in the parking lot with me, I just kept it moving. *Beep, beep, motherfucker*.

After finally getting my license, on the first try by the way, he took me to the car dealer and let me pick out what I wanted. The BMW X5 was by far the hottest whip on the streets and Jamere didn't worry about the price tag.

We bought a townhome in Alpharetta which was a quiet

suburb just north of Atlanta's city limits. Our subdivision was full of children playing on manicured lawns and families grilling in their backyards. It was the perfect place to raise our little girl. I looked forward to giving her the life I never had, full of ballet recitals and Girl Scout cookies.

After settling in, Jamere convinced me to go back to school. College was something I dreamed about when I was a kid but once I got grown, that shit was just a thought lingering in the back of my mind. Then, one day, he came home with an application for Atlanta Metropolitan State College. It wasn't one of the Ivy League schools I pictured myself attending but it was a step in the right direction. As long as I was being productive, Jamere promised to supply my every need. He didn't slack in the least bit.

His business was booming and from the outside looking in, everything was legit. He owned a little storefront near the city's HBCU campuses. Clark Atlanta, Morehouse and Spelman were so close together, I originally thought they were all one school. Students packed his store in droves, buying up any piece of New York they could find. His spot was appropriately named "A Taste of NYC" and sold everything from bootleg DVDs to the latest Funkmaster Flex mixtapes. In fact, it was so popping that he bought the spot next door and made it into a little café grill, where he hired a cook to make burgers, breakfast sandwiches, heros, beef patties with coco bread and all the other greasy spoon type of food typically found in a corner bodega. Jamere literally brought a taste of New York City to the streets of Atlanta.

I turned a blind eye to what he did on the side. We were working hard to escape that life but until we could, there were still bills to be paid and money to be made. He adamantly forbade me to get involved, in any shape or form, with his street hustle. That was fine by me. After so many years of illegal living, I wanted nothing to do with that lifestyle. Instead, I focused my attention on our store. From scheduling street teams to designing promotional flyers, I had found my niche. If it had anything to do with marketing, I excelled at it. In the past, I thought my strength came from the gold mine between my legs. However, Jamere taught me to use the power of my brain instead. Surprisingly, it would get me a lot further in life than any other hustle I knew.

Sometimes, I rolled up my sleeves and worked the counter

in between my own classes or on the weekends. It was hard for me though, because the smell of food made me want to vomit. I was about six months pregnant but I still had bouts of morning sickness that, unfortunately for me, lasted through afternoon and night. On the upside, the baby was making my hair grow like crazy. My curls hung down my back and almost touched my waist. Normally, I wouldn't even need a bra with my bite-sized 34A's but my boobs were so swollen that I was fitting into a full C-cup. Shit, I prayed they would stay that size after the baby was born. As a matter of fact, I was blooming all over the place. My White girl ass was finally getting some plumped 'sistah' curves. Even my face filled out, making me look like a squirrel harboring acorns in my cheeks. I didn't complain, though. I loved being pregnant and Jamere made sure I enjoyed every minute of it.

He tagged along to every last one of my OB-GYN visits. We were having a girl and he was just as excited as I was to be a first time parent. After the doctors told me I might never get pregnant, I cried tears of joy when I missed my first period. It wasn't until after I took three at-home pregnancy tests plus a urine and blood test with my doctor, that I believed it. I was going to be a Mommy. It was bittersweet because I longed to share this moment with my own mother. However, I started praying more and when I did, it felt like I was talking directly to her.

"Did you take your medicine?" Jamere would ask the same question every morning before I even had a chance to reach for my prenatal vitamins. No matter how fat I felt, with my bulging belly, he made sure to compliment my pregnant glow every chance he got. I felt like a princess with him. All the years of loving each other from a distance gave us just the right amount of time we needed to genuinely fall in love.

I had just gotten home after Piper dragged me all over the city looking for baby furniture. She wanted to make sure her goddaughter had the best of everything. Propping a pillow on the bed, I kicked my swollen feet up and decided to take a nap before Jamere got home. Being pregnant made me have the wildest dreams. This night was no different.

CHIGGY

"You make me sick. I can't stand you, stupid," I yelled at my brother as he grabbed the cheese from my hand. "Watch when Mommy get back out here, you gonna be in trouble."

My brothers made it a habit to make my life a living hell, especially when Mommy and Daddy were in the bathroom doing *'grown folk stuff'*. Well, that's what they called it anyway.

I looked in the refrigerator and prayed that some kind of food would have magically appeared since the last time I checked. Despite the fact that my mother had just gotten her food stamps three hours before, it didn't seem like we were going food shopping anytime soon. So, just as I expected, besides the half-empty bottle of ketchup, there wasn't anything in there to eat except that government issued welfare food.

Of course if I was starving like an Ethiopian, I could have had some powdered milk that was so thick and full of lumps, I practically had to chew it to get it down my throat. Surely, I could have broken off a piece of the gigantic blocks of butter that were accumulating as part of the bench-dweller's trade, *"I'll give you a block of butter for a bottle of your honey."*

I never liked any of the surplus scraps they gave us. First of all, it was embarrassing as fuck to have to stand on that welfare line waiting for the church to open to pick up your family's USDA food ration. What was even worse was when you had a conniving ass mother who made you stand in line for every member of your family who had a Welfare Benefits card. I'd be in line and my brother would be standing about ten people behind me, followed by my sister who was like four or five people behind him. Luckily our last name was Adams and since it started with the letter "A" and rations were distributed by your last name, we were in and out of there with the quickness.

Shit, I would have hated to be a Williams.

As soon as we got the food to our apartment, I went straight to the only thing I did like – my weakness was the cheese. The highlight of the semi-annual food distribution was undoubtedly the cheese. They gave us a big block, like the ones they have at the deli. The only thing wrong with that bright idea was the shit wasn't sliced. Since nobody had a fancy deli-style slicer in the hood, we just had to get ill with a knife and cut it straight enough so that it looked better than some plastic-wrapped Velveeta. In reality it looked more like a jagged glob of hardened yellow clay but when you're dirt poor, you learn to use your imagination to see shit the way you wished it to be instead of the way it really was.

It came wrapped in plastic inside of a brown cardboard box with the letters USDA boldly stamped all over it – as if they weren't going to let you hide the fact that you were getting government assistance. My mother had them fooled though. She would take it out of the box, that lacked a listing of ingredients or an expiration dateand put it in a Tupperware bowl instead.

So when my brother grabbed the last piece as I was stabbing my dull butter knife through the block, I could have killed him. He knew I wouldn't eat that other shit.

"Ma, he took my cheese."

I banged on the bathroom door. My parents had been in there for well over an hour.

"All right baby, I'm coming. Me and your father is just talking," she yelled through the wooden door.

I stood there tapping my foot hoping she'd get the hint and come out. She didn't. Instead, she yelled even louder.

"Chaka, get the fuck away from that god damn door right now before I come out there. I said I'm coming out in a minute. Now, go sit yo' ass in that motherfucking living room before we don't go food shopping or no god damn where."

Stubbornly, I stood there, folded my arms and started humming loud enough for her to realize I wasn't going anywhere. If she wanted me to move, she was going to have to finally come out of the bathroom and make me.

"We coming Chiggy Wiggy," my father coaxed, still through the door.

Whenever they were doing 'grown folk stuff', he was always the sweeter of the two.

"All right Daddy but hurry up because they keep bothering me," I whined to my father who was a sucker for his little girl.

"What did I say?" My mother hissed. "Now go on, I'm doing grown folks stuff right now. And I said I'm coming."

"Urrggghhh."

Walking away while stomping my feet in a hissy fit, I sucked my teeth so hard they could've rolled down my throat. I stormed over to the wooden RCA Hi-Fi stereo, that was already tuned to WBLSand blasted Chaka Khan's "What Cha' Gonna Do For Me" from the speakers. The volume was turned up as loud as it would go. If nothing else was going to make my mother come out of the bathroom, I knew that would. I was ready to get a beating if it meant we could finally go get something to eat.

"You always tryna get somebody in trouble, here."

My brother, Khalid, finally passed me the cheese. As always, a little temper tantrum never hurt anybody. I chomped down on my mid-afternoon snack while my little brother Kareem kept banging his walker into the wall. He'd bounce off, start laughing and then bang into it again. In my opinion, that shit looked retarded. I mean, why keep banging into the same wall over and over again? Where's the fun in that?

BAM

I immediately turned toward Khalid, thinking he broke something in the living room which was going to get us all an ass whooping for sure. But my mother's thunderous shrieks from the back of the apartment forced my attention elsewhere. Whatever made that loud sound was a lot worse than anything my brother could've done.

I hopped off the Hi-Fi and ran to the bathroom. Before I could get around the corner and beyond the hallway closet, I saw my father sprawled out on the floor. Remembering my brothers were right behind me, I tried my hardest to push Kareem away before he could see it too. But it was too late. We were all there looking at Daddy with a syringe still stuck in his arm and white foam spouting from his mouth. My mom, in a hysterical fit, couldn't stop yelling.

"FREDDY, GET UP," she screamed. "FREDDY."

Daddy didn't budge and neither did my mother except to smack his face continually as she called out his name. Khalid immediately ran into the room and cowered in the corner while Kareem screamed at the top of his lungs, trying to pull his walker through the narrow hallway leading to the bathroom. As for me, I just stood there shocked and too afraid to move.

"CHAKA, CHAKA, GO GET SOME ICE," my mother ordered.

I heard her but my feet stayed planted.

"GOD DAMNIT CHAKA, GO GET SOME GOD DAMN ICE FOR YOUR FATHER. GO, HURRY UP."

The second time she said it, I went into action. I practically had to jump over Kareem's walker, toppling him in the process and dash to the refrigerator. I opened the freezer and grabbed two ice trays and a bag of frozen peas. I would have grabbed more but that was the only thing in there. By the time I got back to my father, my mother had already stripped him to his underwear. So, not only did I have to watch him having an overdose with a needle still stuck in his arm but I also had to see him half naked.

While my mom kept calling out his name, my little brother furiously wailed and my older brother stayed hidden in our room. I just stood there holding two ice trays and a bag of no-frills peas from Pathmark.

"COME PUT THE ICE ON HIS CHEST, CHAKA."

My body moved on its own as I jumped to Daddy's side and started rubbing the ice on his chest. Every time my mother yelled, I tried to yell much louder.

"DADDY, GET UP. DADDY, DADDDDDDY."

"CHAKA, PUT THEM PEAS IN HIS UNDERWEAR."

What? Did she really want me putting my hands down Daddy's drawers?

My hesitation lasted too long because she grabbed the peas and smacked me across the face with them.

"PUT IT DOWN HIS DAMN DRAWS RIGHT NOW CHAKA. I AIN'T PLAYING WITH YOU," she warned, before turning back to rub ice on my father's neck and face. "FREDDY COME ON MAN, DON'T LEAVE ME."

I closed my eyes, pulled the elastic from the waistband of Daddy's underwear and shoved the peas down. Quickly, I pulled my hand back and continued yelling his name as I spread the now melting ice all over his legs.

In my five-year-old mind, the whole ordeal went on for hours. In reality, it took about three minutes for my father to start snapping out of it.

"DADDY," I squealed, once he started coughing and opening his eyes.

My mother sat him up against the closet door and repeatedly slapped his cheeks to get him to focus. When he did, I heard him whisper to her, "Deb, we gotta go get some more of that shit right there."

My body jerked as I fought to wake up from that nightmare. I hated the flashbacks that crept into my thoughts more and more frequently. Panting wildly, I looked around to make sure it was just a dream. I only calmed down once I glanced over at Jamere, who was peacefully sleeping next to me. I rubbed my belly and said a silent prayer to never let my child go through that type of shit. No matter what I had to do, she was never going to endure one moment of the fear that haunted my memories.

"What's the matter baby?" Jamere slowly sat up and wrapped his arms around me from behind.

"Nothing, I just can't sleep. I can't get comfortable with this big old stomach."

"Hey, watch ya' mouth. You talking about my baby's big old head in that stomach," he said as he kissed my pregnant bump.

Jamere always had a way of making me smile. I would have never thought we'd be having a baby girl and getting married in a few months. Shit has a way of being right in front of you but so far from your sight.

"Come on babe, lay back down. I'll tell you a bedtime story little girl."

"Whatever. Fuck you and your story." I teased. "Just rub my back."

I settled back down while Jamere's hands massaged me to sleep. Had it not been for the slight crack of the staircase leading to our room, I would have stayed in la-la land. But before I could react to the sound, the bedroom door had already flung open.

"You bitch ass motherfucker, get the fuck on the floor," said the voice coming from the person standing before me who was dressed in all black.

It felt like I was watching a movie as Jamere's body was hauled off the bed in slow motion.

"JAMERE," I yelled, before the hand grabbed my jaw and pointed the barrel in my mouth. I felt my front tooth chip as it collided with the gun.

"Oh, you thought I wasn't gonna catch up to you, huh, bitch?"

My eyes sprung open at the sight of the ghost from my past.

How the fuck did he find out where I was? I had been so careful. Nobody knew where I lived. Well, except for my friends, but they'd never tell him. Would they?

From the corner of my eye, I saw Jamere jump up and try to ambush the dude who held me captive on the bed. But what he couldn't see was the other guy coming from behind the dark shadows of the bedroom door. His gun was already drawn and aimed right at the back of Jamere's head. I wanted to warn him but the gat was so far down my throat, I could barely fucking breathe. As I watched the dude with his outstretched arm, slither closer to Jamere, I looked back up at my gunman in disbelief. The pieces of the puzzle were starting to come together.

Damn, I had a feeling he would come back sooner or later. I just didn't think he was coming back so strong.

POW.

I watched as the first bullet flew past my head and lodged into the wall behind me. By the grace of God, Jamere turned around in time or it would have caught him in the back of his dome. As he tussled to get the gun from the dude behind him, the one on top of me leapt toward his partner. With one wrong move, he gave me just enough time to stand to my feet, grab the heavy cast iron lamp from the nightstand and swing it with every ounce of strength I could gather up. It was a one shot deal and the only way I could make sure he didn't attack Jamere, or worse, turn back around and get me.

SPLAT.

It connected and blood splattered from the back of his skull. Grabbing his head, in the exact spot that was gushing blood, he finally crumbled to the floor. Then, that's when I heard it.

POW.

Another shot fired from the gun that Jamere was trying to pry from his attacker's hands. Only this time, I wasn't so lucky. I felt the heat sting through my body. My first reaction was to protect my baby. Wrapping my arms around my belly, it was only a matter of seconds before I got lightheaded and hit the floor with a bang.

How the fuck could this be happening? I saw him get taken down with my own two eyes. Or did I?

After that, I don't remember much of anything else.

Open. Close. Open. Close.

My eyes fluttered, unable to focus on anything in the room. Surrounded by doctors, I scanned every corner to find a familiar face. Blurred vision made it difficult for me to see anything clearly.

Jamere. I tried to call out to him but I couldn't make a sound with the tube stuck down my throat.

From the waist down, I felt nothing. It was as if my body didn't have a bottom half. There were bandages covering my entire left shoulder which looked liked it had swelled about three sizes bigger, thus, giving a new definition to literally having a chip on my shoulder.

I surveyed the room again. Jamere was nowhere to be found. Reaching down to my stomach, I panicked when I couldn't feel my own hands rubbing across my belly. There was a green sheet draped over me with a voice coming from the other side of it.

"Nurse, how far along did they say she was?"

"Six months," said the lady wearing green scrubs who stood on the right side of me.

Her voice was muffled from behind a cloth mask covering her mouth.

"That's not right," the man sitting between my legs, on the other side of the sheet replied. "This baby is full term."

Baby. Still, no sound came from my mouth.

Open. Close. Open. Close.

As hard as I fought, I couldn't keep my eyes open for longer than a second. The room was eerily silent until the sounds of an infant's cries echoed around me.

"It's a girl."

Helplessly, I watched as the nurse moved away from me and grabbed the baby from the doctor. She quickly swaddled her up in a white blanket and rushed her to a small steel countertop. After wiping her down, she put a stethoscope to her chest.

Baby. Mutely, I cried again.

My daughter wailed and I wanted to hold her so badly. However, I couldn't find the energy to move any of my limbs.

There was an image standing nearby. More like an apparition. My eyes squinted as I directed my focus to the presence before me. It looked like my mother but that was impossible. I must have been hallucinating. There was no way she could be standing there.

Mommy. Tears slid from my eyes and rolled back into my ears.

Suddenly, my baby stopped crying. It was as if she saw her too because she stared at the image standing above her and started cooing. It was a happy sound. She then stuck her tiny finger in her mouth and turned her head slightly in my direction. She was the most beautiful thing I had ever seen with a head full of black curly hair and porcelain skin.

Open. Close. Open. Close.

I struggled to stay awake. I had to look in her face just one more time. My baby. My resurrection. Finally, she was here.

From my bed, I could see her big bright eyes as they took in the world for the very first time. I was hypnotized by them. Her gaze pierced through my heart. She had her father's eyes.

Bella Salerno was born weighing seven pounds and seven ounces. She was seventeen inches and came into this world at exactly 7:07 AM. She was my Lucky Number Seven Baby.

Open. Close. Open. Close...

A View of The Top
Book III - The Finale

How will it end?

CPSIA information can be obtained
at www.ICGtesting.com
Printed in the USA
LVHW021645311219
642209LV00016B/306